To all my dental hygienist friends. You make the world's smile brighter!

RING
OF DEATH

RUTH J. HARTMAN

Scrivenings
PRESS
Quench your thirst for story.
www.ScriveningsPress.com

Published by Scrivenings Press LLC
15 Lucky Lane
Morrilton, Arkansas 72110
https://ScriveningsPress.com

Printed in the United States of America

Paperback ISBN 978-1-64917-090-3

eBook ISBN 978-1-64917-091-0

Library of Congress Control Number: 2020949289

Cover by www.bookmarketinggraphics.com.

PROLOGUE

Dorey's short fingernails scraped against the jagged surface of the rock, chalky bits of stone raining down into her eyes and mouth. She coughed and tried to blink away some of the dust. But she didn't dare let go of her skimpy hold on the wall to wipe it away.

The toes of her shoes barely perched on the narrow ledge. Cold air bit into her skin right through her shirt and pants. Is this how it would all end? With her unable to hold onto the wall of the dark cave, her body plummeting to the ravine below?

There didn't seem to be any way out. She'd either fall to her death or stay on the ledge and starve. How had her life come to this?

She glanced up, her heart in her throat. Was he still following her? Would he find her? As if thudding a death knell, her heart rapped against her ribs.

Faint light reflected off the item, which had started the whole nightmare.

The ring.

She wished she'd never seen the stupid thing. That he would have lost it somewhere else.

I never asked for this.

Something flew directly over her head. A bat? Dorey jerked and nearly lost her balance. She pressed tight against the wall, the icy temperature seeping into her cheek. Her whole face hurt from the cold—even her teeth ached. Plops of a loud drip from somewhere nearby made her shiver even more, especially without her jacket.

Her jacket.

The one that Harry had so lovingly zipped up for her before he'd brought her here the first time.

Dorey closed her eyes, hot tears burning their way down her frozen cheeks. *Harry. I'm so sorry. All this horror and destruction because of a ring I found.*

Her ring shone bright again, reflecting the …

Wait … Light?

Had he found her? Dorey gulped in air so fast she got lightheaded. She closed her eyes and took a slow breath. Please don't let him see me. I won't get out alive. Peeking to the right, her movements slow and measured—one, because she didn't want to give her location away and two, she didn't want to fall— she saw a beam of light coming from the mouth of the cave. A lantern?

It was him. Had to be! Who else would be here this time of night in such awful weather?

Something scratched on the rock a few feet below her. A wider ledge was there, but she couldn't reach it without tumbling down into the dark.

No thanks.

More scratching. An animal? Mountain lion? Bear?

Fresh fear of wild creatures doing her harm got in line behind the terror already racing through her veins.

How would she escape the madman who wanted her dead?

1

Eight weeks earlier

Sometimes it didn't pay to get out of bed.

Dorey Cameron should have heeded the warning. Staring down at the woman in the hygiene chair, Dorey tightened her grip on the patient chart. "Excuse me, Mrs. Harkins, but did you just say—"

"You are not touching me. Not even to put that ridiculous paper napkin around my neck."

"I don't understand."

"Young lady, you cannot possibly be qualified to do anything to anyone's teeth."

Unfortunately, not the first time Dorey had been told that. Dr. Conners, the dentist who'd previously run the practice, thought dental hygienists were unnecessary. Since she'd taken the job with Harry, she'd heard from Dr. Conners' former patients that he didn't think hygienists were even qualified to do more than seat the patients.

His interference wreaked havoc with her schedule. More often than not, her patients either didn't show or wouldn't let her near them.

Curmudgeonly old dinosaur.

The fact that Dorey hadn't been able to land a job at any other office was a sign of personal defeat. And she wouldn't even have her present job if Dr. Conners hadn't sold his practice to Harry MacKinley.

At least Harry believed a hygienist was an actual occupation.

Mrs. Harkins had stopped talking. What had she said? Did it matter? It probably wasn't complimentary anyway.

Dorey gripped the patient chart tighter. The thick paper threatened to tear beneath her fingers, but at the moment, she didn't care. "Mrs. Harkins, I assure you I'm quite well trained in—"

The frumpy woman held up her hand, her long fingernails looking like claws with red polish. "Stop. Talking."

Heat traveled up Dorey's face when she sucked in a breath. She blinked, hoping to erase the sight of the woman—lips pulled back in a sneer, looking as if she'd like to bite her.

Mortified, Dorey bit her tongue to keep from shouting out the not so nice words hovering, waiting to pounce. Turning, she stalked from the room. She wanted to run. To flee. Out of the room. The office. Chester, Indiana.

Why couldn't some dentist in a larger city need a dental hygienist? Someone with forward-thinking patients who would be glad to have the services of a hygienist? Who would embrace what she could do for them. How she could help them. Instead, Dorey still resided in her tiny hometown, longing for any escape route she could find. So far, none had materialized.

Face it, you're stuck here. At least for now.

Not for long, if she could help it. When she went home to her apartment every night, she sent her résumé out to a few more dentists. She'd heard back from two with the unfortunate news that they'd already filled their positions. At least they'd bothered to contact her. The others hadn't even acknowledged her inquiry.

Blowing out a long breath, she trudged into Harry's operatory where he had both hands immersed in a full-mouth extraction on Mr. Pemberley. Classic rock, Harry's favorite, played from the CD player in the corner.

Harry glanced up briefly, his safety glasses having slid halfway down his nose. "That was fast. Ready for me to check your patient already?"

She clasped her hands together in front of her waist, trying to hold back her irritation in front of Harry's patient. Be professional. "I'm afraid not."

"Oh." He blinked twice. "I see."

"Yes." *I'm sure you do.*

After removing his gloved hands from Mr. Pemberley's mouth, he held them out, away from his face. "I'm guessing my patient here is ready for a break, anyway." Harry's raised eyebrows were visible over the top of his safety glasses.

With a vigorous nod, Mr. Pemberley agreed. "Yeth. A break would be nith. Thankth."

"No problem." Harry backed his chair away from the patient while the assistant, Luanne, used the suction and water to clean out Mr. Pemberley's numb mouth. Mr. Pemberley let out a sigh, his hands relaxing from their previous fisted stance.

Standing, Harry removed his gloves and washed his hands at the nearby sink. He stepped closer. "Same as before?" he whispered.

She swallowed hard and glanced toward the floor. "Yep."

"Sorry."

"Not your fault." She held his gaze needing him to know she didn't want sympathy.

With a quick peek at Luanne and a glance back at Dorey, he pointed toward his private office. No use having that conversation in front of the nosy assistant. Things were bad enough without her telling Mae at the front desk. Then Mae, in turn, would tell the whole world. Gladly.

She stepped in behind him, closed the door, and leaned against it. "Honestly, I'm not sure what else to do."

"Yeah, I know. But don't give up. I need you."

And she needed the job. Badly. Money for rent, groceries, and cat food didn't happily pop up in her bank account. "I won't give up. It's just ..."

He nodded. "That if Dr. Conners hadn't turned the patients into his way of thinking, it wouldn't be so hard for you."

"For you too. I've seen how he comes in and wastes time talking to your patients, so you can't get your work done." She shook her head. "Frustrating."

"Very." Harry crossed his arms over his chest.

Why hadn't she noticed before how broad his shoulders were? He used to take her for piggyback rides when she was little. Sitting on his shoulders now would be way different. Stop it, Dorey. "So, what do we do?"

"We keep trying."

"I'm not sure that's enough." Mirroring his actions, she crossed her arms. She hadn't gone through years of college to be a trained hygienist to have patients tell her she didn't know what she was doing. And there hadn't been any classes concerning nosy retired dentists who couldn't cut the apron strings from their former patients. If Dr. Conners would leave them alone, everything would work out fine.

Harry relaxed his stance and tapped his finger on the top of the desk. He did that a lot when deep in thought. Did it help him solve anything? She didn't have any better ideas. Might have to give it a try.

"I want you to stay, okay? I'm gonna do everything I can to help." He smiled.

Though he'd always been a dork ever since they were kids,

the man did have a nice smile. Lucky thing, since patients tended to shy away from dental professionals with rotted, crooked teeth. Under the circumstances, Harry couldn't afford to lose any more patients.

"Thanks."

He gave a nod. "Ready to dive back into the shark tank?"

Her laugh came out as a snort. "Uh, you're actually not far off there, Doc. From the tiny glimpse I got of Mrs. Harkins' pointy teeth, shark-like is a good description. I had images of her snapping off my fingers when I got too close."

Harry bit his lip and his nostrils flared. "No fair making me laugh right before I have to see her."

"You started it." Dorey poked him in the shoulder.

With a grin, he opened the door. She stayed right behind him as they made their way back to shark lady. It was a throwback to fourth grade when she huddled behind Susie, the biggest girl in class, during their dangerous weekly game of dodge ball. As a kid, Dorey had been so skinny, somebody with a wicked pitch might have snapped her arm right off. Susie, though, was built like a bulldozer. With the personality to match.

Feeling even more like a kid in trouble at school, Dorey slunk off to the side of the room. At least Mrs. Harkins didn't wield a dodge ball.

Dorey hated to bother Harry with this when he was busy with his own patient. But he'd told her to let him know if it happened again. Unfortunately, it was all too often.

He took a seat next to their patient, the wheels of the chair squeaking when he rolled a little bit closer. "Good morning, Mrs. Harkins." His voice sounded pleasant, but Dorey had known him long enough to recognize the irritation buried in his words. The little inflection he'd put on the word good was anything but cheery.

The woman frowned. "Hello."

Did she not like him any better than she did Dorey? Who wouldn't like Harry? He was amazing. Sweet. Funny. Thoughtful. But Dorey was only slightly prejudiced.

"My hygienist tells me you're a little reluctant to let her do your cleaning."

Reluctant? Try venomous.

"I'll tell you what I told her," Mrs. Harkins said, emphasizing every word with a poke in the air by her finger. "I'll not allow just any old person the liberty of touching my mouth." Her lips thrust out in a sour expression.

The old bat. *Trust me, lady. It wouldn't fulfill my every longing to touch your mouth. I ain't asking you for a date.*

Harry leaned forward, his forearms on his knees and clasped his hands together. "Mrs. Harkins, I assure you that Miss Cameron is very well trained and highly qualified to do your cleaning. Actually, she went to the same school I did and—"

"That means nothing to me. A crumpled-up cocktail napkin stating she's qualified would mean about as much as that framed diploma over there on the wall." The words flew out like they tasted vile and she longed to fling them from her lips.

Dorey longed to yell, it's a license, not a diploma! But she knew that would mean nothing to the woman.

"I see. Then it seems we have a problem." Harry's left eyebrow rose.

"You bet we do." She leaned forward, peering around Harry so she could glare at Dorey. "There is no way that girl is touching me." A visible shiver rippled across her shoulders.

Did she think Dorey was contagious or something? Would jab her with a spear? Burn her under hot coals?

How dare she? Humiliation and anger warred for dominion over Dorey's thoughts. With her arms crossed, she dug her fingernails into the flesh of her arms. A scream lodged in her throat along with an unvoiced rant about how unfair Mrs.

Harkins acted. But it wouldn't do any good and would only embarrass Harry.

He closed his eyes briefly and let out a long, audible breath. "You've made that quite clear, Mrs. Harkins. Are you sure you won't reconsider?"

"Absolutely not."

"That's a shame. I'd hoped it wouldn't come to this. I'm sorry to say, then, I'll have to ask you to leave."

Uncomfortable silence filled the room. Even the sound of crickets chirping would have been welcome.

Shock rolled across Mrs. Harkins' face. "W-what?" Her mouth hung open unattractively, showing her pointy shark teeth to great advantage.

I didn't want to clean your ugly old teeth anyway.

Harry looked the woman square in the eye. "I trust Miss Cameron completely. She's a valued member of my team. I'll not have a patient, any patient, say something negative about her or to her. Do I make myself clear?" He backed the chair away, putting a few feet between them and crossed his arms over his chest. "I believe you know the way out."

Dorey's mouth gaped open. He did not just do that. From his stony expression and rigid stance, no one could have any doubt he was serious. Harry had always been so sweet and funny. Who knew he had a bad boy side?

Snapping her mouth closed, Dorey swallowed, hard. Why would he do that? He'd just lost a patient who'd been with the practice forever.

A deep furrow appeared on Mrs. Harkins' forehead. She stared wide-eyed at Harry. "You ... can't be serious."

"Very serious."

"But what if I have a problem later on ... a toothache?"

"Then we'll be glad to give you a list of competent dentists to call. Mae can assist you with that." Harry cleared his throat. "I have other patients to see, so …" Standing, he extended his arm out to the side toward the front of the office. And waited.

The wall clock ticked, the only sound in the room. Each movement of its second hand progressively louder as time stepped forward. Dorey's heartbeat thrummed in time, somehow choreographed.

What would Mrs. Harkins do? If she apologized, would Harry let her stay? Then Dorey would have to do the cleaning. She would, of course, but boy, would that be uncomfortable.

"I …" Mrs. Harkins blinked, her false lashes bouncing against a vast amount of dark pink blusher. "Well …" With a quick shake of her head, as if not believing what had just occurred, Mrs. Harkins grabbed her purse from her lap and stood. She brushed off the front of her blouse as if wanting to rid herself of any remnant of their office. "You can be quite assured that others will hear about this."

"Good." Harry nodded. "Tell everybody. That way, it might save me the time of having to dismiss someone else from *my* practice who doesn't deserve to be treated here."

"Well!" Mrs. Harkins stomped from the operatory, down the hall, complained loudly at the front desk, and slammed the main office door.

When Harry turned back and made eye contact with Dorey, he gave a little shrug. Didn't it matter to him that he'd just lost a patient and could lose a lot more when Mrs. Harkins started flapping her lips to everyone?

Rushing over to him, Dorey narrowly missed the footrest of the patient chair as she skirted past it. She grasped his shoulders tightly. "Why did you do that?"

"I had to." His muscles tensed beneath her fingers.

"No, you didn't."

"Yeah, I did."

She gritted her teeth and muttered, "Stop arguing with me. I'm having flashbacks to seventh grade."

"You know that a lot of Dr. Conners' patients acted as if he created the moon. If I don't stop this now, it won't go away. I didn't take over this practice to have to convince patients my staff is competent. I came here to do my job."

"You might not have any patients left to see." She dropped her hands to her sides.

"Then I'll get new ones." He didn't seem particularly concerned. Sure, it was a busy practice. Now. But if people kept leaving, it might not stay that way. Didn't it bother him that he had bills coming in the door? Student loans to repay? Mortgages on his house and the office?

She leaned closer and lowered her voice. "You didn't have to do that for me."

"Yeah, Dorey." His glance slipped down to her lips, lingered for a few seconds, and then worked its way back up. "I did." Giving her a pat on her arm, he left her alone in the hygiene room.

She shook her head. Why did Dr. Conners have to cause so much trouble? Working on patients when they didn't want to be there in the first place seemed hard enough without him meddling. Harry worked so hard. Was such a good dentist. But some of the patients wouldn't even give him a chance. They were too loyal to Dr. Conners.

With slow movements, in turtle mode, Dorey pulled on gloves and began to clean her room for her next patient, who hopefully wouldn't spew venom at her and would consent to allow Dorey to do the job she was trained for.

She jerked to a stop, the patient napkin dangling from her fingers like a windsock. Before, when Harry told her he'd had to get rid of Mrs. Harkins for Dorey's sake, he'd stared at Dorey's lips. Her lips. What did that mean? She knew what it meant when other guys did it. But Harry? The dorky brother of her sister's husband? The goofball who always teased her?

She sputtered a laugh. No. Way.

A few hours later, Dorey gratefully closed the door behind her, glad to be home. How come trying to find something to keep her occupied at work was more stressful than working? She glanced down. Weatherby wound around her ankles, meowing pitifully.

"Yeah, I know." She bent down to pet him. "You're starved. Haven't eaten for twenty-seven days. The usual, right?" Actually, he'd been gone three days this time.

Her cat froze and stared up at her. Eerie how he did that. Like he understood her. Even when she used sarcasm.

"Okay, sorry. Come on and let's get you fed."

The dark gray cat took off like someone had pinched his long skinny tail and raced to the kitchen. Dorey wasn't far behind, but Weatherby sat next to his empty dish, scowling.

"I'm right here, dude." Dorey filled the dish, then sat on the floor. Weatherby crunched the dry food fast and loud, like a starving man gorging on potato chips.

She ruffled the soft fur on his head, but he didn't look up. "Weatherby, I have a problem. Patients aren't showing up, and it's making me crazy. And when they do show, sometimes they won't let me do my job. What should I do?"

He ignored her, except for a purr. Just kept on chewing, his face buried in the dish up to his whiskers.

Sighing, she crossed her arms over her chest. "It would be nice if you at least pretended to listen, you know. You could—"

The cat jerked his head from the bowl and whipped it toward the doorway.

Dorey frowned. "What?"

His fur bristled and stood on end. With an arched back, he hopped sideways, then took off like a shot toward the front door. Before Dorey could grab him, he'd climbed through the kitty door.

"Wait. What's wrong?" She ran after him.

When she flung the front door open, the cat stood on the

small front cement slab, back still arched like a buffalo's, tail slashing left to right.

Dorey glanced around but didn't see anybody. The parking lot was empty except for two cars parked at the other end. "Cat, what's gotten into you? Why are you so freaked?" Unlike other cats, Weatherby ran toward possible confrontation, not away.

He gave a long howl, worthy of any self-respecting wolf.

"Stop that. You're scaring me." She knelt and touched his back.

Finally, he quit howling.

Ah ... quiet.

"Dorey." Not a shout, but a whisper, making the hair on her arms stand up like Weatherby's fur.

She gasped. Who said that? No one was around that she could see. It might be one of her neighbors calling through an open window. Did someone need help?

No. As far as she could tell, no one close by was even home. At the very least, she couldn't see anyone hanging out any windows, trying to get her attention.

"Dorey."

She stood up. Who called her name? She looked around again, still not finding the source. Why couldn't she see the person trying to get her attention? Was someone playing a joke? Hiding where she wouldn't notice them?

"This is getting too weird for me, Weatherby."

Rubbing her arms, she went back inside but waited just inside the doorway. After a few more seconds of continued vigilance, her cat joined her.

With the door now securely locked, Dorey tried to relax. There was no one there. Nobody called your name.

But someone had, hadn't they?

Am I losing it?

2

Dorey checked out the schedule the following week. It had been so nice and pretty and full of patients. Now it had more holes than a victim in a gangster movie. "What happened to it?"

Mae replied, "They're dropping like drunken mosquitoes at a beach party."

"How come?"

"Don't know." She shrugged. "Might have something to do with Dr. MacKinley telling everybody off." Her gray eyebrows, resembling furry caterpillars, rose over the top of her glasses.

No surprise Mae had heard all about it. Not only did she hear everything patients had to say when they left the office, she brazenly asked them pointed questions to get the scoop on things. The woman lived for gossip.

Dorey pointed at the phone. "I can try to call someone from my list."

"I've already tried calling several to move them up from later in the month. No luck."

With nothing else to occupy her, Dorey took it upon herself to do a deep, thorough cleaning of her room. The staff did a good job of cleaning surfaces with disinfectant between patients, but things like corners and tiny crevices around the equipment that patients didn't come in contact with got overlooked sometimes.

When the schedule was busy, Dorey could barely run to the bathroom between appointments. That was especially bad if she'd consumed the super-large size of diet soda. Her weakness for those had gotten her in hot water more than once.

After snapping on disposable gloves, she dusted out the inside of her cabinets and drawers, the baseboard corners, and tiny cracks between the metal pieces of her equipment.

She eyed the chair. Sure, it had been reupholstered, but several patients had been there since then, and sometimes small items disappeared deep down between the seat and the back. One time she had extra fun cleaning out bright blue glitter a teenage girl had worn sprinkled all over her clothes.

Like a minuscule Marti Gras.

Dorey crammed her hand down into the tight space in the chair, barely able to move her fingers around. She pulled it back out. No glitter, thankfully, but she did find someone's toothpick. Gross. Grimacing, she threw that away and tried again.

Nothing … nothing …

Wait. What's that?

Something wedged in deep. Dorey couldn't see it. Could barely graze the edge with her fingertips. She yanked her hand out, removed her glove, and grabbed a pair of forceps from her drawer. With the glove back on, she eased the forceps carefully down, not wanting to scar the chair's new fabric. The item had slipped way far down.

Would she be able to get it? She hated leaving it down there. Mostly because, now that she knew the thing existed, it would bother her until she'd removed it. Did she have a little OCD?

Yeah, okay.

Something pinged against the forceps. Metal? Had someone

lost a hairpin? Loose change? Two more tries and she grabbed the very edge.

And pulled out her hand.

Held precariously between the tips of the forceps perched a ring. Very pretty. And turquoise—her favorite color.

Her grandmother had given her one several years ago, but Dorey had lost it one day at the beach. She'd been so stupid to take it off and leave it on her towel when she'd put suntan lotion on. When she'd come back from a dip in the water, someone else had helped themselves to her favorite ring.

Dorey had always wanted to replace it but never found one she liked well enough to buy.

This one, though, was perfect. A dainty stone set in a silver setting surrounded by what appeared to be tiny diamonds. When she turned it back and forth, it caught the light. It appeared old, tarnished, and valuable.

What should she do with it? Leave it with Mae for lost and found? Nope. Better ask Harry since it was found in his office. And the ring was more valuable than some little kid's left shoe kicked off during their cleaning.

After rinsing off the ring at the sink, she set it aside, removed the gloves, and washed her hands.

She knocked on the doorframe of Harry's office and stepped in, closing the door behind her. He sat behind his desk.

"I saw you cleaning in there when I walked by earlier." He leaned forward, elbows on his desktop. "Thanks. But you never were one to stand around and do nothing."

"If I don't stay busy, I feel like I'm cheating you since I'm getting paid anyway." She shrugged.

One side of his mouth rose.

Uh-oh. She knew that look. She crossed her arms, tapped her toe, and waited for his teasing.

As if reaching back in his mind for old memories, he peered up at the ceiling. "Yeah, I remember you playing with all those stuffed animals of yours. Mostly cats. Lining them up on your parents' couch and telling them they had to clean their rooms, and do a good job at it, or you'd tell your mom."

Dorey smacked her hand over her eyes for a second. "Why do you have to drag out all those weird things I did when I was a kid?"

"'Cause it's fun."

"Maybe for you."

He shook his head slowly. "Oh, come on, Dorey. You like the attention."

"Not when you refer to me like I'm nine years old. In case you hadn't noticed, I'm no longer the kid you used tease."

"Believe me. I've noticed."

"Oh." Panic set in when he pushed away from his desk and stood. What was he doing? Why did he stare at her like she was on the dessert menu and he had a yen for a chocolate sundae?

Slowly, he walked around the desk, then leaned back against it and crossed his arms. "Is there ... something you needed?"

"Um, needed?"

"You did come in here. So ..." He pointed to the door.

She blinked. Why did she ... "Oh." Dorey reached into her pocket and pulled out the ring, relieved to have something to break the tension. "I found this down in my chair."

"Wonder whose it is?"

"No clue. Not sure what I should do with it. Could we put a notice in the paper about it? Maybe the patient who lost it might see that and come to collect it."

"Hmm." He eyed the ring in Dorey's hand. "If we do, every crackpot out there will swear the ring is theirs and show up or call. Mae wouldn't be thrilled to have her phone line clogged up when she's scheduling patients." He glanced away.

Her eyes widened. "Wait."

"What?"

"Are you afraid of Mae?"

"You've met her. Aren't you?"

She laughed. "Yeah, okay. Um, what about an ad saying someone left it in the office and the person has to identify it to claim it?"

"We could, but ..."

"What?"

"I don't want to use my advertising budget for that. I need to place an ad for new patients."

Dorey sighed. "Right. 'Cause I can't seem to get anyone in to get their teeth cleaned." All those years of training and she barely got to use her skills.

"No, I didn't mean ... It's not your fault. I don't blame you. You know that, right?"

She nodded. But did she really know it? Guilt crept over her. She put the ring back in her pocket and gazed up at him. Hard to look him in the eye, so she spoke to his left ear instead. "You know ... if you don't think it's working out ... I mean, if you can't afford a hygienist right now, I—"

"Stop." He stepped forward and placed his hands lightly on her shoulders. "You're staying, okay?"

She shrugged and turned her head.

Harry placed his finger beneath her chin and angled her head, so she had no choice but to make eye contact. "Okay?"

"Yeah." She swallowed hard. Time to change the subject. "Maybe I can look through the schedule, see if there's a likely candidate for the ring, in the recent patients we've had."

"Good idea." He squeezed her shoulder. "That way, not everyone would have to know about it. And ... let's keep the ring between you and me for now."

"Um, sure." Her fingers fidgeted at her sides.

"Well ..." He tilted his head toward the door. "Somebody else might want it for themselves."

"You think?"

"You've seen the jewelry those two wear."

Both women did sport a ton of hardware. Dorey was surprised Luanne could get gloves on over her huge rings. When she did, her hands resembled one of those dinosaurs with the spikes on their backs.

A knock came at the door. She jumped back, like she'd been doing something wrong. She'd always considered Harry as a big brother. Why did it feel different now? Like some tide had shifted and they'd discovered new territory.

The door opened and Mae stuck her head in. She lifted one eyebrow when she spotted Dorey but shifted her attention back to Harry. "Dr. MacKinley, your next patient is here." She glanced at Dorey. "Sorry. No one for you yet." She turned away without closing the door. Had she left it open on purpose?

I feel like my mom just caught me with a boy in my bedroom.

"Well," Harry said, heading toward the doorway. "Gotta go."

She desperately wished she had someone waiting to see her too. "I'll get back on the phone. Surely, someone out there won't mind coming in this week."

He gave her a smile and left.

With nothing else to do for another hour until the next scheduled patient, she sat down at Mae's second computer out front and scrolled through the past few weeks. Maybe a name would pop out at her of someone who might have lost the ring. She could pretty much rule out blustery old men. Probably any men. Focusing on the women patients and teen girls, Dorey started making a list.

"What are you doing?"

Dorey jumped. "Uh ..."

"I already called to confirm the patients for tomorrow."

"Oh, I... wasn't doing that." She knew better. Mae acted like a territorial dog guarding its food dish.

Mae leaned over to see the computer screen. "If you're looking for someone to call in, it won't do you any good to look at people who've already been here."

"No, of course not." Her face heated. *Mae must think I'm some kind of idiot.* Dorey stood and went back to her room. She'd have to try to use the computer when Mae wasn't there. Though that wouldn't be easy. The woman rarely left her post, afraid she might miss something.

What other way could Dorey get the names? She'd remember some of the patients she'd had over the last few weeks but not all.

Ah ... A slow smile formed on her lips. She could file patient charts for Mae. The receptionist would never turn that down. Filing was her least favorite thing to do.

Dorey was just being helpful, after all. When Mae looked away, she could jot down the names for later.

She hurried down the hall and ended up in the reception area again. Mae turned and eyed her suspiciously. "What's up?" After questioning her for looking at past patients for future appointments, Mae was guarding her domain even closer than usual.

"Nothing. Just ... had some time on my hands—" She flipped her hand in the air for emphasis. "—and thought I'd file some charts for you."

Mae blinked slowly. "Oh. Thanks."

Why hadn't Dorey thought of this before? She picked up a stack of charts that Mae hadn't filed yet. The receptionist often whined about hating to file things, obvious by the large pile of charts stacked off to the side, close to tipping over.

The phone rang, taking the older woman's attention and giving Dorey a chance to jot down some names. She'd already filed several for the male patients and had left out the women. Working quickly, she hoped to get all the names she could to figure out who might be the ring's owner. If the ring had been hers and she'd lost it, she'd want it back.

After making note of the ones that might be candidates,

Dorey went back to her room. She took the paper out of her pocket and stared at the names.

Now what?

Did she just start calling people? Would that be weird? *Hello, I have a ring.* Did you lose a ring?

Lame, Dorey.

But she had to do something. It didn't feel right just hanging onto the ring.

"What'cha doin'?"

Dorey nearly leaped out of her skin and smacked her hand against her chest. "Harry!"

He stepped closer. "Startled, are we?"

"Maybe a little."

"More like a frightened cat."

She let out a breath, trying to calm down. "My cat hardly ever acts like that."

"Since when do you have a cat? Didn't think you'd had one since you moved out to go to college."

"Since he showed up a few weeks ago. He comes and goes. I'm never sure when to expect him. Weatherby isn't the most trustworthy."

"So, the name means something? You always used to name your stuffed animals—"

As she narrowed her eyes, she said, "Are we back to that again?"

He laughed. "Can't help it. Anyway, what's it mean?"

"Weatherby. Because he sits outside in all kinds of weather. Doesn't seem to care if he gets wet or not. I've never seen a cat like that. The weird thing is, he gets wet often, but his white paws always look grungy."

"So far, I haven't heard anything that makes me want to meet him."

"Oh, he's great. When he decides to show up. I love him, but let's just say that if he were human, his occupation might be thief. I'm never sure what he'll drag home next."

"Like what?"

"The latest was a long black sock with a hole in the heel. Before that, he brought home someone's nearly empty toothpaste tube. Who knows where he gets this stuff. I think he's part retriever."

"You lead such an exciting life." Harry smirked.

"Don't I know it?"

Harry slid a glance to the counter and back. "So, what's goin' on?"

She held out the list. "These are the most likely ones who might own the ring. I thought maybe I should call them and ask. I'm sure the person would want it back."

"Good idea. Then if none of them is the owner, maybe you should wear it."

"But—"

"Maybe the owner will see it. And if no one claims it in say, a month, it's yours."

"Are you sure? That doesn't seem right." Although, she liked the idea of keeping it herself. It wasn't the one from her grandmother, but it might give her pleasant memories of the one she'd lost.

He tapped his finger against the paper. "No one's called about missing one, have they?"

"Well, no. And I'm sure Mae would have said if they had."

"Right. So, it might not be that important to whoever lost it."

"What about Mae and Luanne?"

He leaned close. "I think it would look better on you," he whispered.

Dorey sucked in a breath. When he'd moved toward her, she'd had the craziest idea he meant to kiss her. *Are you serious? It would be like kissing your brother.*

Except, she didn't have a brother.

3

M ae pointed to the schedule. "Some people seem to be in dire straits."

With her hands on her hips, Dorey asked, "What does that mean?"

She pursed her red lipstick-covered lips and looked over her reading glasses at Dorey, looking every bit the disappointed teacher when a student answers incorrectly. "Dire straits is defined as—"

"No, I know the definition. I mean, why do you say that? Is there some strain of flu going around?" Why did Mae always treat Dorey like an underachieving wayward granddaughter?

"Nothing as mundane as flu."

"What, then?" Dorey almost wished she could take the words back, not wanting Mae to delve into the definition of flu.

"Well, like I said, a few gave the excuse of not wanting to see a hygienist because of what Dr. Conners said. But a couple of them ..."

Dorey lowered her eyebrows.

"It seems" —Mae gave a quick shake of her head— "There's some rogue person going around wearing masks."

"Like Halloween?"

"I guess."

"What kind of masks?"

"Someone wearing a hideous clown mask peeked in a patient's living room window and scared her so bad she didn't want to leave her house."

"I do understand the whole aversion to clowns thing. But I wish the patient would have come in anyway. Are there more patients like that?"

"There's another one who said a person in a mask knocked on her door, and when she answered, he ran away."

"I take it this mask was scary too?"

"A zombie."

"Ugh."

"Precisely. I don't know what the world is coming to, but I'm not sure I like where it's headed. I feel like I should be wearing garlic around my neck to ward off the curse." Mae tapped her throat twice.

Not cursed, at least Dorey didn't think so. But something was going on. How bizarre that a couple of their patients saw a person in a scary mask on the same day? Did things like that happen during a full moon?

Halfway down the hall to her room, Mae hollered her name, and Dorey hurried back to the front desk.

Mae held out her phone. "Guy on the phone says he needs to talk to you."

"Who is it?"

"Wouldn't say. Just that it's important."

Dorey shrugged and took the phone. "Hello? This is Dorey. How can I help y—"

The phone clicked. Then, a dial tone. Dorey frowned and gave the phone back. "Weird. Nobody there."

Mae shrugged. "Maybe a wrong number."

Dorey nodded and turned. Wait. How could it be a wrong

number if they'd asked for her specifically? She shook her head and ambled back down the hall. Whatever. Some weirdo just wanting to cause trouble. Who knew?

There had to be someone she could get to come in. She turned the corner toward her room. Half her day was shot. Harry wouldn't blame Dorey for the cancellations, but he wouldn't be amused either. She wanted to help his practice, but so far, the hygiene schedule wasn't cooperating.

Hurrying past his operatory doorway, she hoped he wouldn't see her. What would she tell him when he found out about the world's fastest crumbling dental schedule? Try to make light of it? Say something funny to make him laugh? After his dealings with Mrs. Harkins, he might not be in the best mood when it came to uncooperative patients. Maybe she could get some others to fill in the gaps before he found out.

The middle drawer of her right-side cabinet held her printed schedules for the next few weeks. Although, they'd need to be reprinted before the scheduled days. There would be too many changes to simply use a pen and do the occasional cross-out and write in.

Dorey opened the drawer and peered inside. Where was it? She always kept it there for when she had to try to call someone in. She rifled through the pamphlets on tooth brushing and flossing where her list usually was, then frowned. No one would have taken it. Harry, Luanne, and Mae wouldn't have a use for her list. Nobody else knew she kept it there. Weird.

Luckily, she remembered some of the names, so she recreated the list as best she could. Maybe someone would be able to come in. Someone … anyone …

After updating that day's lineup with who hadn't shown up, she laid her new list of potential people next to it on the counter. With any luck, she'd get several to commit, and Mae could print out the updated schedule for her. Then Harry wouldn't even have to know how bad it had been. He'd never been in the habit of checking her schedule, only his, trusting her to take care of it. By all appearances, she wasn't doing a bang-up job.

Dorey tapped in the phone number of the first name on her list.

"Mrs. Campbell? Hello, this is Dorey, the hygienist for Dr. MacKinley. We have some openings today, and I'm checking to see—"

"I'm sorry, Dorey. We're in a bit of a snag right now. Angelique ran away."

"Ran away?" She frowned, trying to remember if they had a daughter with that name. It didn't sound familiar. "Angelique …"

"Our pedigreed poodle."

"Oh, my goodness, well, I hope you find her."

"Him. Angelique is a boy." Indignation flowed down the phone line.

Okay … Maybe the dog ran away to escape his embarrassing girly name. Poor mutt.

"He was out in the yard and got scared off by a man wearing some hideous mask."

Mask?

"Until I find Angelique, I won't be able to concentrate on anything else."

The phone clicked in Dorey's ear. She was almost afraid to call someone else.

Don't be silly. These are flukes. What were the chances that other people would have something similar? She hadn't heard any news stories about crazy people in costumes, but then she did tend to retreat into her own little world with her cat once she left work for the day. Sometimes he got a little possessive with her time and grumbled if he didn't receive her undivided attention.

Harry's deep voice floated in from down the short hallway,

laughing at something Luanne said. Very soon, sooner than Dorey would like, he'd finish his patient and come talk to her. Then, she'd have to tell him about the schedule.

Unless he already knew.

No. If he knew, he might have said something.

Dorey grabbed the phone again. I have to find someone to come in.

Footsteps came from the hallway. Harry walked in, his eyes taking in the empty patient chair. "What's up? Somebody not show?"

"Make that nobody." She set down the phone.

He tilted his head. "How's that?"

Dorey fidgeted with the pen in her left hand. "You may as well know ..."

"What?" He took a step closer, concern etched on his face.

"We're having lots of trouble getting patients in. I hate that. I feel so bad that no money is coming in when you have tons of bills to pay. I even noticed one from the upholsterer on Mae's desk earlier today."

"Don't worry about it."

"The schedule fell apart. Disintegrated." She touched the arm of the chair, feeling terrible that he'd spent so much money on upgrading it, yet no patient sat there.

He waved his hand. "It happens."

"Yeah, if there's a flu epidemic or six feet of snow. Neither of which is happening right now."

He shrugged. "I guess it's to be expected when word got out what I said to Mrs. Harkins."

"That's not all of it."

"How can you be sure? That is one rude woman. And after all, I did tell her to spread the word, hoping to keep out the fellow evil-doers."

"Because I doubt even evil Mrs. Harkins is running around

town in masks scaring people enough that they are afraid to leave home." She crossed her arms.

His eyes widened. "What?"

"I know. Strange, huh? That happened to some of our patients, but only to ones on my schedule."

"Only on yours?" He narrowed his eyes. "Hmm. I knew you were trouble the first time I met you."

"Um ... what?"

"Ever since you were little, problems seemed to follow you."

Her mouth dropped open. "That's not true."

Harry stared at her for a second then sputtered out a laugh. "Joking."

Sometimes the guy's timing for humor wasn't the best. She huffed out a breath. "Let's hope it's not true. I can't believe all the hygiene patients who aren't showing. It's unreal. They're dropping like swatted gnats."

"So ..." He leaned closer and gave a loud sniff, sounding like a bloodhound on the hunt.

She backed away, her butt slamming into the counter behind her. "What're you doing?"

"You take a shower today? Maybe, you know, word got around that you ..."

"You are such a guy." She smacked his shoulder.

He grinned.

"Yes, I took a shower, so I don't stink. And no, I'm not wearing patient repellent."

He cuffed her on the side of the head, lightly. Just like he did when they were kids. She hated that.

Pushing his hand away, she frowned. "Seriously, Harry, what are we gonna do?"

"Don't call me that."

"It's your name."

"Not—" He glanced out into the empty hallway. "—at work."

"Why not?"

"After the Mrs. Harkins debacle," he pointed toward Dorey's patient chair with his thumb, "I need all the credibility I can get. Harrison sounds more respectable than Harry. Maybe it would make a difference to a patient still not sure about me."

"Whatever. I am not going to call you Harrison. I've never called you that. Neither did anyone else except your mother. And that's only when you'd done something extraordinarily bad."

He dropped his mouth open in mock surprise. "Insubordination? From my own employee?"

"Sometimes they refuse to grow up." She shook her head and walked toward the door.

4

Phone calls to everyone on Dorey's list with vague mentions of lost jewelry had failed to yield the owner of the ring. Since she had Harry's blessing to wear it, she started the next day. Normally she didn't wear jewelry at work, but the ring was so dainty, it didn't snag her gloves when she put them on. Plus, she just loved wearing it.

The day her grandmother had given her the first turquoise ring, Dorey had been fourteen, and Grandma had taken her shopping. Just the two of them. They'd had lunch and taken a drive through the park, then they'd gone to the mall.

Dorey had admired the ring beneath the glass case in the jewelry store but didn't think much about it. She walked over to look at some necklaces across the store. A few minutes later, Grandma bought her the ring. Dorey tried to refuse, saying it wasn't her birthday or anything. But her grandmother insisted.

Grandma died four months later.

That Dorey lost the ring caused a lot of guilt for a long time. Maybe that's why this ring was so special. It made her think of a woman who was so sweet and caring, she'd bought her granddaughter a present—just because.

When she got to work that morning, she checked the schedule right away, as usual. Knowing who was, or wasn't, coming in helped her to plan for the day. She leaned down to get a better look at Mae's computer screen. Hallelujah. Her day was mostly full. Several harder patients, which would be more work for her, but she was thrilled just to have warm bodies to fill her chair.

Mae came into the reception area. "Good morning."

"Morning, Mae."

"Didn't think you liked jewelry."

"What?" She glanced down to where Mae was looking at the turquoise ring. "Oh, yeah, I do."

"Never saw you wear any before. Thought maybe it was a religious thing or something."

"Uh, no." Dorey bit her lip, trying not to laugh. As much jewelry as the receptionist wore, she must be totally anti-religion.

"Well, anyway, it's pretty."

"Thank you." Time to change the subject. No use having to answer a lot of questions about it when Harry didn't want Mae and Luanne to have dibs on the ring. Dorey pointed to the computer screen. "Looks like we had some calls for patients wanting in?"

"Several called right at the end of the day yesterday. Like we were running a sale. Never know what gets into people."

"Whatever their reasons, I'm glad someone will be here."

Mae nodded, her glasses sliding to the end of her nose. "Me too."

Four long appointments later, Dorey was worn out and ready for lunch. She'd had two men, one woman, and a little boy who kept throwing fits and trying to kick her. Dorey escaped without a black eye, but it had been touch and go for a while. Thank goodness people had shown up. How refreshing to be able to do her job.

Time for a break. Dorey grabbed her purse and headed toward the door.

"Dorey?"

She turned.

Mae held out the phone. "Another call for you."

Who this time? Her family always called her cell number. With a sigh, just wanting to get out of the office for a while, Dorey took the phone. "Hello? This is Dorey." She waited but heard nothing. What was going on? Just as she started to take the phone away from her ear, she heard it.

A high-pitched keening, like someone in terrible pain. The screech went right through her, making her shiver. "Hello? Do you need help? Can I—"

Click. The dial tone buzzed.

Mae sat there, frowning. "Who was it?"

"I don't know. Just someone making a strange sound."

Mae shook her head. "We seriously need Caller ID around here. Then we'd know who was wasting our time with crank calls."

Dorey nodded. Why was everyone acting so odd lately? Scaring people with masks, making prank phone calls. Whatever. She was too tired to care now.

She was almost to her car when Harry caught up with her. "Hey, since we have a little extra time for lunch, I was gonna get some pizza. Wanna go?"

When Dorey was little, if Harry would have included her in his plans with his friends, she'd have leaped for joy, done cartwheels and backflips. Now, little flutters of nervous excitement trotted up her spine and her palms were sweaty. Why would she be nervous? It was Harry, for Pete's sake.

"Yeah, sure." She smiled, hoping he wouldn't notice her anxiety.

They hopped in his truck and headed for a pizza place six blocks away. Once seated and with their food, Dorey got nervous again. This is so weird. Sitting here, just the two of us.

Harry leaned closer to the table. "You got quiet. What's up?"

"I'm fine." She fidgeted with the napkin in her lap.

"No, really. Is something wrong?"

That was the problem, wasn't it? Harry knew her too well. Since she was seven. Maybe hanging around him and her now-brother-in-law in her younger years was back to bite her. Since seventeen-year-old Gordon had been at their house so often to see Dorey's sixteen-year-old sister, Eva, twelve-year-old Harry migrated to wherever his older brother had been.

When Harry looked at Dorey now, did he see a little giggling girl who pestered him constantly and followed him around begging for piggyback rides? Or a woman in her twenties who …

Who, what? Why was she questioning her relationship with Harry now? Nothing had changed except she worked for him. And they were still friends. Nothing more. Even though she wished it were more.

"Dorey?" Harry's frown told her she'd daydreamed a little too long.

"Sorry, just … a lot on my mind, I guess."

His glance lowered to her hand. "The ring?"

"The … oh. Yeah." She looked down. "Just thinking about who it belongs to." Glad for something to do, she twisted the ring around on her finger. Why were her hands shaking? She let go of the ring and stuffed her hands in the pockets of her scrubs.

"Like I told ya, hang onto it, and if no one claims it in a few weeks, consider it yours. Besides, it looks good on you." He winked. He'd been doing that lately. Had he done it before? She couldn't remember.

Heat crept up her neck to her face. Harry was doing that more and more. Giving her compliments. Teasing her, but not always like he used to. Sometimes when he paid her attention now, she got all quivery inside, like when she'd been dating—

Whoa. Dating? Harry? That would be like dating her—

Dorey, he's not your brother.

She studied him for a minute as he tucked into his meal. He really was handsome. Had he always been, and she'd been oblivious? But it's Harry. True, he was the same guy she'd followed around like a puppy for all those years.

But ...

Now when she looked at him, there was something different. Something more. A quiet strength. A baritone voice. A masculine square jaw and wide shoulders. His dark eyes looking right into hers. And those lips ... how would it feel if he were to kiss—

"So anyway, I told her to just fill it in with whoever."

"Uh ... what?" Dorey blinked.

He raised one eyebrow. "Mae ... the schedule? Where did you go just now?"

"Sorry." She picked up her drink and took a sip from the straw.

Harry raised one corner of his mouth.

Here it comes ... the teasing. She should have known he couldn't resist.

"Well, isn't that just fine?" He sighed dramatically. "Take a girl to lunch and get ignored."

Dorey laughed. Inside, though, his words burrowed into her mind and wouldn't leave. Take a girl to lunch. Did Harry think this was a date?

Did she?

But he didn't mean it that way. He was her boss. Her friend. Harry was just being silly in saying take a girl out. Being nice in asking her to lunch. She relaxed and finished her pizza.

Harry and her on a date ... She sputtered a laugh.

His grin reappeared. "What'd I miss? Something funny?" He

leaned closer. "Come on, I could use a good laugh. My second patient this morning chomped down on my finger." He flexed his hand. "I don't think he meant to, but you never know."

Dorey bit her lip. She couldn't tell him what she'd really been thinking. "Oh, it was nothing." *What can I say?* Instead, she gave a shrug. If Harry knew her real thoughts, she'd be mortified. Better not to say anything at all.

Checking his watch, he said, "Hey, we'd better go. Let me go pay real quick."

Dorey nodded and stood. "Sure." Biting her lip so she wouldn't grin, she followed him outside to the truck. She had to stop herself from laughing out loud at her ridiculous thoughts. That they'd been on a date.

"You sure look happy, Dorey. That excited to get back to work?"

Darn her expressions. Harry could usually read them like a cheap novel. "Nah, just happy thoughts."

"Hmm." He turned his attention to driving them back.

Dorey was relieved he hadn't said anything more as they walked into the office. Her discomfort level went skyward at the thought. Why was she obsessing about whether it had been a date or not?

You know why. Because you wished it had been.

Shaking her head, she forced away the image and went to her operatory.

Mae appeared in the doorway. "Your patient, Mrs. Johnson, is here."

"Thanks." Dorey nodded. "Be right there."

She put her purse away, washed her hands, and went out to greet her next appointment. Then groaned. There sat Dr. Conners, chatting away with her patient. Now Dorey would be behind from the start. Great.

Even though Harry didn't like it when Dr. Conners came in to just hang out and cause trouble, Mae thought he was wonderful and would never tell him he wasn't welcome. Maybe Mae would prefer to have Dr. Conners back and Harry working somewhere else.

The retired doctor sat there, patting Mrs. Johnson's hand. "Now, don't be afraid when you go to see that girl. If you don't want her to clean your teeth, which of course she's hardly qualified to do, just tell her so."

Mrs. Johnson smiled. "Thank you, Dr. Conners, for your advice. I had no idea that hygienists were so undertrained."

They obviously hadn't spotted Dorey yet or they would have stopped their conversation. She backed up a step and hid around the corner, hoping Mae wouldn't pick that moment to appear. Dorey felt like a fool, naturally, but she was also livid. How dare he do that?

She'd have to tell Harry about it, though she didn't want to. He was already furious with the older man's interference. But he was trying to stop Dr. Conners from spreading his venom to the patients, so Dorey would have to fess up about it.

A few deep breaths to calm down and she rounded the corner. "Good afternoon, Mrs. Johnson." Barely glancing at the man, she said, "Oh, hello, Dr. Conners." Maybe her tone would get across the point that he wasn't welcome in the office.

He glared at Dorey and stood. "Miss Cameron." Turning back to the patient, he said, "Don't forget what I've told you." Without another word or glance at Dorey, he stomped out of the waiting room.

Where did evil dentists go when their missions had been accomplished? Did he have a lair somewhere? Dorey heard the main office door open and close.

Thank goodness. Now she could get on with—

Uh-oh. Mrs. Johnson was frowning. The afternoon should be loads of fun ...

Mrs. Johnson, or as Dorey referred to her in her mind, Mrs. Prune-face, finally allowed Dorey to do a cleaning. Well, she let her polish her teeth but not scale off the tartar. So, they were really only half clean, which Dorey hated. Made her feel like she hadn't done her best.

When Dorey had done all she could get away with, she left the operatory and got Harry's attention. He followed her into the hall, and she told him she hadn't been allowed to do everything and that Dr. Conners had made another unwelcome visit.

He nodded. "All right. I'll say something, but I guess we should be glad she let you do anything after what Dr. Conners probably told her."

"Yep."

The entire time Harry did Mrs. Johnson's exam, she frowned. When he mentioned he'd really like Dorey to scale the teeth too, her answer was an unequivocal *No*.

With a sigh, Dorey waited as her patient left, muttering something not very nice. Then, Dorey cleaned the room for her next patient.

Mrs. Goins stepped into Dorey's room, with her mouth turned down at the corners.

Not again. Dorey groaned. She pasted a false smile on her face. "Hi, Mrs. Goins." Would she not let Dorey do a cleaning either?

"Hi." She plopped down in the chair and set her purse in her lap.

After putting the napkin around the patient's neck, Dorey asked, "How've you been?" Then, she held her breath and waited.

Mrs. Goins flipped her hand. "Oh, fine."

Fine? That was an improvement. She leaned the chair back. "Any problems?"

"I do have a concern, but I'm guessing you meant about my teeth."

Dorey blinked. "Um, yes."

"I got the strangest phone call right before I left the house to come here."

Dorey let out a breath. Maybe Mrs. Goins wasn't upset about being at the office. "So, was the call bad news?"

"Not exactly. Well, what happened was, someone called claiming to be from your office."

"Oh?" Those calls she'd gotten, when no one had said anything when she'd answered and the one with the screeching noise ...

"But I was pretty sure he wasn't."

"Dr. MacKinley doesn't usually call patients at home unless it's post-op after an extraction or something, to check on them."

"That's what I figured. It's always Mae who calls about things like that, and I'd know her voice anywhere. I asked the person some questions. Told him I wasn't sure he could be from the office. That I didn't appreciate some prank caller wasting my time for no good reason. Gave him a good piece of my mind."

"Who was it?"

Mrs. Goins gave a shrug. "I never found out. He kind of stuttered something unintelligible and hung up."

"Hmm. Weird." Why were all these rude, strange people calling and hanging up all of a sudden?

"Exactly."

Relieved that the woman didn't seem to be having qualms about being there, Dorey started to open the sterile packet of instruments. As she pulled them out of the pack and laid them side by side on her tray, she paused. Could it have been Dr. Conners calling her? He would know all the patients and could easily find their numbers in the phone book.

No, that didn't make sense. Mrs. Goins would have known his voice from being his patient before. Plus, he wouldn't have had time to call her if he was sitting in the reception area talking to someone else. Then who in the world would have done it?

She finished the cleaning, Harry did the exam, and Mrs. Goins left the office, smiling.

Game over. Check and mate.

Her next patient was Mr. O'Leary. Good grief. Another grumpy one. Maybe he would be in a better mood than usual today. By the law of averages, he had to be pleasant sometime, right?

No such luck.

Mr. O'Leary frowned when she asked him to follow her to the room, placed the patient napkin on him, took X-rays, and started the cleaning. What a moody man. He grumbled and complained with a vengeance, as if he were trying to win an award. Where were the nice people? She knew they existed because she'd met some. Thank goodness for Mrs. Goins.

Dorey finished the cleaning, took off her gloves, tossed them in the trash, and washed her hands.

"That ring …"

Mr. O'Leary's voice startled her as she dried her hands.

"I think I've seen it before. Where did you get it?"

Shocked that he'd notice her jewelry, she stammered, "I, um … found it."

"Found it? A ring like that?" He glared at her. "That doesn't sound likely."

Was he calling her a liar? What would a grumpy old man know about women's rings anyway? She crossed her arms over her chest.

"Something like that belongs to a person who *deserves* to wear it." He slid a glance sideways at her, making it clear she didn't fit his description.

Dorey's heart plummeted. Maybe it belonged to his wife, and he'd seen her wear it but now couldn't place where he'd seen it. Dorey tried to remember exactly when Mrs. O'Leary had last been into the office.

"It's the strangest thing. That ring …" He scratched his head.

Dorey waited for him to say more, but he didn't. She hoped she was wrong. That it wasn't his wife's. If the rightful person came to claim it, she'd have to give it up.

Mr. O'Leary didn't say anything further, but kept giving her dirty looks, as if she were a thief not good enough to wear such a nice-looking ring. At least he hadn't laid claim to it for his wife. Yet.

That evening after her shower, she changed into sweats and relaxed on the couch. Weatherby had shown up after being gone for two days and had eaten everything in sight. Now he was curled up in her lap, bathing his paws. Had been for ten minutes.

"Honestly, Weatherby, your paws should be clean by now." She lifted one, earning a growl from the cat. "So, why do they still look dingy?"

He scowled at her and washed the paw one more time, as if her touching it had tainted it somehow.

"Whatever." She laughed.

The cat gave her the stink-eye, jumped down, and ran out the kitty door. Ten minutes later, he was back.

Dorey frowned. He had something yellow hanging from one side of his mouth. A piece of paper? "Come here, Weatherby. Let me see."

He growled when she tried to take it. It ripped down the middle. Before Dorey could pry the rest from his teeth, he took off again.

Dorey looked down at the paper. The edges were wet with cat spit. It had some writing on it, but part of it must have also been on the half Weatherby still had. She spread the small piece of paper out on her lap.

NG BACK.

NG? What was the other part of that word? Or did the two letters stand for something?

Feeling silly, she shook her head and grinned. Who knew

where her cat had gotten the paper or who it belonged to? Probably had nothing to do with her anyway. Might have been something a neighbor had dropped outside. Or else, Weatherby had gone dumpster diving again behind the apartments. It could have been worse.

5

"What happened this time?" Dorey stared at the same schedule the next morning. The one that had looked so promising at the end of the previous day. No holes. Just nice and smooth.

Mae peered over her glasses. "More bizarre excuses. One is stranger than the last. I'm getting worried about it. I mean about the money that isn't coming in the door to pay the bills." She raised a single eyebrow. Was she indicating Dorey getting paid even when her patients didn't show? That was standard, though, for lots of offices. Ones that didn't work on commission.

Still, Dorey worried about that very thing. Maybe she could convince Harry to switch her to commission. She'd make less money, but at least she wouldn't have anything to feel guilty about. And Mae would stop needling her.

Even though her morning had crumbled, her first patient was, so far, still supposed to come. That was a relief. If it made the day seem long when she had a lot of openings. It was even worse when the day started with one.

When her patient didn't show at fifteen minutes past the appointment time, Dorey chalked it up to yet another no-show.

With a sigh, she looked around. She'd recently restocked her room. The lab. Harry's operatory. Filed charts for Mae. And thoroughly cleaned the room and chair over and above what they did after each patient.

That left the job of sharpening her instruments. Her least favorite duty on the planet. But Dorey literally had nothing else to do. And she wasn't going to just stand there. She opened the drawer and pulled out the first packet of instruments, ready to tackle the drudgery.

"Dorey." Mae stood in the doorway. "Your first patient just now showed up. He apologized for being so late. But since you don't have anyone now, do you want to go ahead and see him?"

Relieved, Dorey nodded. "Definitely. Go ahead and send him back. I'm all ready."

A few seconds later, Mr. Anderson rounded the corner. "Good morning, young lady."

She'd always loved his cheery greetings. "Same to you, Mr. Anderson. How're you doing?"

He pulled a handkerchief from his back pocket and mopped his forehead. "Well, I've been better, but definitely worse."

Dorey blinked and waited. She knew there'd be more coming. He always had a story.

He sat down on the edge of her patient chair. "You see, I was on my way here this morning, on time, mind you, and I had a bit of a mishap."

Uh-oh. "I hope everything's okay." She placed the patient napkin around his neck and set the clasp.

He turned, settled his legs on the chair, then slumped against the back. "It's the strangest thing. I had parked a few blocks from here and planned to walk the rest of the way. I do that on purpose. Doctor says it's a good way to get exercise. Anyway, I was stepping off the curb to cross the street when I heard squealing tires. I turned around to see a white van racing by, horn honking, really close to me."

Dorey gasped and touched his shoulder. "Oh, my goodness. But you aren't hurt, are you?"

"Just my pride. And my belt."

She raised her eyebrows. "Belt?"

He pointed to his pants. Sure enough, there wasn't a belt. Instead, he wore a bungee cord used to secure things in the backs of trucks so they wouldn't blow away.

"I … see." She bit her lip. The bright red bungee cord was quite the fashion statement with his yellow shirt and faded blue jeans.

"When I dove for the sidewalk—quite the feat at my age, let me tell you—my belt snapped right in two. I didn't want to show up here with my drawers around my ankles, so I grabbed this here cord from my truck."

Her nostrils flared as she tried not to laugh. She patted his shoulder. "I'm just so glad you weren't seriously hurt."

"Yep. Just my pride."

"And your belt."

He gave her the thumbs-up sign. "You got that right, sister."

She leaned the chair back and put on her protective gear. "So, the van—I take it the person didn't stop to see if you were all right?"

"No. The person kept right on going, like he'd chased nothing more than a squirrel off the road. The van windows were tinted. I couldn't see who was driving."

"That's terrible." He must have been so scared.

He nodded. "If things had turned out differently, not only would I have missed this appointment, I'd be in the morgue. The van didn't hit me, just scared me. But what if I'd cracked my head when I fell on the sidewalk?"

Dorey shivered. He'd come within inches of death. She glanced down at him, thankful he'd come out unscathed.

Except for his pretty belt.

After Dorey cleaned Mr. Anderson's teeth, she told Harry

she was ready. He was sitting in his chair just chatting with his patient, so he excused himself and followed her back to her operatory.

Harry shook hands with Dorey's patient. "Good to see you, Mr. Anderson. How goes it for you?"

Unfortunately, Dorey hadn't had time to fill Harry in. Besides, Mr. Anderson would be able to tell it a whole lot better than she could.

His mouth turned down at the corners as he told Harry his tale. "I really did like that belt too. It was handmade. My brother had brought it back for me from a trip to Greece. It had these little Greek symbols carved into it."

The man was more upset about that than nearly being run over?

Harry's eyes widened. "Wow. I'm so glad to see you're in one piece."

"Yep. 'Cept for the belt."

Harry shook his head. "Any idea who it was? Any markings on the van?"

"Well, I don't think so, but then, I was running for all I was worth, so there wasn't much time to take a gander at any writing there may have been."

Harry nodded. "Of course." He patted Mr. Anderson's shoulder much like Dorey had done. "I'm relieved you weren't injured."

"Except my—"

"Belt, yes, of course."

"There was one thing, though." Mr. Anderson frowned. "Right as the van took off, the window lowered a crack, and something flew out. It was some sort of mask."

Dorey widened her eyes. What was going on? Too many crazy people in the world.

Harry leaned Mr. Anderson back in the chair and did the exam. "Looks good as usual."

"Thank you. Your girl here does a good job."

"Thank you." Dorey smiled as heat rose up her face.

Harry gave her a smile and then turned his attention back to Mr. Anderson. "She does at that."

"Pretty to look at too."

Harry gave Dorey a sly grin "No argument there."

Mr. Anderson chuckled and got up from the chair. He ambled out of the room. A few seconds later, Dorey could hear him telling Mae about his *new* belt.

Whenever she got embarrassed, her skin turned a bright red. No need letting Harry see it if she could help it. Dorey covered her face with her hands.

"Hey." Harry's warm hand connected with hers, tugging hers back down. "You okay?"

She nodded. "Um, just embarrassed."

"Why?"

She shrugged and started to clean up. Now that she had Harry here, though, she needed to bring up her idea of him paying her commission instead. When she turned around, Harry leaned against her counter with his arms crossed.

"Dorey, what's goin' on?"

Stepping to the doorway, Dorey peeked out. Mae was sitting at her desk, but she wasn't on the phone. She didn't really want the receptionist to hear her personal business. "Got a minute?"

"Sure. Let's go to my office."

As Dorey followed Harry, her face heated again. If another man suggested getting her alone in a room, he might have something in mind. But not Harry. Though Dorey wished he would.

Stop it.

She closed the door behind her. "Sure you have time? Because it can wait if you don't."

"Mrs. Hanover's getting numb. What's up?"

"It's just that ..." Dorey wrung her hands and paced in front of him. "With a lot of the patients not showing up and me still making—"

He held up his hand. "Is this about money again?"

"Yeah." She focused on him. "Because I feel so guilty about making money when I'm not seeing patients. Maybe you could pay me on a commission basis instead. If the cancellations happened just every now and then, that would be something different, but this has been days and days of me hardly seeing anyone, and I—"

"Don't worry about it." He stepped forward and grabbed her upper arms.

"But I—"

"No. Let me worry about all of that. You do a great job. You heard Mr. Anderson just now."

"It's only that—"

"I want you here. I like having you around. And things will pick up for you."

"How can you be so sure?"

He dropped his hands from her arms, and she was suddenly chilled. "Our patients will stop having such rotten luck. Besides, there must be a lot of patients who won't listen to Dr. Conners."

"You make it sound so easy."

"It is. It'll be okay. Believe me?"

Dorey lifted one eyebrow. "Hmmm. Believe you? That's a trick question. I'm remembering all the times you wanted me to believe you, and I found out later you were telling me a bunch of fibs."

His mouth dropped open as if he was really insulted. "Like what?"

"Like when I was little, and you were in middle school and you told me you'd learned how to tie your shoes that special way when you were in the army. I didn't remember you ever being gone long enough to have been in the army, but I believed you, because you were you."

He snorted.

"And the time you convinced me that those walnuts each had a prize inside, so I'd smash them open with a hammer. Then you ate them, and I never found a prize." She stomped her foot. But she wasn't seven years old anymore. She glanced down at her shoe and back up. How embarrassing.

"That's just stuff boys tell girls to try to sound important." Harry smirked.

"How do I know you're not doing that now? Or just saying it to make me feel better?"

"Because we're not kids anymore." He stepped close again and rubbed his hand up and down her arm. "I promise, I'll never lie to you again. Got it?"

She nodded.

With a sigh, he said, "There's something else you want to say."

In the worst way, she wanted to insist that he pay her commission. That it would be fairer to him when she wasn't busy. Her hourly wage was nothing to sneeze at. It wasn't like she made minimum wage, for Pete's sake. But once Harry made up his mind, that was that. If she tried to argue, he'd only end up teasing her about something again.

With a quick shake of her head, she said, "Nope. Nothing. Nada."

"I'm not sure I believe you, but I'm guessing you have a good reason for not saying it." He checked his watch. "Listen, I gotta go. Remember, if you need to tell me anything. I'll listen."

She wanted him to stop trying to take care of everything. But a tiny part of her heart warmed that he wanted to.

6

After her shower, Dorey changed into comfy pajamas and vegged out in front of the TV. She eyed the kitty door for the tenth time. Where was Weatherby? She knew she shouldn't worry about him. He did stay away for a couple of days at a time pretty often. Still, she wished he'd show up. Maybe if he got enough to eat out on his own, hunting for mice or whatever, he might stay away longer.

Then, there was always the possibility that he was mooching off other people too. Dorey snorted. Yeah, that sounded like him. A sneak and a thief. Still, she did love the conniving little furball.

She grabbed a handful of buttered popcorn from her bowl. Not the best diet, and a hygienist certainly knew better. But hey, she lived alone. Who was going to tattle on her? Besides, popcorn was cheap. And she still hadn't been to the grocery.

A loud squeak came from her entryway. The kitty door. Dorey set down her bowl and turned.

Weatherby came trotting into the living room. He eyed her as if she were a landing strip, then leaped up in the air and gracefully perched on her lap.

Dorey eyed his paws, as she always did. "Dirty again. And don't tell me that once you wash them, they'll be white. 'Cause I know that's not true. Maybe your tongue is defective."

Weatherby had his head turned and chin pointed down so she couldn't see his face very well. "Hey there, you need to look at Mama when she talks to you."

Her cat mumbled something incoherent. Nothing like his normal wail that was his version of a meow. Dorey gently turned his head until she could see him.

"Weatherby. What's that in your mouth?" He angled his head away again.

Leaning down, Dorey saw it was something black, a few inches long. "What in the world do you have this time?"

Ignoring the cat's growl, she tugged the object from between his jaws. It was a wadded-up piece of cloth. She tossed it in on the floor, intending to throw it in the trash later.

"What were you doing with that? And where did you steal it from?" She shook her head. "I don't know what to do with you, young man."

The cat stopped licking his paw suddenly and stared right at her. Weird. It was as if he understood her. He meowed so loud, so pitifully, that the hairs on the back of her neck rose. Yeah, that sounded more like his usual squall.

She scratched under his chin. "Don't worry. I wouldn't do anything. I love you, you silly cat." Weatherby purred, turned in a circle, and plopped down on her lap with a solid whump.

Dorey went back to watching the movie but couldn't really get into it. The hero looked way too much like Harry for her comfort. She switched it off and set down the remote.

"Maybe I'll just read." Reaching for her mystery novel on the end table, she turned back to find Weatherby merrily munching on popcorn.

With a frown, Dorey eyed the popcorn bowl on the coffee

table, a good foot away from the couch, to her cat on her lap. He hadn't budged from his spot. So how did he get it?

"You are just a little magician, aren't you?"

Weatherby looked up at her and gave what looked for all the world like a great big grin.

Dorey laughed. "I sure am glad you came home tonight. I missed you." His dish needed food, but she longed to hold him a little bit longer. Besides, he was filling up on popcorn. The more she petted his back, the louder his purr boomed from somewhere deep inside.

Rolling onto his side, he peered over the edge of the couch, then slid off Dorey's lap and hopped back up. In his mouth was the black cloth.

Dorey shook her head. "What is so interesting about a piece of material?"

He whipped his head vigorously back and forth, like the cloth was live prey he needed to shake the life out of. When he opened his mouth to meow, the cloth dropped in a wet hunk, right on Dorey's chest.

"Gee, thanks for that." She grimaced, plucking the soggy mess from her shirt. When she turned to give it a toss, something caught her eye. Another color, muted but different, like a shade of dark gray, edged around a tear in the cloth. Curious, Dorey peeled apart the material. A second rip was there with the same gray surrounding it. When the fabric was pulled all the way taut …

Not rips in the cloth. Two eyeholes. It was a mask! Dorey sucked in a breath.

She dropped the thing like it was contagious. Another mask? Why would anyone—?

Her cell phone rang, and she jumped. Not many people had that number. Was it the person who'd been trying to scare everyone with masks? Heart thumping hard, she picked it up from the table. Caller ID said it was Harry. She let out a long, slow breath. "Hello?"

"Hey, Dorey."

"Hey …" Thank goodness it was only him. She gave herself a little shake. Stop being so paranoid. So, her cat found a mask. Big deal.

"Listen, a few of the other dentists in town are going exploring at one of the caves tomorrow.

"Okay …" But was it only coincidence that her cat had found one right after her patients had been scared by masks too? Maybe—

"Wanna tag along?"

What? Jarred from her previous musings, Dorey frowned at the phone. Didn't tagging along make her sound like a little kid again, wanting to go everywhere that her sister and Harry and his brother went?

"Dorey? You there?"

"Um … well …"

"Don't feel like you have to or anything. It sounded like fun. Tomorrow is Saturday, after all. Unless …"

"Unless what?"

"Maybe you have plans. A date … or something?"

A date? Ha! She couldn't even remember the last one. "No. I don't have any plans."

"Great! How about I pick you up at ten tomorrow morning?"

Was that emphatic great because she didn't have a date or because she was free to go with him?

Dorey laughed. "I don't remember saying I would go."

"Oh."

She could picture his smile faltering, his eyes turning done at the corners.

"Hey, listen, no pressure, I just—"

"Sure. Ten is fine."

"Really?"

Now his face was probably lit up, eyes wide, big smile.

She smirked at the phone as if Harry could see her. "Yeah, 'cause I don't have anything better to do."

"Hey."

"Joking."

Harry laughed. "I knew that."

"Sure, you did."

"Okay, see you at ten."

She held up her hand. Why? It wasn't as if he could see her. "Oh, Harry?"

"Yeah."

"Just one thing."

"What's that?"

She drummed the fingers of her other hand on the side of the couch. "Sometimes I get sort of, uh, nervous ... in caves."

He sputtered a laugh but stopped when she didn't join in. "Are you serious?"

"Uh-huh." No sense telling him she'd rather have a tooth yanked without anesthesia than go inside one.

"Then why did you say you'd go?"

"'Cause you got all sad-sounding, and I didn't want to hurt your feelings." *And because I'd jump at any excuse to spend time with you. Even in a cave.*

He didn't speak for several seconds. "That's sweet." He cleared his throat. "Don't feel like you have to go or anything. But if you do, I promise to keep you safe in the scary cave."

"See you at ten." Dorey chewed on her bottom lip.

She clicked off from the call and put the phone on the table. *What did I just do?* Though the caves had always been a local attraction, she'd avoided them ever since she was little, and her dad had taken them there to explore. She hadn't realized at the time it would be totally dark once deep inside, and there were bats. Blech.

After taking a deep breath and letting it slowly out, she

closed her eyes and rested her head back on a pillow. *You can do this, Dorey. You're not a little kid anymore.* Besides, it would be a great excuse to stand extremely close to Harry.

Why did it seem like he was asking her to do more and more things with him lately? Or was it her imagination? They'd always done things together. Maybe the difference was that now, Harry didn't act as if he minded having her tag along. Was he doing it because he felt sorry for her? Because she lived alone? But he lived alone too. He didn't even have a pet.

No, something was definitely changing between them. At least on her part. While it was true she'd always wanted to be wherever he was and had a crush on him, the feelings she had now were deeper. Truer.

Adult.

Dorey slunk further down on the couch and pressed Weatherby against her chest. What if Harry still considered her as his brother's much younger sister-in-law? Someone to keep an eye on and take care of. Hadn't he said that very thing about tomorrow? That he'd keep her safe?

With a sigh, Dorey picked up her book. Maybe if she read about someone else's mysterious adventures, she could stop thinking about wanting to kiss Harry.

7

Harry showed up at exactly ten. As he stepped inside the apartment, Weatherby launched himself right at Harry's chest. Lucky for both of them, Harry caught the cat before getting scratched. "The infamous thief?"

"Yeah. Meet Weatherby." She hopped on one foot as she struggled to get her other shoe on, then took the cat from him and set him on the couch.

Weatherby, a disillusioned expression on his face, flipped his tail in her direction and promptly made his way to the kitty door and outside.

"I'll have to pay for that later." She pointed her thumb toward the door.

"Pay for?" Harry raised his eyebrows.

"You've never had a cat. They're kinda high-strung."

Weatherby stuck his head back inside the kitty door, hissed in their general direction, and left again.

"Ah." He eyed her as she yanked on the stuck zipper of her windbreaker. "Need some help?"

Here we go. I'm a little kid again. "If you wouldn't mind."

Harry stepped closer and grabbed the end of the zipper. "It's stuck."

Dorey snorted. "Brilliant deduction, Doc. No wonder you were at the top of your graduating class."

"You want my help or not?" He gave her the stink-eye.

Unable to hold back her grin, she nodded.

He smiled back and tried the zipper again. "What the heck did you do to this? The teeth are all crowded together in that one spot."

"Of course, you'd compare this to teeth."

"That's what they're called. Zipper teeth." He pointed to her midsection.

Though Dorey knew that already, hearing Harry say it in such a serious tone sent her into a fit of giggles.

"What's so funny?"

She sputtered another laugh. After slapping her hand over her mouth, she said from between her fingers, "N-nothing."

Harry gave a long-suffering sigh. "Honestly ..." He bent down and studied the zipper more closely. He raised back up and ran his hand through his hair. "I need leverage."

"Uh-oh."

"What?"

"When I hear you use that term at work, it usually means you're gonna rip some poor unsuspecting patient's wisdom tooth out."

"I wouldn't say unsuspecting. I mean, they do make the appointment for—"

She held up her hand. "Anyway, what did you mean ... about the teeth, the zipper teeth?" She bit her lip as another giggle threatened to pop out.

"Turn around."

"Huh? Why?" She put her hands on her hips.

"Why do you have to question everything I say?"

"Why do you have to be so bossy?" She tapped her foot on the floor.

Harry leaned close enough she could smell his aftershave. "'Cause I'm your boss."

"Ha-ha."

"I'm trying to help you so we're not standing here all day. Turn around."

She raised one eyebrow, remembering all the times he'd said those words, she'd complied, and then she was sorry. One time she'd turned her back on him, and when she peeked over her shoulder, he'd slipped on a scary monster's mask. Mask. Why did she have to think of that? Lots of other times, he'd grabbed her and tickled her ribs the moment she'd turned away.

"Nope." The man was hard to trust.

"Dorey ..."

She didn't want to, but Harry did have a point. If they didn't get going soon, his friends would have to wait for them at the cave before going in.

"Fine." She turned away, not knowing what in the world he'd do.

But when he came up behind her, pressed his front tightly against her back and wrapped his arms around her waist, she nearly melted in satisfaction.

"Ahhh ..."

"Hmmm? You say something?"

"No." She straightened, bumping into him.

He let out a long breath. "Okay, maybe don't pop your head up like that. I'd like to keep my chin intact."

Still in the throes of ecstasy of being held by him, the ache on the top of her head was delayed. "Sorry."

She raised her hand to rub her head, but he caught her by the wrist and lowered her arm to her side.

"Let's try that again. Hold still and I'll see if I can get a good hold on that tongue."

She bit her lip. *There he goes again with dental comparisons.* But she forced herself not to move. Or laugh. Harry's arms snaked around her again. The heat built up in the nearly nonexistent space between them, and it was all Dorey could do not to wilt.

Something popped and zinged.

"There ya go." He dropped his arms and pulled away.

Now Dorey was cold. *Come back. I liked it where you were before.* Instead, she turned to face him. "Thanks."

He shrugged. "It's what I do."

She tugged the zipper up and down to test it. "Repair stuck zippers?"

"Take care of you."

"Hey, I've told you before I can take care of—"

His hand shot up fast, his fingers covering her lips. "We can talk about it later. Right now, they're waiting for us at the cave. Ready to go?"

She nodded, but a chill ran down her spine. In all the hullabaloo of getting her jacket fixed and standing so close to Harry, she'd forgotten where they'd planned to go.

Bother.

They headed out to Harry's truck. Once inside, he waited, refusing to start the engine until her seatbelt was securely fastened. She rolled her eyes.

"What would I tell your sister and parents if you went flying out the window on our drive? They'd never invite me over for supper ever again. No more fried chicken. Or pumpkin pie. It would be quite the tragedy."

"Just drive." She punched him in the shoulder.

He laughed as he pulled out of her apartment parking lot and onto the street. The grouping of caves was twenty minutes away. Harry had turned on the radio and was warbling to a song she kind of knew but was considered old by the time she was in high school. She shook her head at him and then watched the scenery go by as they made their way out onto the nearest highway.

The closer they got to the caves, the more Dorey's stomach threatened to revolt. She wrapped her arms around her middle. *You'll be fine. You can do this.*

Harry pulled the truck into the parking lot situated near the entrance to the caves. He grinned and hopped out, then came around to open her door. Dorey forced herself to let go of her middle and step out of the truck.

Slowly, she tilted her head back as she surveyed the dark mouth of the nearest cave. Her legs trembled. She checked to make sure Harry hadn't noticed. No, thank goodness. He was waving at three other guys, maybe in their thirties to forties. Dorey had seen them at local dental meetings but hadn't met them before. She looked around.

Is this it?

Was she the only girl?

When Harry had said other guys, she'd assumed he'd lumped in guys and girls, maybe if some of them brought wives or girlfriends or that some of the dentists were women. Guess not. Then why did Harry make such a big deal about wanting her to come? Wouldn't he have rather spent time with just his friends?

She smiled and shook hands with the others when Harry made the introductions. Forcing her gaze away from the cave, she took deep, slow breaths.

"Ready?" He patted her on the back.

No. "Yes." Dorey had already told Harry on the phone that caves bothered her. No sense in bringing it up again since they were already here. She followed the guys up the short trail that led to the first cave.

The path inclined slightly as dirt changed to rock. The men all reached into pockets or backpacks and removed flashlights. Wait! She hadn't brought one. Now she'd really be left in the dark. Why hadn't she—?

"Here." Something nudged her hand. She looked down at a long yellow flashlight Harry held out.

"Thanks." Harry really was so sweet. He always took care of everything. She switched it on.

"You're not going to wait until we're inside?" Harry lowered his eyebrows. "You'll wear the battery out."

They were almost to the cave. If the battery ran out that quickly, they had problems. She shook her head quickly. "I want to be prepared."

He gave a one-shouldered shrug. "Suit yourself."

"Don't I usually?"

He laughed. "Always."

Dorey was last as they entered the darkened mouth of the cave. An instant drop in temperature made her glad for her warm long-sleeved tee-shirt beneath her windbreaker. And also, that her jacket was now zipped. *Thanks, Harry.*

She grabbed the back of his jeans at the belt loop. With the glow from her flashlight, she caught his bewildered expression as he peered over his shoulder at her.

"Need something?"

"Nope." She clung tighter to the rough denim and stayed with him, step for step. *He's going to scold me any minute for standing too close.* But he didn't.

The beam of her flashlight caught on something dark on a far wall above a narrow ledge. "What's that?"

Harry stopped and aimed his light in the same spot as hers. "Can't tell. Looks like ... a heart?"

"Could someone have carved it?"

"It wouldn't have been easy in stone, but I guess it's possible."

Dorey sighed. "Sweet. Maybe it was someone in love and he—"

"What makes you think it was a he?"

"I don't know." She tilted her head as she studied the carving. "I could just imagine a guy doing that for the girl he loves."

Harry snorted. "Not any guy I know."

Dorey stuck her tongue out at the back of Harry's head, remembering all the times she used to do the same thing when they were kids.

Well, he deserved it.

The path descended. Dorey had to balance herself with her arm along the slick, cold stone of the wall so she didn't tumble forward. But she still held onto Harry with her other hand.

When the path narrowed, the walls appeared to close in. Dorey gritted her teeth together. Don't think about that.

"Incoming!" yelled one of the guys up ahead.

Dorey jumped. Incoming what?

Harry ducked, so Dorey did too, coming face to face with his backside. Somehow, she still had her stranglehold on his belt loop, although barely.

"What was it?" She glanced around. "I never saw anything."

"Bat." Harry stood up straight again.

Dorey lost her grip on his jeans. "Bat?"

The memory of the one from her childhood, the black, squeaky thing that actually made contact with her hair as it fluttered around them, came back full force.

Dorey shrieked.

"What?" Harry stopped in his tracks and turned.

"The-b-bat."

He leaned around and looked behind her, using the beam from his flashlight to check things out. "I don't see it anymore. It's gone."

"O-okay." She tried to swallow but her throat was too dry.

"Dorey?" Harry stepped closer.

Without thinking, she leaned forward and pressed herself against his chest. His arms came around her shoulders.

"You—you're afraid of bats?"

She nodded into his jacket front, not caring that it would give her hair static electricity.

Harry turned a little and said over his shoulder. "Go on, guys. We'll catch up in a minute."

One of them said, "Sure."

The sound of footsteps decreased as the other men left them.

Harry pulled away and tilted Dorey's chin up. She could barely make out his face with the dim light from their flashlights. But she saw enough to know he was concerned.

"Dorey, what's going on?"

"I told you. I don't like bats." She huddled close again.

"Is that all?"

"Isn't that enough?" Their beady eyes, squeaky voices, creepy flapping wings.

"What I meant was, is there anything else you don't like about caves? You'd said before they make you nervous."

Oh, just everything. "No. That's it."

He pressed a comforting kiss to the top of her head. "If you're sure."

She nodded against his mouth. *Let's just stay right here. Your friends can figure out a way to edge around us when they head back this way, right?*

"All right, then." He took her free hand as she clung to her flashlight with the other. "That better?"

No. She nodded.

"Remember, I can't see you."

"Oh, uh. Yes. Better." *No. I don't mean it. Let's go back.*

He held onto her hand. They walked side by side when they could, but eventually she had to walk behind him again, clutching his hand. He had to be uncomfortable with his arm reaching back like that but never complained.

The air grew colder as they got farther into the depths of the cave. Dorey scrunched her shoulders and buried her chin inside her jacket. Voices carried from ahead, the sound bouncing all around them. It was hard to tell how close the other guys were.

As the path dipped, Harry stepped down.

Dorey tried to follow but her shoe slipped on a slick spot. "Harry!"

He let go of her hand as he turned and tried to catch her. Her weight and the downward path made that impossible. Dorey crashed down on top of him as his back smacked against the path.

"Oof!" Harry's breath released loudly.

Afraid to move for a few seconds, Dorey held still, listening to her own breathing, Harry's, and the constant drip of water from somewhere to their right.

"Not hurt, are you?" Harry's arm reached up and curled around her back.

She raised her head from his chest and peered down, though she couldn't see him very well. Both of their flashlights had gone flying off to the left, and only a faint shimmer was visible from them. "I think I'm okay. You?"

"I'll be sore tomorrow, but everything important is intact."

"You mean you have body parts that aren't important?"

He chuckled, his warm breath a welcome comfort against the cold air.

When his breath brushed across her lips, all she wanted to do was kiss him. No, that wasn't right. She needed to quit thinking like that. Bracing her hand on the rock beside her, she rolled off Harry, landing on the hard ground.

"Dorey?"

She heard the fabric of his jacket rustle, and the location of his voice told her he'd sat up too.

"What—"

"Nothing. Fine. I'm ..." She struggled to stand but couldn't find a good foothold.

"Wait." A few seconds later, Harry was standing, and his hand found hers in the darkness. "Hold on a second." Their hands nearly lost their grip.

What was he doing? She jumped when something was placed in her hand.

Oh, it was her flashlight. "Uh, thanks."

"You sure you're not hurt, Dorey?"

"I'm fine. Uh, maybe we should find your friends. Wouldn't want them to worry where we are."

He exhaled loudly enough for her to hear. "Yeah, let's keep going."

Harry took a trail that veered off to the left. How did he know where to go? There was more than one choice. She'd be toast if she was here by herself. But she never intended to be, so not a problem.

After a few minutes of zigzagging and stumbling, Dorey heard voices again. Harry must have been right. She smiled at the back of his head. Not a bad guy to have around in a crisis.

Or any other time.

The trail widened and then opened into what looked like a large room.

"Cool." Harry gave a wave to the other guys who were sitting on some sort of ledge. It looked like someone had carved a little couch into the wall. It really *was* cool.

But she still didn't like caves, overall.

They reached the guys. One of them—was it Dr. Vernon? — stood and gave Dorey his seat.

She glanced up. "Thanks."

"So," he said, looking between Dorey and Harry. "What happened back there?"

"Dorey's not fond of bats." Harry smirked.

"Was that all?" Dr. Vernon crossed his arms. "Thought maybe you two just wanted to be alone."

"No. I can see Dorey anytime at work." Harry laughed and shook his head.

Oh, he could, could he? Dorey fumed. Thanks a lot, Harry. *Makes me sound like a piece of your dental equipment.*

Dr. Vernon chuckled. "Yeah, well, I wouldn't mind some alone time with *my* hygienist."

Harry scowled. "Aren't you still married?"

"Probably wouldn't be a good idea then, huh?" Dr. Vernon shrugged.

The other guys laughed. Dorey wanted to sink into the floor. This was precisely why it wasn't a good idea for her to be the only female. Guys tended to act differently if they were alone. She eyed Harry. If Dorey wasn't here, would he be cutting up about women like they were? She hoped not.

Laughter echoed around them. If Dorey could find her own way out, she'd already be gone. As it was, though, she was pretty much stuck listening to them ridicule women or talk about them like they were playthings.

Not good.

Harry was smiling and nodding. Did he agree with them? Or was he just being polite? Either way, it would have been so much better if he'd never invited her along.

Invited? He'd practically begged. But why?

Dr. Vernon caught Harry's attention and pointed to Dr. Cortez. "He's married too. See, it doesn't matter." He elbowed Harry and lowered his voice.

But Dorey still heard every word thanks to the echo.

"Lucky for you, you won't be cheating on a wife when you fool around with your hygienist."

"Listen." Harry coughed and stood up. "Dorey and I should probably be heading back." He looked pointedly at her. "You did have that thing to do today, right?"

So, he didn't want to hang around either? She nodded. "Yeah. Don't want to be late."

Harry turned to the other men. "You guys stay, hang out if you want."

"Nah," said Dr. Vernon. "My wife gets a little crabby if I'm out too long on a Saturday where she's not invited."

Dorey's eyes widened. Then, it wasn't that his wife had been busy—he hadn't even invited her.

They left the rock room and headed back. Dorey was still disoriented and gladly went last, behind Harry again.

Soon, but not soon enough for Dorey's taste, they reached the mouth of the cave.

Once outside, Dorey squinted up into the bright sunlight. She peeled off her jacket, which suddenly felt hot and oppressive.

Harry did the same. Amazing how much the temperature had dropped in there. He talked to the other guys for a minute, and then they went their separate ways.

"Hey, sorry about all that. Some guys are jerks. I wish they wouldn't have said those things." He shrugged. "Ready to head home?"

"Sure."

8

The following Sunday evening, Dorey was still sore. She could only imagine how Harry felt, since she'd fallen on top of him and—

Don't go there.

She still couldn't believe she'd very nearly kissed him. It didn't mean anything. It couldn't. Maybe she was wrong. Maybe what she'd experienced was ...

What? What else could it have been?

Stop thinking about it. If she didn't, she wouldn't be able to look him in the eye any time soon.

He's like a brother ... like a brother ...

To get her mind off him, Dorey dragged out her many containers of beads. Maybe making some new bracelets to give away would help. Since Weatherby was a no-show for now, it was a good time to do it. Cats and tiny beads that roll across the floor weren't good companions. At least not for Dorey. Weatherby, on the other hand, would think he'd landed in a feline soccer match.

The squeak of the kitty door announced her cat's arrival.

"There you are." He was dragging something long and white across the floor. It bounced merrily behind him on the carpet.

"Uh-oh. What have you stolen this time?" Dorey bent down and tugged it from his mouth, earning her a glare. Well, at least it wasn't a mask. It was a bra. A very long, very large-cupped bra. "Weatherby. You're a thief and a pervert? Or is that purrvert?"

She sighed and tossed the garment in the small trashcan by her door. She had no idea who it belonged to, and whoever it was might not want it back anyway if a mangy-looking cat had slobbered on it.

"I'm going to work with these beads now." She sat back down at her coffee table and gave him a stern look. "Be good."

Weatherby winked.

"All right, at least think about trying to be good."

His meow sounded like a chortle. Good thing she loved him. If he were human, he'd be serving a ten-year sentence somewhere for his many crimes.

Working on the bracelet wasn't helping her not think of Harry. Sure, she'd always had a crush on him. But that would be normal under the circumstances, wouldn't it? He'd always been at her house, conveniently there for Dorey to follow around. Something was changing, though. Now when she was close to him, all she wanted to do was kiss him. Really kiss him.

The crazy thing was, she'd gotten this vibe from him lately that he wanted the same thing. But that couldn't be true. Or could it?

She threw her hands in the air, and pink and white beads went flying. "I don't know!"

Weatherby, startled by her outburst from his attempted nap on the couch, bolted from the room and ran through the kitty door. The door swung in and out several times before coming to a rest. As fast as he was running, he could be in Mexico by dark.

Dorey slumped her shoulders. "Ugh." She'd hoped to spend the evening with him. He might be a sneaky thief, but at least he was a good listener. And he really loved to cuddle. Since she'd scared him off, it was just her again. She didn't particularly want to be alone with her thoughts. They hadn't been playing nice lately.

Beading wasn't working. Maybe she could try reading. That might help. She sat down on the couch and grabbed her book. It was a good mystery, but she couldn't concentrate. Her mind raced, not lighting anywhere for more than a few seconds. Now her head ached.

Her house phone rang. Before she could reach it, the machine kicked on. Dorey waited. Nothing. Was it another stupid caller who just hung up? But wait, this wasn't at work. How would someone know to call—

A raspy hoarseness, like a person with something stuck in their windpipe, rose eerily from the phone. A cold tentacle of dread wound around Dorey's spine. Someone was breathing heavily into the phone. Wasn't that only in horror flicks? This had to stop.

She hurried to the phone and lifted the receiver before she lost her nerve. "Listen here, you jerk. I'll—"

The dial tone was the only reply.

Dorey let out a long, loud breath and replaced the receiver. Hopefully, whoever was making these prank calls would get tired and stop. Soon.

She went back to the couch to hopefully read some more. A few minutes later, her doorbell rang. Maybe it was Harry. They could sit and talk and then she'd feel better. As long as she didn't give in to her compulsion to push him down on the couch and not let him up until he'd thoroughly kissed her.

She rushed to the door and flung it open, a smile on her face. But her grin slid off when she saw who stood there. Marie was one of her friends from high school that she still hung out with occasionally. One of those natural blondes with blue eyes and fair skin. She was pretty and knew it. Not exactly the person Dorey wanted to spend time with right now.

Dorey held onto the edge of the door, hoping the other girl didn't want to come in or anything. "Hey, Marie. How are you?"

"I'm good." She practically bounced inside the apartment without being invited. "I was going to take a quick walk in the park. Wanna come?"

Dorey had no desire to walk in public next to the beauty queen. But hadn't she just wished she had some company? Maybe it would do her good to take a stroll in the fresh air. It had to be better than sulking alone in the apartment, didn't it? Dorey squelched the sigh that longed to work its way out of her lips. "Sure. Let me get my shoes."

The park was only a few blocks away. It was still light enough out that several people were there, walking, jogging, and sitting on benches, talking. Dorey went often, but usually alone. At least that way, no one would compare her to someone like Marie. She slid a glance to her left, marveling at how the girl didn't appear to have any physical flaws. Not one.

Marie set a quick pace. Dorey was determined not to lag behind, even though they were practically running, and Dorey had trouble catching her breath. Why was Marie going so fast? Train to catch? Late for an appointment? Dorey had never seen the fascination with jogging. A walk, sure, but when she bounced around until she might throw up the contents of her stomach, not so much.

A few high school age guys were playing football. Dorey and Marie barely dodged getting slammed into a tree by a few of them when the ball headed their way.

"Yikes!" Marie grabbed Dorey's arm.

Did she think Dorey was going to tackle the huge boys? Protect her so her perfect hair didn't get mussed? Dorey gently pried Marie's fingers from her arm, and they continued walking.

A man and a little boy were tossing a Frisbee back and forth. A large dog barked and jumped, trying to catch the Frisbee every time it passed over his head.

Something crashed through the leaves somewhere behind them. With all the little kids around, not to mention the dog and squirrels, Dorey didn't even turn around to see.

But Marie did.

"Oh!" She grabbed Dorey's arm again and walked even faster, practically dragging Dorey through the grass.

"What? What's wrong?" Were the football guys hurrying after them? Had someone's huge dog gotten loose and ran free? An angry squirrel thinking they'd stolen his walnut?

"Don't slow down unless you want it to catch you. Hurry! Go faster!"

"It, what?" Dorey's breath came in short bursts.

Marie lowered her voice but kept her quick stride. "There's something—I think it's a weasel—running after us. Come on. Save yourself, Dorey. Don't end up being rodent bait."

A weasel? In the middle of the public park? Didn't seem likely. But then, Marie did tend to overreact to any woodland creature. Once outside during their gym class period, Marie had even climbed a tree to escape a chattering squirrel. Dorey still wasn't sure what Marie thought that would accomplish. It surprised her that Marie even suggested going to the park today in the first place.

Dorey peeked over her shoulder. A flash of dirty gray zipped across the clearing as Weatherby dove behind a tree. Then he poked his head around the side, paws clutched to the bark of the tree, eyes scouring the park for possible enemies. Did the cat think he was on a reconnaissance mission? Or was he spying on Dorey?

She took in a long breath, trying to get some oxygen to her screaming lungs. "Don't panic. It's not a weasel."

"How do you know? I mean, those things carry diseases, don't they? Aren't they sometimes rabid? I don't want to get bitten. I'm only twenty-seven. I have plans and dreams for my life. I want to live."

"I told you, it's not a weasel."

"How can you be so sure?" Marie's voice rose higher with each panic-stricken word.

"Because it's my cat." My weird, misguided, neurotic cat.

Marie's eyes widened. "I have cats at home. That's not a cat."

"He is too."

Marie stopped and stared at Dorey. Was she trying to tell if Dorey was pulling her leg?

"Well, in that case, it's the ugliest, er—" Her face reddened as she seemed to realize she'd just insulted Dorey's pet.

As Marie cleared her throat, she glanced away. "Uh, there actually was something I wanted to ask you when I stopped by your apartment." She took a lock of her long hair and wound it around her finger, something she always did that when she wanted a favor.

Ah ... Now they were coming to the reason for Marie's sudden interest in spending time with Dorey when she hadn't even made contact for at least six months. It never failed. The girl was always after something. Usually, whatever Dorey didn't want to give. She stifled a sigh. "Okay. What?"

Eyes lit up, she smiled. "Well, it's about your boss. Dr. MacKinley."

"Oh, sure. Why? Do you have a toothache? I'm sure Mae could squeeze you into the schedule. Are you in pain? We didn't have to take a walk tonight. Just call the office first thing tomorrow and—"

Marie laughed. It was one of those musical giggles that

Dorey had always wished for. Instead, she had the pig-like snort.

"No, silly." Marie lightly smacked Dorey's arm.

That was something she did a lot too.

"I'm not interested in what he does. I'm interested in *him*."

"What for?" Marie had never actually met Harry. Had probably seen him before if he'd been hanging around with Gordon at Dorey's house and Marie was there, but as far as Dorey knew, that was it.

Then, the light clicked on in her mind. Oh …

"I think even you could figure that out, Dorey."

What was that supposed to mean? Was Marie insulting her intelligence or her capacity to understand men?

Marie sighed and gazed up at the sky. "He's so handsome. So built, and, well, let's face it. He *is* a doctor."

So much for not caring about what Harry did. Some women just wanted to hook up with someone with a prestigious-sounding job. Did Marie think Harry was rich? Dorey crossed her arms. "What would you like to know?"

I should tell her that Harry is a weasel. Rabid. Would bite her. Then she wouldn't live, even though she's only twenty-seven. But lying to her wouldn't be right.

Marie started walking again but at least slowed her pace enough that Dorey wasn't panting. She twirled another long lock of her hair around her finger. "Is he … seeing anyone?"

Dorey blinked. Was he? He'd never really said if he had a girlfriend or not. Why hadn't Dorey ever asked? They talked about most everything else. Even if she had asked, would he have told her? She shrugged.

"Not as far as I know." If Harry was seeing someone, Dorey might not want to know. Because that knowledge would effectively squash any dreams Dorey had about him and her.

"Oh, that's good news. Think you could put in a good word for me? Make sure he knows how handsome I think he is. That I think his physique is awesome. Oh, and tell him all my good qualities. How I'm a size four and am an expert at doing my hair and make-up, that he and I would make such a cute couple."

Marie's eyes took on a dreamy quality. "You could even let him know what things I like, in case he wanted to buy me a gift. I know you won't mind doing that, you know, since we've been good friends forever." Marie blinked her huge eyes, her smile growing larger.

A kid on her birthday. *Oh! Is that present for me?*

Dorey tried hard not to wear one of Weatherby's famous scowls, although it was dying to appear on her face. Smiling at that point was not an option. Since when had she and Marie been close? They'd been friends, sort of, but only when Marie didn't have anything better to do or anyone more popular to hang out with.

In high school they'd been at opposite ends of the spectrum. Marie, cheerleader. Dorey, science club. Marie, homecoming queen. Dorey, lab partner to the teacher since they had an uneven number of students in the class.

Marie stopped again and grabbed Dorey's arm.

Why did she keep doing that?

"It would really mean a lot to me, Dorey. I'd consider it a personal favor."

As opposed to what, a corporate one? But she knew her friend would only bug her until she got what she wanted. Might as well get it over with.

"Yeah, I guess." Why hadn't Marie asked if Harry was dating Dorey? Was it such a foreign concept that he might be interested in her? Yeah, it would be. Especially to perfection such as Marie.

Marie's high-pitched squeal startled a pair of doves from their perch on a nearby tree branch. "Thank you!" Marie turned suddenly. "I suppose I should be getting home now. I'll walk you back to your apartment." Then, she actually clapped.

Not saying much out loud, but doing a lot of internal mumbling, Dorey stomped the whole way back to her apartment while Marie jabbered incessantly about Harry. His eyes. His hair. His supposed income. What kind of car did he drive? Did he live in a fancy house? Have extravagant parties?

They were just about to the entrance to the apartment complex when someone called out Dorey's name.

With a groan, she turned. Harry. Worse timing there could not have been.

Marie grabbed Dorey's arm again.

She was really tired of being mauled.

"It's him," squeaked Marie. "Dr. MacKinley. What should I do? Should I say hello? Tell him how cute he is? Ask if he likes how I have my hair? Talk about the weather? Tell me what to do, Dorey."

"Just be yourself."

Squealing again, Marie jumped up and down.

Dorey rolled her eyes and waited for Harry to reach them from the parking lot, hoping Marie would calm down before he got there. "Hey, Harry."

"Hey. I was gonna see if you wanted to hit the park, but ... I'm guessing you already have?" He eyed her tennis shoes and then what was her— she assumed—flushed, sweaty face.

"Yep. We just got back." She watched Harry carefully, glad that he wasn't staring at Marie.

"Oh, okay." He waited for a minute.

Did he want to meet the blonde bombshell?

"Maybe another time."

Marie yanked on her arm. Again.

"Oh, right. Uh, Harry, this is Marie Carlton. A ... friend."

Before Harry could say anything, Marie jumped forward, grabbed his hand, and held it to her chest.

Dorey's mouth dropped open when Harry's face reddened.

Slowly, he extricated his hand from hers and took a half step back. "Nice to, uh, meet you, Marie. I'm—"

"I know all about you, Dr. MacKinley." She batted her long eyelashes.

If this exchange had taken place in an earlier century, it would also have been a good moment for her to swoon so Harry could catch her and hold her in his arms while he professed his undying devotion.

"Ah. You do? Um ..." He took another step back. "I need to be going now. I'll ... see you tomorrow, Dorey. And, Marie, was it? Nice meeting you." He spun around and nearly sprinted to his truck in the parking lot.

Marie turned to watch him go. "He's so dreamy." Every few seconds, she let out a breathy sigh, her chest rising and falling dramatically.

Finally, when Harry's truck had turned the corner and was no longer visible, Marie focused on Dorey. "Well, it was really nice to see you. Please let me know what he says about me tomorrow, okay? You're the best. Bye!" With a little wave and a giggle, she left.

Why me? Dorey groaned and headed toward her apartment. Her sulking had been delayed by the walk, but now she'd give in to it, whole hog. The fact that Marie was salivating after Harry would add that much more fun to the mix.

Something rustled from a nearby bush. Weatherby popped his head out and stared at her, green eyes wide, whiskers twitching against the leaves.

"Now you show up. Perfect. But I guess the good thing was, you scared poor Miss Marie when she thought you were a rabid weasel. So, thanks for that."

Weatherby crawled out of the bush and rubbed against her leg. Yes, a true friend did try to frighten away beautiful interlopers from a guy a girl secretly loved.

9

As soon as Dorey walked into the office, she glanced to the waiting area. A gorgeous woman, maybe thirty or so, sat there with a leather briefcase. Ah, a drug rep. They had a certain look about them. Cheerful. Perky. Well-dressed. And almost always attractive. Hopefully, the woman was here to see Harry and not Dorey. She hated spending so much time listening to their marketing spiels instead of working.

Wait. Maybe she shouldn't hope the woman was there to see Harry. The less he saw of gorgeous females, the better. Dorey didn't need any more competition than she might already have.

That reminded Dorey of Marie. She'd be expecting Dorey to question Harry on what he thought of Marie after meeting her last night. Might as well get the unpleasantness over with. She'd pester Dorey until she did.

Loud, cheerful whistling accompanied someone in through the main door.

Harry.

Dorey hurried to catch him in his private office before they got started on patients for the day or before he got waylaid by the pretty thing sitting out front. As much as Dorey didn't want to tell him what Marie had said, she had to. Because if Marie asked her—and she would—Dorey would have a terrible time lying.

Darn her pale skin that turned a lovely hue of pink whenever she attempted a falsehood.

What if Harry was interested in Marie? Had found her to be beautiful, wanted to ask her out? Not only would it crush Dorey's heart, but it might also mean there would never be a chance for them in the future if Marie got her hooks into him and he succumbed. Something unpleasant tumbled around in Dorey's stomach. If he did say that, she might not be able to keep the contents of her tummy inside.

When Dorey got to his office, he was hanging up his jacket.

"Oh, hey, Dorey."

"Hey, yourself." She walked in and closed the door.

He glanced at the door and back to her. "Hmm. A closed door. Either it's something serious or you want to have your way with me." He jiggled both eyebrows up and down.

Way with me ... Warm kisses ... soft caresses, leading to—don't go there. "Ha! You wish." Dorey crossed her arms over her chest, hoping he wouldn't guess her thoughts just now.

"Maybe I do wish." He laughed. "Oh, before I forget, my brother called last night. They're coming into town this weekend. Kind of a last-minute thing. He wanted to know if I could get some of our old friends together at the local lodge for a party. You wanna come?"

Since when had she been invited to their parties? She frowned. Usually they'd said she was too much younger than them to hang out. But if she didn't go, would he want to ask Marie? "Um ... I don't know."

"Got other plans?"

"No." Why did she just blurt it out like that? It made her sound like she didn't have any social life at all.

I don't.

Unless she counted Weatherby. He was the only male in her life she gave kisses to.

"Aww, say you'll come." Harry was giving her those sad, puppy-dog eyes she found hard to resist.

"I won't know anybody besides you, Gordon, and Eva."

"That won't matter. Will you do it? For me? I want you there."

She huffed out a breath. If it would keep him from taking someone else, she'd better go even though she had no interest in being there. "Fine. I'll come."

"Don't sound so thrilled about it." He laughed again. "I have to get there way early to make sure everything is set up for food and music. I can pick you up beforehand, and you can wait at the lodge with me or—"

Getting ready for the party would take all the free time she could get. "I'll just meet you there."

"You sure?"

"Yep."

"Okay, so really—" He pointed to the closed door "What's up?"

She didn't want to do this, but it wouldn't go away. Marie was very persistent when she wanted something. *Just do it.* "Well, last night when you found me in front of my apartment building with Marie—you remember Marie …"

He blinked. "Uh, yeah. It hasn't been that long in the past."

Dorey twisted her hands in front of her. "Anyway, she and I had taken a walk in the park."

"Right. You told me that last night."

"So, Marie, um …" *I don't want to do this.*

He placed his hands on his hips. "Dorey, what's going on?"

"All right, I'll just say it. Marie thinks you're hot, and she wants to know what you think of her."

He sputtered a loud laugh. "Think of her? Are we in middle school again?"

"If you'll remember, you and I weren't in middle school at the same time, oldster."

He ignored her jab. "You're serious. She thinks I'm ..."

"Hot."

"And wants to know what I think of her?"

"Yep." Dorey rolled her eyes.

"I don't even know her. How can I have an opinion about her?"

"True. Okay, what I'm asking is, do you think she's, well—"

"Hot?"

Did he think so? Dorey stared at him. Marie was gorgeous. Flawless. Built. What guy wouldn't think so?

Harry came closer and tapped her nose with his finger like he did when she was little.

She grabbed his hand. "Stop. You know I hate that."

"Why do you think I did it?" He grinned. "Listen, this girl ... Marie?"

Dorey bit her lower lip and nodded.

"I guess she's pretty, if you like that sort."

"What sort? What's not to like? She's perfect. Did you notice her complexion? Her hair?"

What am I saying? Have I lost my mind? I don't want him to like her. Stupid, stupid tongue for blurting out the very thing I didn't want you to.

"All I meant was, she's not my type."

Type? Harry had a type? Why hadn't she known this? Dorey looked at the floor. "Oh. Then ..."

"Then ... who is my type?"

She gave a single nod but couldn't meet his eyes. She wanted to hear it so bad but was scared to death too. What if he said his type wasn't anything like Dorey? What if he said it was?

She swallowed hard and tapped her shoe on the floor, waiting.

"Why so interested in my love life, kid?"

"I'm not a kid."

"It's a term of affection."

"No, it isn't."

"Yeah, it is."

"Stop arguing with me. I'm having flashbacks to—"

"Seventh grade? So, you've said before. Dorey, why are you trying to push this teenage girl at me?"

"Teenage girl? She's my age."

He tilted his head. "If you hadn't told me, I never would have guessed."

She studied him closely. Was he serious? "Actually, she's three months older than me."

With a shrug, he looked her over slowly from her face to her shoes and back again. Dorey felt like she'd been put on display somewhere public. A chill snaked up her arms, over her shoulders and down her back.

He leaned closer. Was he going to kiss her? Her heart rate sped up. Did she want him to? *Of course, you do. Stop being an imbecile.*

"Dorey," he finally said, "I don't know why, but lately…"

"Lately, what?" *Don't keep a girl in suspense!*

"You just seem different."

That was it? Different? Was that good? Bad? Weird?

"How?"

"I can't really explain it. I-I don't know."

He opened the door and left. The sound of his footsteps grew faint in the hall.

Wait …

He never answered her question about who his type was.

10

Dorey stressed over everything while getting ready for the party. Hair up or down? She wore it in a ponytail at work for the sake of convenience. Definitely down, then. Needed something different. Outfit? She eyed her choices. Not much to go on. Not only did she wear scrubs at work and jeans and casual shirts at home, her rent was due, and she didn't have the funds for retail therapy at the moment.

So, she'd to go with her usual standby. The pink V-neck sweater. It was old, but still looked okay.

With only one good pair of jeans without any small holes or tiny stains, that choice was a no-brainer.

Makeup? She hardly ever bothered with much. Maybe just a little eye shadow this time. Would Harry even notice?

Why are you wondering that? You're not his type. But did she really know that? He hadn't said. Had only told her what his type wasn't. Someone like Marie.

Rats. She'd never called Marie back after the four voicemail messages the girl had left on her home phone machine. Glad she hadn't given Marie her cell number. Then she might get calls at work about whether or not Harry liked her.

She glanced at the clock and hurried to finish getting ready. Oh, no. She was running late. Her stomach formed knots hard enough to double her over. Dorey preferred sticking to a schedule. Knowing what would happen when. Who would be there at what time. Somehow the uniformity of it provided safety. Comfort.

Maybe that's why she liked working in the dental office with its strict timeline for who was supposed to be there at a certain time. If everyone were like her, the world would run like clockwork. Nice and orderly. She sighed. *I sound like someone's grandmother. Not very exciting, am I?*

Get over it. Go to the party. Have a little fun for once.

She was halfway to the door when her phone rang. Already late, she decided to just let the machine get it. Dorey jerked to a stop when the machine picked up, and some sort of old-time music sounded. Wait, she knew that song. After a few seconds, she recognized it.

Ring around the roses. It was a song they sang when she was in kindergarten. Why would someone call her and—

The machine clicked off.

Frustrated at the annoying call, she was now leaving even later than she'd planned. She grabbed her purse and headed out to her car.

Weatherby sat outside close to the parking lot, eyeing a small hole in the dirt. Probably a mole or something. She shuddered. What were the chances there'd be a tiny dead body in her apartment when she got back? Hopefully, it wouldn't be waiting for her on her pillow tonight. Blech.

Before she unlocked her car, she pointed at her cat. "I'm leaving for a while. Be good." Realizing the futility of her request, she shook her head, gave Weatherby a wave, and headed across town to the lodge. She finally had to force herself to stop checking her reflection in the mirror on the way. Having a wreck wouldn't be anybody's idea of a party.

When she pulled up in front of the lodge, it took her a while to find a spot to park. How many people had he invited, anyway? The loud drumbeat from the music inside the building was likely to have one of the neighbors calling the police due to excessive noise.

Dorey smirked, imagining her perfect sister trying to talk her way out of being hauled to the police station, saying it wasn't her party, it was her brother-in-law's. Would Eva throw Harry under the bus?

As she walked up the cement porch steps, she nearly tripped on the top one. Taking a quick glance around, she was relieved no one saw her. She opened the squeaky door and stepped inside.

A cloud of smoke attacked her lungs as soon as she walked in. She coughed and tried to wave it away. Wonder where Harry was? She stood on her tiptoes, trying to find him. The sea of crowded humanity was so loud. But then they'd have to be, to hear each other over the music.

"Dorey!"

She turned and saw her sister waving from the entrance to the kitchen. Eva motioned for Dorey to come to her.

Sure, I'll climb over sixty-three people. No problem. Be right there. Dorey started out politely asking people to move so she could get through, but she wasn't getting very far. Having tugged on sleeves, poked people in the backs, and yelled, "Excuse me!" several times, she just elbowed her way through.

From the silly grins and laughter, it looked like most of them would be too toasted to notice anyway. And nobody would remember anything tomorrow. How long had some of them been here? Maybe they started drinking before they'd come.

"Hey." Her sister hugged her. "Good to see you."

"You too."

Eva eyed Dorey critically. "Haven't I seen that outfit before? Like lots of times?"

"Don't start." Dorey held up her hand. "I don't have any disposable income at the moment."

"Why? Isn't my brother-in-law paying you? Might I need to have a talk with him?"

"No. Don't do that. Everything is fine. Harry is ... He's a great boss."

Her sister eyed her over her drink of something red and fruity-looking and then shrugged. "If you say so. Still, I'm glad Dad had that talk with Harry before he and Mom moved to Florida."

"What talk?" Dorey frowned.

Her sister waved her hand. "Just making sure Harry would keep an eye on you. Take care of you. No biggie."

Take care of you. So maybe that's really all she was to Harry. A project. A burden. Someone to look after, like a pet. An unwanted one.

Eva glanced down at her cup as if just noticing it. "Hey, you need something to drink."

"I'm okay, really."

"Don't be so boring, Dorey."

"I'm not boring. I just don't drink."

"Well, it's a party. Tonight, you shall drink." She laughed way too much. And too loud. How much had she had? How long had she and Gordon been here?

"I don't want any. Okay?"

"This is my ... oh well, I've lost count of how many I've had." Eva tugged Dorey's purse away and swung it back and forth.

"No joke."

Her sister didn't seem to notice Dorey's sarcasm. "I'm so glad you're here. I've missed you." She swung Dorey's purse in a higher arc, like little girls playfully holding hands.

"I've missed you too."

The purse went up a little too high, and the contents spilled out onto the floor. Dorey sighed. Perfect. The one time she hadn't zipped it closed. She was usually so careful about that. She bent down and tried to retrieve her stuff before someone stepped on it.

Eva knelt beside her. "Oops." She frowned at the mess on the floor. Her expression said, *Did I do that?*

Dorey glared at her. *Yes, you did that.*

Eva sat on the floor but didn't help Dorey pick things up. "Listen, I've been meaning to ask you something."

"What?" Dorey grabbed a Chapstick that had rolled a couple of feet away, narrowly avoiding having her fingers crushed by some guy's boot.

"I haven't heard you talk about any guys lately. Are you seeing anybody?"

Dorey shook her head. Not for lack of trying.

"Well, it's high time you did."

"What? Um—"

Eva popped up from the floor as if startled, part of her fruity drink landing on Dorey's hand. "Daryl, come over here!"

Dorey turned and looked up. To her horror, a guy, all smiles, and if his crooked gait was any indication, exceedingly wasted, headed toward them. She grabbed the rest of her stuff and crammed it into her purse before standing.

The guy came and planted himself next to Dorey. Way too close. "This must be the little sister, huh? You didn't tell me how cute she was." He looped his arm over her shoulder and pulled her close. "I'm Daryl."

"I'm Dorey." She frowned and tried to extricate herself, but alcohol must have given him a vice-like grip.

"Dorey … Funny name."

Her sister piped up. "It's short for Doris."

"What a cruel thing for your mother to do. Doris." He threw his head back and laughed.

"Why do you think she uses a nickname?" Her sister elbowed Dorey.

Dorey fumed and glared at her sister, who seemed to be ignoring her. She'd been wondering about Eva throwing Harry under the bus. She didn't guess it would be her instead.

"Well," said Eva, "I have a few people I want to talk to so, see you two later." She winked and left.

Left?

Wait. Had her sister planned on introducing her to Daryl all along? What was Dorey supposed to do now?

She finally ducked down low enough that Daryl had to let her go. He nearly stumbled in the process. Too bad he didn't just fall down and take a nap or something.

He grabbed her chin in his fingers, which smelled like smoke. "How about we go find some privacy?"

Her mouth fell open. What a letch. "I don't think so."

"Aww, come on.

Ew. She gasped and smacked his hand away. "Get lost." She turned to leave.

He laughed and caught her from behind, wrapping his arms around her waist. She squirmed, but he wouldn't let go.

"Help! Somebody!" Either because of the noise, everyone else being so drunk they didn't notice or care, no one offered to lend her a hand.

Dorey lost her balance as Daryl dragged her backward. "Stop. Hey!" She hit his arm as hard as she could, but the goon wouldn't release his grip.

"Let me go!" Dorey tried to kick back behind her but couldn't connect with his leg. She looked over her shoulder and saw where they were headed. The stairway.

Struggling harder, she heard a loud rip. Glancing down, she saw her sweater now had a little more *V* at the neck than it had before. Which meant she showed more cleavage than she ever did. But what really made her mad was the tear in the fabric. *This is my favorite sweater!*

Nothing she tried worked. Daryl kept dragging her toward

the stairs. No one seemed inclined to help Dorey. Instead, the ones who actually took notice cheered Daryl on.

When they got to the bottom of the steps, he shoved her down. Her back thumped painfully against the edge of the hard wood. Daryl crawled on top of her. Before she could yell, his nasty mouth slobbered all over hers.

Help! Anybody?

She tried to roll out from under him, but he was too big. Too strong.

"What are you doing?"

Daryl stopped kissing her and slowly lifted his gaze to the voice. "Oh, hey Harry."

Harry?

As relieved as Dorey was to see him, she hated for him to see her lying under this creep.

Boots that Dorey recognized as Harry's favorites appeared on the step next to Dorey's head and kept going down the stairs. "Daryl, I'm thinking Dorey's not really into being mauled on the stairs."

Daryl laughed. "I'm trying to get her upstairs, but we fell."

"The rooms are locked." Dorey couldn't see Harry's face past Daryl's chest but heard the jingle of keys.

"Oh. Well, then she and I can go out to my van. Plenty of room in the back."

"Get off me." Dorey struggled against him.

"You heard her. Get off," said Harry.

Daryl frowned and looked down at Dorey. "But she likes me. I can tell."

Before Dorey could say anything, Daryl was suddenly lifted off her. She sat up and wrapped her arms around her middle. Harry had a hold of the back of Daryl's collar and belt. Without saying another word, Harry unceremoniously escorted him out the door, giving him a swift kick in the butt for good measure.

Quickly, Harry came back to her. "Are you okay? Did he—"

"I'm okay." She brushed her hair out of her face. Her hand trembled.

"You're not okay. I'm taking you home."

"You can't leave, Harry. It's your party."

He sighed. "No. It's my brother's. I didn't know it would be this kind of party. I'm so sorry I invited you to come to something like this." He stood and reached for her hand. "Come on. Nobody will even know I'm gone."

She let him help her up, then pulled her hand free, needing to tug her sweater down over her exposed stomach. She'd forgotten about the tear in her sweater and rolled her eyes when her cleavage showed even more. When she looked back up, Harry was staring at her chest. But his expression wasn't one of lust. It was of rage.

"Come on, Dorey." He took her hand again and forced people aside to make a path to the door. Once outside on the wide concrete stairs, Dorey had to step over Daryl, who was passed out on the bottom step, snoring.

Harry glared down at him, looking like he wanted nothing more than to kick the guy again. "He'll sleep for a while but will be sore tomorrow." He shrugged. "Not that I care."

11

L ate Sunday morning, Dorey heard a noise outside her apartment door. By the time she got there and opened the door, no one was around. Right before she was ready to go back inside, she looked down.

Six red roses, their heads chopped off and lying next to the stems, had been placed on her welcome mat. She blinked. *What in the world?* She bent over to see them better. Who would have done that? And why?

Some of the red petals of the roses were strewn about on the ground, looking very much like large drops of blood.

Dorey shuddered. Peering around in both directions, she was glad not to see anyone else nearby. She grabbed her broom and dustpan from her coat closet just inside the door and hurried to clean up the mess. As quickly as she could, she shut and locked her door and tossed the remains of the decapitated flowers into her trashcan. Like throwing a body into a grave.

Dorey, get a grip. It was just a prank. Right?

Her heartbeat kicked up a notch. Who in the world had sent them? Was it the same person who was messing with her patients? But that didn't make any sense.

She thought of Daryl from the night before. Slobbering all over her, trying to drag her to an upstairs bedroom at the lodge. No doubt he was mad this morning. Both from her trying to fight him off and Harry literally kicking him down the front steps. Maybe Daryl left the roses to send a message.

Her landline phone jangled, and she jumped. Hardly anyone ever called that line. Usually it was Mae, if she couldn't get Dorey on her cell and wanted to leave a message. But Mae wouldn't call on Sunday, would she? Or it could be Marie, wanting to know about Harry's opinion of her. Or a pesky sales call.

Dorey let the machine pick up, not in the mood to talk to any of the above now.

Just when she assumed the person wouldn't leave a message, a deep muffled voice sounding as if the caller had a scarf over his mouth said, "Did you like my gift, Dorey?" The machine clicked off, and a loud beep followed, indicating the message.

It hadn't sounded like Daryl unless he had altered his voice somehow. But why would he do that? No, it had to be someone else. But who?

The hairs on the back of her neck rose. Suddenly chilled, Dorey rubbed her hands over her bare arms. It was early enough she was still in her pajamas. The top was skimpy and didn't cover much. She turned to go get her robe.

A loud knock on her door caused her to scream. She smacked her hand over her mouth. *Dorey, you've got to calm down.*

Someone pounded on the door this time. "Dorey?"

Harry? Dorey ran to the door and unlocked it. Before she could open it, Harry did it for her. His large frame filled the doorway. Sunlight from behind him caused his face to fall into shadows. It was hard for her to see his features very well.

"I heard a scream. Are you—" He scanned the room as if

looking for some intruder. "What happened? Are you alone? Did you fall or something?"

"I …" Her mouth went dry, and her words stuck in her throat.

"Are you okay?"

She found her voice, although her words came out sounding like a croak. "Fine." She swallowed. "I'm fine."

"Why did you scream when I knocked?"

"Sorry. It just startled me."

Harry lowered his eyebrows and skimmed his gaze over her face. "Are you sure that's all it was? You kinda freaked me out."

"Come on, Doc. Now you sound paranoid." She forced a laugh.

He ran his hand over the back of his neck. "I was worried about you after last night."

"Yeah. About that. Thanks for … Well, thanks."

"You don't need to thank me, Dorey." He gave her a crooked grin. "Taking care of you is what I do."

While she normally would have found the comment a little irritating but mostly funny, Dorey couldn't take it that way this time. After what Eva had said at the party, about their dad having a talk with Harry about watching over Dorey, she felt like some unwanted appendage Harry didn't quite know what to do with.

"Don't worry about it."

"I'm not. I just wanted to see if you were all right after what that jerk tried to do." Harry's hands fisted at his sides. He was still upset, obviously.

Dorey placed her hand on his shoulder and looked him in the eyes. "I'm fine. Really."

He narrowed his eyes and shook his head. "I don't think so. Something happened, didn't it? People don't scream like that unless they're really scared."

There he goes again, acting the mighty protector. It was

exactly why she didn't want him to find out about the roses. But if she didn't fess up, he'd keep haranguing her until she told him. She let out a frustrated breath. "All right. I found some dead flowers outside my door."

His head jerked back. "Dead? Why would someone—"

"I have no idea. But that's all it was. Honest."

Harry lowered his voice. "Dorey, you screamed when I knocked. You were freaked out."

"It was just someone's idea of a silly prank."

"Who?"

"I don't know. For a little while, I'd wondered if it was you." She playfully poked him in the chest.

While she'd expected him to laugh at her joke, hoped it would take the edge off their conversation, he didn't even crack a smile.

"Are you in some kinda trouble?"

"Of course not." She put her hands on her hips. Why did everyone think she couldn't take care of herself? "It's like I said. Just some prank. I'm not worried about it, so you shouldn't be either."

Harry's shoulders slumped as if accepting the fact that she wasn't going to tell him anything more. He glanced around the small living room. "So, you have plans for today?"

"Oh, I'm behind on some laundry. I don't have any clean scrubs to wear tomorrow. I don't think the patients would appreciate me showing up in my pajamas."

Harry's gaze slid down. Dorey actually felt it. Her skin warmed. She self-consciously crossed her arms over her chest.

That seemed to snap Harry out of some daze. He gave a nod. "All right ... I'll see you tomorrow."

"Sure. Tomorrow."

As Harry walked to the door, Dorey couldn't get her feet to move. She waved as he said goodbye and then finally closed the door behind him.

If she didn't get a grip on herself around Harry, he'd be sure to know how she felt about him. It was getting harder and harder to hide it. And working with the man several days a week sure wasn't helping.

Maybe it was time to check on the job situation again. See if anyone in a nearby town, hopefully someplace larger than this one, had a need for a hygienist.

Spending so much time with Harry when she was so attracted to him was tough. And it didn't seem like it would get any easier as time went on. Just the opposite.

It wasn't until a few minutes later that Dorey replayed Harry's words. Asking if she had plans for the day. Had he planned to ask her to do something with him? Well, she'd blown that.

Dorey, you're an idiot.

12

Monday, Dorey was not in the right frame of mind to work. But she went, of course, because she wasn't a slacker. Hopefully, she'd have several patients to see and take her mind off the disaster of the weekend. Her sister called her late Sunday evening to see how her date had gone. Dorey told Eva what happened, but Eva thought she was joking.

She'd said, 'Okay, fine, if you don't want to kiss and tell, fine with me.' It was all Dorey could do not to throw her phone across her living room. Obviously, her sister hadn't witnessed what Daryl had tried to do. Or maybe she had but was too drunk to remember it the next day.

And the fact that Harry knew about the roses … Dorey really wished he didn't. Maybe Dorey's explanation of it being someone's idea of a joke satisfied him. She hoped so. Because she wanted to believe that's what it really was.

Even more, she desperately wished she wouldn't get any more flowers.

If she got lucky, maybe there wouldn't be any new ones. But what about those beheaded roses? What could it mean? Who'd done it? She'd suspected Daryl until she'd heard that voicemail.

Whoever it was hadn't sounded anything like him. And Dorey hadn't gotten the impression that he was clever enough to find some way to alter his voice over the phone or to even think up the idea to try it.

She said hello to Mae and went straight to her room, not feeling like making small talk at the moment. There would be plenty of opportunity for that when, if, she had patients show up. After stowing her purse in a cabinet, she turned around to check out the schedule posted on the opposite wall.

And froze.

A huge bouquet of roses sat in a clear vase on the counter.

Red roses.

A scream threatened to come from her throat. Dorey clutched her neck, hoping to keep it from escaping. Wouldn't that be wonderful? Screaming in her apartment and Harry hearing it was bad enough. But at work?

Flowers. First dead ones, now live. What did it mean? She took several deep breaths, trying to calm down. It wouldn't do to hyperventilate and pass out on her first patient's chest.

She hadn't received flowers from anyone in years. And now twice in two days. It seemed too much of a coincidence that when she did, it was the same color and type of flower that had been outside her apartment door. Even though these still had their heads.

Maybe Harry had gotten them to cheer her up after the awful scene at the party? That sounded like something he'd do. Sweet. Thoughtful. She let out a breath feeling better already. Wait. Would he have sent her the same kind of flowers she'd gotten before? Had she even mentioned that the flowers had been red roses? Maybe—

Harry walked in. "Hey, Dorey." His gaze followed hers. "You got flowers? Who from?"

Not Harry, then. "I …" She cleared her throat. "I'm not sure."

"Is there a card?" He tilted his head toward the vase.

How stupid. She hadn't even looked. "Uh, I hadn't gotten that far yet. Just got here."

He leaned forward like he really wanted to know whose name was on the card, dying to find out who'd sent her roses, but his feet stayed still. Dorey rushed to the counter to look. At least then she'd know and could finally calm down a little before her patient arrived.

The card had a familiar logo on it from a local florist. She scanned down to the message:

Thanks for last night. Can't wait to do it again. I'm hoping you're free next weekend. Daryl.

It was followed by a drawing of someone's large, red lips forming a kiss.

Dorey nearly choked and dropped the card on the counter. She backed away, feeling like the thing was as dangerous and frightening as a viper.

"Hey, what's wrong? Who—"

She pointed to the card, indicating he should look.

Harry took a few long strides across the room and snatched up the card. His eyebrows lowered.

"Harry, you saw him … what he tried to do. I never wanted him to. Why would he send those? And say … that? He made it sound like we—"

Harry held up his hand. "Yeah, I know what it sounds like." The muscle in his jaw formed a solid ridge as he clenched his teeth together. "Do you wanna keep them? The flowers?" He glared at them as if they themselves had written the vile note.

"No."

"Want me to do something with them?" He tightened one hand in a fist, like he wanted to tear them to bits.

"I don't—" Dorey shrugged.

Mae came around the corner. "Ah, I see you got the flowers the florist brought by. Red roses are my favorite."

Harry caught Dorey's eye and angled his head toward Mae.

Dorey nodded. "Listen, Mae, why don't you take them?"

"What? No, I couldn't. They're yours." But her gaze floated back to the vase.

"I'm quite sure at least one of Dorey's patients today is allergic to them." Harry pointed at the schedule. "You'd be doing us a favor."

"If you're sure." Mae looked at Dorey.

"Yes." Dorey smiled and nodded. "Please do."

Mae's face brightened. "Well, thank you. What a nice treat." She took the large vase in both hands and carefully carried them out of the room.

Dorey let out a long breath. "Thanks," she whispered so Mae wouldn't overhear. "Your suggestion about someone's allergy helped."

"No problem. It's what I ..."

She glanced up, waiting for him to finish. It's what I do. But he didn't. Maybe when she hadn't laughed the last time he'd said it, he'd gotten the message that she didn't want to be teased about him taking care of her.

Gotten the message.

What kind of message was someone sending her with those dead flowers? And now that Harry knew about them, would he leave the subject alone, or would he bring it up later? Bug her about who might have sent them and why?

Harry came closer, stood just a foot away, and leaned his hip against the counter. He crossed his arms but said nothing.

"What?" But she knew what. He'll want to discuss all the roses. Dead and alive.

"Aren't you curious to know if all the flowers were from the same person?"

"No." She looked anywhere but at him.

"Come on. You're as nosy as that cat of yours."

"I-I don't need to know. I don't wanna talk about it."

"Is there something you don't want me to know?"

She shook her head. "Haven't you ever heard of a person's right to privacy?"

"Sure. But with all the stuff that's gone on the last few days, I'm concerned about you. I want to make sure you're okay. That you're—"

"What? That I'm looked after? Taken care of?"

He lowered his chin and stared at her. "Why are you being so hostile?"

She leaned forward until her face was inches from his. "Because my dear sister told me the truth."

"About what?"

"That dear old Dad had a talk with you before they moved. About me. Watching over me."

Harry let out a breath. "I won't deny it."

"That's it?"

"What about it? They were moving across the country, and you were just getting out of college. Would be living on your own for the first time. He just wanted—"

She held up her hand. "I know it all by heart. Because you're always reminding me. It's what you do. Look out for Dorey. Take care of Dorey because she's incapable of taking care of herself."

His eyes widened. "Wait a minute—"

"I am an adult, you know."

"I realize that."

"Do you?"

He reached out and grasped her hand. "Oh, yeah. I'm fully aware. Believe me." He gave her hand a squeeze and left.

Dorey slumped against the counter, partly from having argued with the person she cared about most and partly because he was aware of her adulthood. What exactly did that mean?

13

I t had been hit or miss with patients showing up. The ones
who did were new additions, since some of the originally
scheduled ones were still having catastrophes of the weird kind.
Honestly, Dorey had never heard of so many people having so
many strange accidents occurring all at once.

But since she knew Harry didn't have feelings for her, maybe
it would give Dorey the push she needed to find another job.
Sure, she'd sent out lots of résumés, but for the past several
weeks, she'd let it lag. Since learning Harry watched out for her
at her dad's request, the hope she'd harbored in her heart for
him to have more than brotherly feelings fizzled.

Now she could move on, find something new and not look
back. No regrets. You can't lose something you never had to
start with.

She glanced around the room one last time, making sure she
had everything cleaned and put away. Satisfied, she got her
purse and turned out the light to her room. The reception area
was empty, and she hadn't heard Luanne's voice for a while
now. Dorey checked the clock above Mae's desk. Good grief, six

o'clock. No wonder no one else was there. *Guess I have to lock up.* She dug in her purse for her office keys.

Footsteps sounded behind her, and she gasped. Whirling around, she nearly wilted when Harry came around the corner.

"Dorey? Your face went white."

"You scared me."

"Sorry. Didn't realize I wore my scary face today."

Normally they both would have laughed at that, but after their argument that morning, they'd hardly said much to each other all day. Apart from necessary conversation pertaining to their patients, at least. And that had been stilted at best.

"I was just going to lock up." Dorey jangled her keys. "Thought I was the last one here."

Harry nodded. "I'll walk out with you. I'm all done too." He flipped out the lights, plunging the room into darkness. A faint light showed outside the front window. Red streaks on the horizon would fade to darkness in the next hour or so.

They walked outside and Dorey bent down to lock the door. Harry stood a few feet behind her, silent. Dorey hated the bad feelings between them. Hated it. But she wasn't sure how to fix it. To give in completely to Harry's point of view would be for Dorey to stay in the role she'd always had with him.

Little sister. Tag-a-long. Someone he had to deal with.

But that's not what she wanted. What she longed for in her heart, she couldn't have. It was clear now Harry didn't return her romantic feelings. And why should he if he still saw her as a kid? Though he said he saw her as an adult, his actions didn't prove it. Sometimes the way he talked to her or acted like she couldn't be trusted to take care of herself, she might as well be back in middle school again.

No thanks.

"Well," said Harry. "Have a good evening. I'll see you tomorrow."

"See ya."

With a tired sigh, Dorey walked down the steps to her car. It was dark enough now she could barely see to put her key in the lock. A cold chill ran down her back. After finding those dead roses and hearing the voicemail, Dorey wasn't thrilled about being out here in the dark. What if whoever had done it was watching her? At least Harry was close by this time.

Stop it. That's what gets you into trouble. Depending on him. It's no wonder he thinks he has to protect you from everything.

A phone rang. Dorey glanced up to see Harry answer a call on his cell. He got in his truck but didn't start it. Who called him? Was it a friend? Harry might even be dating someone, who knew?

It's not your business.

She got in her car and started the engine. Putting it in reverse, she frowned when the car acted sluggish, like it didn't want to go anywhere. What was up? She checked the gas gauge. Nope—half a tank. She pressed harder on the gas and tried again. The car moved, but she heard a thump.

Thumps and cars did not mix well.

Maybe she didn't have it all the way in gear. Opening her car door so the light would come on, she peered down at the gearshift. Nope. It was in reverse. Hopefully, the car wasn't on its last leg because she really didn't have the funds to replace it right now.

Harry pecked on her window, and she jumped.

"Got a problem? I was on the phone but noticed your car was acting funny."

Here we go again. I have a problem, and it's Harry to the rescue.

But Dorey knew next to nothing about cars, and she really didn't want to walk home. Grateful Harry was still there, she answered, "Yeah, something's wrong. I put it in reverse, and the car is really slow. And something thumped back there somewhere." She pointed toward the back of the car.

Could she have sounded any more lame?

"Let's take a look."

She got out and shut the door. Harry crouched down near the rear of the car. "Here's your problem."

"What?' She walked toward him.

"Your tires have been slashed."

"What?"

He stood and walked to the other side. "All four of them. We'll need to file a police report and call your insurance company."

Dorey let out a huff. If it wasn't one thing … "Are yours okay on the truck?"

"I better check. I hadn't tried to back out yet." It was a few seconds until he went to his truck and then came back. "Mine are fine. Weird."

She shook her head. "Oh, no."

"What?"

"It's the patient thing again."

"Huh?"

She stared up at him, his features in shadows from the near-dark. "Think about it. Only my patients have the strange incidents. Not yours. Only my tires are slashed. Not yours."

He waved his arm in the direction of the parking area. "This neighborhood has gone downhill the past few years. Some sort of random vandalism, maybe."

"But they didn't touch your truck. Your patients haven't been kept away from the office because of weird occurrences." He'd teased her that day about keeping patients away because she needed a shower. If he joked about it now, she'd slug him.

"You're freaking me out." He stepped closer to her.

"I'll admit I'm freaked out too."

He held out his arms, and she went willingly. Though he was only being thoughtful, she could pretend, at least for a minute, that the hug meant more. She pressed her face into his clean shirt — he'd changed clothes before he'd left the office — and gave out a small sigh that she desperately hoped he hadn't heard.

Why couldn't Harry feel about her the way she did him? Was it her age? It had to be. Or ... maybe he just wasn't attracted to her. Though she knew what his type wasn't, he still hadn't told her what was. Obviously, she wasn't it.

It could also be that he was so used to taking care of her—and she let him—that he couldn't think of her any other way.

The blame for that was partly hers too.

He released her and stepped back. "Come on. I'll drive you home."

"Thanks." She nodded. "What about my car?"

"It will have to be towed."

"I was afraid of that."

"We can call tomorrow from the office. I know a good place just a few blocks away." He pointed his thumb behind them. "They're very reasonable."

"Okay."

He tapped her hand. "Listen, if you don't have the funds right now, I could always—"

"No." She crossed her arms. "You don't need to do that."

"I know I don't need to. I want to."

"I can handle it. Really."

"I know that. But if I make sure it gets done quickly, I'll have my hygienist at the office when I need her. I'm not gonna let you be a slacker, Dorey." He smirked.

"Uh-huh, that's me. Lay around in the dental chair when I don't have a patient."

"So, Mae wasn't kidding when she told me that."

"She ... what?"

He raised his eyebrows, and one side of his mouth quivered, longing to grow into a full grin.

Dorey smacked his shoulder. "You are such a guy."

"You say the sweetest things." He laughed. "Come on."

They climbed into his truck and he backed out. "I was going to get takeout pizza for supper since I'm out of groceries. You game?"

She smiled, glad they were friends again. "For pizza? Always." Besides, her pantry was nearly bare at home.

"True. What was I thinking? When it comes to pizza, you're a..."

"A what? Were you going to say pig?"

"The term that came to mind was hog, but yeah."

She slugged him again.

"Hurt your hand?"

"No." She rubbed her knuckles. "Maybe a little."

They picked up their food and took it back to Dorey's apartment. Once inside, Harry took the pizza into the kitchen.

Dorey kicked off her shoes and put her purse on the end table by the front window. Something moved out on the windowsill. Was someone out there, watching them? Had the person who'd slashed her tires followed them? Or had the person who left the dead roses come back? Dorey leaned forward, pressing her forehead to the glass. Two glowing eyes stared back.

Dorey screamed.

Harry ran to the living room, his eyes wide.

"There's a-a—" She pointed to the window.

Harry flung the door open. Dorey heard a scuffle in the bushes but was too scared to move. What if he was hurt, or worse?

"H-Harry? Are you ..." She took a couple of steps toward the open doorway.

Harry let out a few unintelligible words and then stomped back in. "Here's your culprit."

Caught in Harry's grasp, Weatherby scowled and wiggled, trying to get free.

Dorey let out a breath. "Honestly, Weatherby. A thief, a pervert, and now a peeping tom?"

Harry set Weatherby on the floor and shut the door. "Pervert? Do I wanna know?"

She shook her head at her cat. "Sometimes he brings stuff home. I'm never sure if I'm supposed to be in awe of his hunting skills, grateful for him providing for me, or horrified at what he drags in."

"And he brought..." Harry wound his hand in a circle.

She sighed. "A bra."

Harry sputtered a laugh. "What?"

"Yep." She held her hands out from her chest. "A big one. I don't know where he snatched it from or who it belonged to, but some poor full-figured woman is walking around without her undergarment."

"Wow." Harry looked at the cat. "Not sure if I should be impressed at his prowess or—"

"Horrified?"

"Right."

Dorey laughed. "Well, now that the skulker has been found out, I'm going to change out of these clothes."

"Well, hurry up, 'cause I'm starved."

14

When Dorey got home the next evening, there was a message on her machine. *Should I listen to it? What if it's him again? What if it's not?* But she knew that blinking light would plague her until she found out. Her hand shook as she pressed the button.

"Hey, Dorey! It's Marie. We have to get together. I'd love to do something tonight. Call me."

Dorey groaned. Not only was she tired from work, but she really, *really* did not want to spend time with perky Marie. Still, she'd promised to talk to Harry about her and then report back and so far, Dorey had ignored Marie's voicemails.

Might as well get it over with.

She called back, having to hold the phone away from her ear when Marie happily squealed. After a quick shower and change, Dorey headed out to her car, thankful the garage had been able to replace her tires that afternoon. She'd cringed at the cost but refused Harry's offer to pay for it. Maybe her insurance would at least cover part.

Dorey wanted to visit the new section at the museum on prehistoric animals. Marie wanted to go clothes shopping. But

Dorey didn't have enough money for that after paying for new tires. Plus, she had a free coupon for the museum.

Game over, Marie.

If Marie didn't like it, she could go squeal at someone else.

When Dorey parked in the museum lot, Marie was standing outside the building, looking gorgeous, as usual. "I should have put on some makeup," Dorey muttered. "I'll look like a frump next to her. Too late now."

She hopped out of her car and reached Marie, who hugged her. "I'm so glad to see you!"

"Hey, how are you?" Dorey had to physically force herself not to roll her eyes.

"I'm pumped." Then she actually pumped her fist.

"Oh … uh, great."

Marie grabbed Dorey's arm and nearly yanked her off her feet. Why was she always in a hurry? The museum had been there for decades. It wasn't going to run away now.

They trotted up the long, wide staircase and stepped inside the darker interior. A pack of noisy kids tore past them toward a display of toys from around the world. Dorey was finally able to extricate her arm from Marie as they got to the check-in booth.

A stern-looking man, who looked old enough to have personally known the dinosaurs, motioned them forward. "That will be eight dollars each."

Dorey held up her coupon good for two free passes.

Mr. Tyrannosaurus Rex frowned. Even his wrinkles had wrinkles. "Let me see that." He snatched it away from Dorey's hand and glared at it. With a harrumph, he stamped their hands and told them to step forward. Dorey started to head toward the back, where she knew the prehistoric exhibits were.

"Just a minute," he called from behind them.

Dorey turned. Maybe he wanted to introduce her and Marie to his contemporaries in the exhibit personally?

He pointed a gnarled finger at a middle-aged heavy-set woman whose white button-down blouse could have used a few more inches of fabric. "Go over there."

Dorey frowned. "Oh, okay." She gave Marie a shrug, and they walked ahead a few feet. The woman, not even as friendly as the old man, snarled, "Empty your handbags, ladies."

"Why?" Marie stomped her high-heeled boot on the floor. "It's a new purse, and I recently got all of my makeup tucked away in the cute little compartments, just the way I like it."

The woman raised one eyebrow. "If you want to enter the exhibits, you'll empty your purse. We don't want anyone walking out with something from one of the exhibits. We check everyone now on the way in and out."

"Why are you checking people on the way in?" Marie pouted. "A person wouldn't smuggle something into the museum, would they? Don't you think it would make more sense just to—"

Dorey elbowed her in the ribs and tilted her head toward the counter. Both of them upended their purses. She cringed when the florist's card that had been attached to the roses in the office floated out and landed near Marie's tube of lip gloss. Why didn't she throw the stupid card away?

Marie stared down at it. "Oooh. You got flowers? Who from?"

Dorey grabbed it before Marie could read it. Then she glanced at the woman. "Oh, um, are we allowed to put our stuff back in our bags now?"

The woman did a quick glance at the contents strewn on the counter, took a peek inside their purses, which took longer with Marie because of all the cute little compartments, then deemed them officially allowed to reclaim their items.

Dorey took a few steps before she realized Marie wasn't beside her. "Hey, um, the prehistoric exhibit is this way."

Marie's eyes were opened wide, nearly glazed as she stared

at a small room off to the left. "Just look at those Victorian gowns."

"Hmmm. Yes." Dorey glanced down at her jeans and cotton shirt. Right. As if she'd have any interest in those. But ... She glanced at Marie. She did have to give her some bad news about what Harry had said after meeting her. Maybe she could tell her, get it over with, and console her by looking at the dresses afterward.

"Listen," said Dorey, "let's go sit over on this bench for a minute."

Once seated, Dorey placed her purse on her lap. She waited for Marie to settle her own purse on the bench, check her makeup in her mirrored compact, and flip her hair over her shoulder—twice.

"Marie, I did ask Harry about you and—"

"Oh." She grabbed Dorey's arm again. "He's sooooo cute. And he's a doctor."

"Yes, I think we covered that the other day. Anyway, while he thought you were pretty—"

She bounced on her seat.

Dorey grabbed Marie's hand. "Listen, I'm sorry, but Harry isn't interested." She hated to be blunt, but giving Marie false hope wasn't fair.

Marie's face fell. "Oh." She turned her head away.

"But don't feel bad, I mean, he did say you were attractive and—"

Marie gasped.

"What?"

"Look at that tour guide who just walked into the military exhibit room. Let's go meet him!"

Dorey's mouth dropped open as Marie actually jogged across the carpeted foyer and into the other room.

Well, guess I don't need to feel bad about Harry not liking her.

"Imagine meeting you here."

Perfect. She glanced up and swallowed a groan. "Hello, Dr. Conners." Couldn't she escape the annoying presence of the man and the trail of trouble he left behind for Dorey with her patients? She busied herself with fastening her purse, which she'd forgotten to do after it was searched. That could get a girl in trouble.

"I wasn't aware hygienists were cerebral enough to be interested in something as educational as a museum." He narrowed his eyes as he studied her.

She smiled sweetly. *I wasn't aware that evil dentist ogres were let out of their cages after dark.*

He glared at her as if she'd said it out loud. "Having a little trouble staying busy at work these days?"

"Nope." Dorey crossed her fingers behind her back. "We're busy. Can hardly keep up."

"That's not what I've heard."

"Then you're listening to the wrong people, Dr. Conners."

He leaned forward and pointed his gnarled finger at her. "Don't get glib with me, girly."

"I'm not your girly."

"I'll not stand here and be sassed by a glorified cleaning lady."

Dorey clenched her fist at her side but kept her mouth shut. She wouldn't do Harry any favors by saying anything else. Though she wanted to.

Really bad.

"You'll be sorry." He pointed his impossibly chubby finger at her again.

How had he fit those mitts into people's mouths?

He stormed away, nearly knocking over a couple of kids caught in his wake.

Dorey fumed. *How dare he tell me I'll be sorry? Why I'll just—*

Wait.

You'll be sorry?

He'd just threatened her. Did that implicate the curmudgeonly dentist as being behind the dead roses? Would he have sent them to intimidate her? Try to scare her enough that she wouldn't want to leave her apartment to go to work? But anyone could have sent them. And left that voicemail. Maybe it was a coincidence that he seemed a good possibility for both.

Or maybe it wasn't.

"Dorey!" Marie waved her arms over her head like an air traffic controller.

Dorey hurried over so Marie would stop. People were starting to stare.

"What took you so long?" Her question was for Dorey, but Marie's focus was a few feet to their left.

Ah yes, the tour guide.

Marie grabbed Dorey's arm. She really needed to stop doing that.

"Come over and meet Armand." Marie leaned close and whispered, "He's French."

Dorey listened to Armand giving a bunch of older women simply fascinating facts about the type of buttons used on military uniforms through the ages. It didn't sound like he was French. More like from New Jersey. He finished his talk, smiled at the gushing women, and gave them a wave. Then, he came to stand by Marie, who had dropped Dorey's arm, thankfully, and clutched his.

"Armand, meet my friend, Dorey." Marie smiled up at him.

Dorey nodded. "Hello, Armand."

He inclined his head. "*Bonjour.*"

"Uh, *bonjour* right back at ya." Dorey nearly choked.

"I just love foreign dignitaries." Marie sighed.

Dorey bit her lip. Poor misguided, easily duped Marie.

Armand gave Marie a wink and then took her hand and kissed it. Marie's knees buckled a little, and she leaned into Armand.

Well, as long as she's happy. At least now she'd stop asking about Harry.

Armand whispered something to Marie and then left.

"He has to go back to work, poor thing. It's tough having to earn money so he can get his visa." Marie sighed.

Dorey widened her eyes. "Sure. Say, how about we go visit that Victorian exhibit you wanted to see?"

"Okay." Marie grabbed Dorey's arm, but this time Dorey was ready and didn't stumble.

They walked through the room as Marie gawked at dress after dress. Dorey, frankly, was bored, but Marie acted interested, so she could put up with it for a little while. But she would see the prehistoric animals before she left.

Marie reached out to touch the fabric of a frilly gown before Dorey pointed out a small sign that said not to.

"Oh, poo." Marie frowned but kept looking at the dress. "Ohhhh. Look at the pendant they have draped around the mannequin's neck. Simply stunning. I wonder how much something like that might cost."

Probably much more than a visa for a French dignitary from New Jersey.

Marie turned and gave Dorey the once-over. "Why don't you ever wear jewelry?" She moved her wrist up and down, and four metal hoop bracelets jangled.

"I do. I'm even—" She glanced down. No, she wasn't. She'd been in such a hurry to shower, change and meet Marie, she hadn't put on the ring. She shrugged. "Sometimes I do."

"You know, Dorey, if you want to catch the attention of a guy—" she gave a quick glance across the foyer to Armand "—you might have to step it up a little. You know—makeup, some nice clothes. I'm only saying this because I'm your friend."

Dorey bit the inside of her cheek and then forced a smile. "Awww, aren't you sweet for thinking of my welfare?"

"It's what friends do." Marie latched onto her again and tugged her toward another grouping of mannequins in long, drab dresses.

15

The next morning, Dorey was dragging. She rarely did anything in the evenings during the week, preferring to relax at home with Weatherby, who, by the way, had been none too happy when Dorey got home to feed him at 9:00. How was she to know he'd pick that night to show up?

Harry met her at the counter. "Have fun last night?"

Dorey frowned. "Um, yeah, I guess, why?"

"One of our patients who came in to pay a bill was at the museum. She told Mae she saw you talking to Dr. Conners in the lobby." He leaned closer, even though Mae wasn't at her desk. "How did that go?"

"Let's just say he's even less friendly outside of the office than in." Dorey made a face.

"Wow. Pretty bad, huh?"

She waved a hand. "Nothing I couldn't handle." She gave him a look that said, *just like I can handle other things in my adult life.*

"Well, good. Glad it wasn't terrible for you." He clapped his hands once, then placed them both on the counter. "Okay, listen …" He leaned toward her.

What was he doing? Dorey leaned back.

"Not only did you have more cancellations . . ."

Dorey groaned.

"But I had a big case I was supposed to work on this morning, and my patient has the flu."

"At least he's not canceling because of being scared by a clown. Or run off the road by a van. Or having his male poodle Angelique run away."

Harry raised an eyebrow at the dog's name. "Anyway, because we have extra time, we're gonna do our twice-yearly office staff cleanings and checkups."

Dorey rolled her eyes.

He touched her arm, and one side of his mouth rose. "I know it's not what you'd planned for today, but our cleanings have to happen at some point, right? Might as well get it done while we're all free at the same time. I mean, how often does that happen?"

"You're right. It's rare." Dorey let out a sigh. "Okay, let me go get set up. I don't care who wants to go first for a cleaning. You guys can fight over me." She grinned.

Harry laughed and turned toward the hallway as Luanne and Mae came in the main door together.

A few minutes later, Luanne strolled in. "Hey Dorey, guess I drew the short straw." She winked.

"At least you get it over with first. I have to wait for Harry to clean and check mine at the end. Glad we don't have like twenty employees to wait through." She pushed the button that reclined the chair and waited as Luanne's head lowered.

She nodded. "Say, I've been meaning to ask. I noticed you have a new ring you've been wearing."

"Yep." Dorey glanced down at her hand. She could barely make out the shape of the stone beneath her glove.

"It's turquoise, right?"

"Uh-huh."

"Any chance you'd be interested in selling it?"

"Um ..." Dorey moved her focus from Luanne's mouth to her eyes.

"It's just that I love turquoise. I'm always on the lookout for something unique, ya know?"

Dorey almost laughed. She did smile, but with her mask on, Luanne wouldn't be able to see it. Mask? Why did so many things point toward them? She forced her attention back to her patient. If Luanne wore any more rings, necklaces, and bracelets than she already did, she'd look like a walking jewelry counter. As it was, Dorey could hand her a tambourine, and she could moonlight as a gypsy right now.

Dorey nodded. "Well, thanks for your interest, but I really like it. I think I'll hang onto it."

"No problem. Never hurts to ask."

"Of course." Dorey smiled.

Luanne was a smoker, so her cleaning took longer than some to remove the stain. Good thing Dorey had plenty of time to work on her. When her patients actually showed up, and there were several in one day like Luanne, Dorey would go home with sore hands.

Finally, she finished. "If you wanna relax here, I'll go get Harry."

Luanne put her hands behind her head and crossed her legs at the ankles. "Suits me just fine." She grinned.

Dorey found Harry in his office reading a dental journal with a picture of a molar on the cover. "Gee, Doc, that looks really exciting. Think I could tear you away to do Luanne's exam?"

"Gladly." He tossed the magazine on his desk. "If I ever can't sleep, that's the kind of thing I grab to read."

"Don't let the dental society hear you say that," she said over her shoulder as she stepped out of the room ahead of him.

"I'm not too worried. I'm guessing they use it as a sleep aid too."

Harry sat down, put on gloves and a mask while Dorey stood beside the counter, ready to make any necessary notes in Luanne's chart.

"Any pain anywhere, Luanne?"

"Nope." She pointed a bejeweled finger at him. "And don't go finding any problems in there, ya hear?"

He chuckled. "I'll do my best not to." And he didn't.

Next would be Mae. As soon as Dorey's room was clean, the receptionist came in and sat down in the chair. She patted the seat. "I always forget how comfortable these things are. Maybe I should keep them in mind if I ever need a nap."

Dorey lowered her voice conspiratorially, "I have it on good authority that our boss does that from time to time." She winked.

"Wouldn't surprise me a bit." Mae cackled.

Mae's cleaning took no time at all since half of her teeth were replaced by a denture. Within fifteen minutes, Dorey was at Harry's door again. She held out her hand toward the hallway. "We're ready."

He hopped up, looking like he had too much energy and didn't know how to use it. They all hated not being busy. Unfortunately for Dorey, that had been most of her workdays lately.

Mae's exam took just a few minutes. She got up from the chair and mumbled, "Guess I get to go back to filing."

Dorey rolled her eyes at Harry, and they both grinned, aware it was Mae's least favorite job.

"You want next, or you want to do me?"

Harry raised both eyebrows at her words 'do me.'

"I didn't mean, um. Well, what I meant was …" Dorey opened her mouth, then closed it, wincing when heat traveled up her face.

"Sure you want to rephrase your question? It sounded interesting the way you said it." He took a step closer.

Her mouth fell open. "Getting kinda forward, aren't we, Harry?"

"Forward can be fun." He shrugged and leaned closer like he was going to kiss her or something.

Dorey held her breath and stared at his lips. Just when she thought he would actually do it, he stood up straight.

"You can clean mine next. Let me know when the room is ready."

She nodded, unable to form words as he left the room. Harry was silly, teased her, and had hugged her. But this was out and out flirting. She fanned her face with her hand.

Grabbing a plastic cup from the dispenser, she got a drink of cold water. Might do her more good to just pour it over her head, but she'd have a hard time explaining why her shirt front was wet. And then Harry might look there and ...

No. That wouldn't be good.

She put on gloves and grabbed all the disposables, throwing them in the trash, then cleaned the chair and all the equipment. The dirty instruments went into the lab to clean later.

When she came back, she got out supplies and fresh instruments. It was always weird to clean Harry's teeth. But even more awkward this time after what he'd just said.

Dorey's hands were shaking. She couldn't clean Harry's teeth. Not in this frame of mind. Maybe if she cleaned his last, there'd be enough time for her to calm down now while she sat in the chair. She'd just tell Harry she'd changed her mind and he could do her first.

Don't say it like that.

She hurried to tell Harry the room was ready and then rushed back to her room, wanting to get in the chair before he got there. She grabbed the patient napkin from the tray and clipped it on. Then she could ensure he'd have to check and clean hers first.

Footsteps came a few seconds later. He stepped in and stopped. "Oh. I—"

"You don't mind, do you?"

He came closer, glanced over his shoulder, and back at her. "I thought maybe you wanted me to sit in the chair *with* you," he whispered.

"Nah." She forced a laugh. "With our combined weight, the chair might break."

"Might be worth it." Harry raised one eyebrow.

What had gotten into him?

She clasped her hands tightly together in her lap as the head of the chair began its descent.

Wanting to talk about something work-related, she said, "So I never heard. What were the reasons for all of my cancellations today?"

Harry shrugged.

She looked up at him, only being able to view his eyes above his mask and nothing else. "Harry?"

"More of the same."

"You mean weird stuff? And people who've been listening to Dr. Conners?" She tensed, waiting.

He patted her shoulder. "That's why I wasn't gonna tell ya. Didn't want you to be upset."

"I can't help it. Even you have to admit that it's odd, only being my patients. And the fact that you've been paying me my regular salary all this time and—"

"Dorey. Stop talking and open your mouth so I can do the exam."

She let out a frustrated sigh but complied. Her skin must have been super sensitive or something, because she'd never noticed before how warm Harry's hands were even when he had gloves on. And how long his eyelashes were.

Her mind jumped to someplace it shouldn't have. To her and Harry, alone in the office, the lights turned out—

"Dorey?" He sat back and removed his hands from her mouth. He held up a scaler. "Did I get you with my instrument?"

She eyed the metal piece about as long as a pencil as if it had offended her. "No, I'm fine."

Dorey's heart thumped hard in her chest. This was getting ridiculous. Calm down.

He laid down his instruments and picked up the handpiece and prophy paste for her polish. "Didn't see any cavities."

"That's good."

He loaded some cinnamon paste on the hand-piece brush but didn't start her polish yet. He cleared his throat. "About the patients not showing up ... I know I've said more than once that I don't want you to worry about it. I meant that. I'm really not worried about paying you even when they don't show up."

"But if you paid me commission, then it would be fair to both of us."

"Dorey, if you only got commission these past few weeks, your paycheck wouldn't be enough to pay your rent and buy food."

"I don't care. I feel awful that—"

His hand on her shoulder silenced her. "Please, let me do this for you. I-I want to, okay?"

She looked up into his eyes and could see he did indeed mean it. Her vision blurred as tears threatened to form. "Thank you."

16

After her shower and changing into sweats, Dorey walked into the living room. Weatherby lounged on the couch, giving himself a tongue bath. How he could lick his paws for an hour and still not be clean continually amazed her. She eyed him. "Maybe you need a proper scrubbing. I could give you one in the sink. Use some nice bubble bath. Then you'd smell all pretty."

Weatherby gave her the stink-eye.

"Don't worry." She laughed. "I wouldn't. I value the skin on my hands and face too much to try that."

Seemingly offended, Weatherby jumped down from the couch and dove through the kitty door.

Great. Now who knew when he'd be back? As she headed toward the couch to watch TV, the squeak from the cat's door surprised her. "Back so soon?"

Her cat ran in and leaped in the air, landing on her lap.

"Wow, what's all this? Decide to forgive me already? That must be a record."

She rubbed the top of his head and then reached under his chin to scratch him there. And recoiled. Something furry that was not Weatherby had touched her hand. *Ick!* With care, and ignoring his growl, she lifted the cat and put him on the floor. He put his front paws on the couch as if to jump up there again.

"No," she said sternly.

Sitting back down on his haunches, he glared at her over the tiny body in his jaws. A mouse? She couldn't see its head very well, so she wasn't sure. Either way, it wasn't something she wanted in her apartment.

She stood and rushed to the kitchen, where she kept a box of disposable plastic gloves. Didn't every hygienist have some? When she came back, Weatherby had dropped his prey on the carpet— thanks a lot— and was licking its fur.

"Okay, cat, I'm going to have to confiscate your prize."

Weatherby slapped his paw over the rodent.

"Now listen. You can't keep that thing in here." She tilted her head. He'd only been outside for a matter of seconds. He was quick, but she'd never known him to catch something that fast.

Slowly, keeping her voice steady and slow, she reached out her gloved hand. "Now, honey, let Mommy see what you brought her, okay?"

Weatherby backed up against the couch and growled, rolling the small animal toward him with his paw.

"Weatherby, Mommy needs to see what you have."

She reached out again only to be rewarded with a hiss. So much for slow and steady. With her right hand, she grabbed her cat by the scruff of his neck, to render him temporarily immobile without hurting him. With her left hand, trying not to gag, she grabbed the rodent.

It was definitely dead. In fact, it was so dead, it was ice-cold. For the first time, it registered what color it was. White. This was no ordinary field mouse. More like something she'd seen at a pet store.

Dorey frowned and stood, letting go of Weatherby as she did. The cat jumped in the air and came close to nabbing the mouse again, but Dorey raised her arm just in time. Once the dead body had been properly stuffed in the kitchen trash can and her gloves tossed in after it, she scrubbed her hands. After tying up the bag, she ran the trash outside, tossing it into the nearest dumpster.

How weird that Weatherby had found something dead right outside her door. And it had to be no farther than that because he hadn't had time to go any greater distance before he'd brought it back inside.

Hopefully there wasn't blood or any body parts on the cement in front of her door for her to step in the next time she went out. Cautiously, she opened the front door and peered down. No blood or intestines. But there was something red tied to the outside corner of Weatherby's kitty door.

Dorey stepped outside and crouched down, trying to see what it was. A note tied with red ribbon.

Did you like my gift?

Her eyes widened. It was from the same person that had left the headless flowers. It had to be. Same wording. She was sure of it.

Looking around, she didn't see anyone, but still felt like she was being watched. Snatching the paper off the kitty door so no one else would see it, she hurried back inside, closed, and dead-bolted her door. Her breathing was ragged as if she'd just run a couple of miles.

The messages and roses could no longer be brushed off as a bunch of pranks. Leaving something dead, even though it was a rodent, was going too far.

She started to throw the note in the trash and changed her mind. Now that things were sizing up to be more than a practical joke, should she go to the police? She reached in and captured the very edge of the note between her thumb and finger. The paper slipped and floated to the floor, face down.

There was more writing on the back. She squinted to read the very tiny letters.

If you go to the police or tell anyone, you will regret it.

Shock rolled through her. It was as if whoever had left the note had read her mind.

The creep factor of the whole ordeal just climbed a notch higher.

She backed away from the paper on the floor as if it might reach out to grab her ankle. What should she do now?

Should she call Harry? No. The note said not to tell anyone. Would whoever sent it hurt Harry if he knew what was happening?

The thought of something happening to Harry nearly made her queasy. She couldn't risk it.

I can't just walk around that spot on my kitchen floor forever. She quickly grabbed the note and tossed it in the trash. Even though there'd been nothing visibly staining the note, such as rodent blood, she scrubbed her hands again. As she dried them off with a paper towel, it was as if she tried to scrub away the thought of what the note said. With a shudder, Dorey balled up the paper towel.

A crash came from the living room. Dorey shrieked and ran, afraid something had happened to Weatherby.

Her cat was there, all right, perched on top of her TV, his tail puffed out like a squirrel.

"What happened?" Her heart raced. "What was that crash?"

Her gaze darting crazily around, she finally saw it. Broken glass on the back of her couch. With a frown, she rushed over and parted the curtains. And there, low on the picture window, right above the sill, was a gaping hole several inches wide.

Hands shaking, she carefully peered over the back of her couch. Dorey gasped and slapped her hand over her mouth.

Down on the carpet, sitting in a sea of shattered glass, sat a brick.

Her mouth went dry. Who had done it? Were they still outside? Everything in her wanted to run in the opposite direction. Hide under her bed with her cat and never resurface. But she also had to find out who the culprit was. This had to stop.

Shoving aside her fear, Dorey hurried to the door and flung it open. A scan to her left showed no one. To her right was—

"Hey, Dorey."

She jumped and screamed.

Harry ran the few feet separating him from her door. He reached out and grabbed her shoulders. "What's wrong? Are you hurt?"

No words came out as she shook her head.

"Talk to me. What happened?" He lowered his eyebrows, his gaze seeming to take in every inch of her face.

Still unable to speak, she blinked and swallowed hard. Instead, she backed up into her open doorway and inside the apartment.

Harry followed. She pointed to the general vicinity of the couch and window.

"Dorey, what—"

She closed her eyes, waiting for him to see it.

Harry looked over the back of her couch, just like she'd done a scant few minutes ago.

"When did this happen?"

"J-just now. R-right before you came."

He took her in his arms and held her close. Pressed against his chest, Dorey could have sworn their heartbeats raced together, matching beat for beat.

"Honey." He stroked his hand down her hair, still damp from her shower. "Are you sure you're all right?"

"I think so." She burrowed into him more, tucking her head under his chin, wanting to stay there forever. Never move.

Never have to think about anything except Harry. His warmth. His comfort. His protection.

They stayed that way for a while, though not nearly long enough for Dorey. She sighed as he pulled away.

"Dorey …" He took her hand and led her to the kitchen. Forcing her onto a chair, he grabbed a clean glass from her dish drainer and filled it with water. "Drink this."

She wasn't thirsty. Didn't want the water. But the look of determination in Harry's eyes caused her to comply. She drained the glass and handed it back.

"Good." He set it on the table and knelt in front of her. "Now … You're not hurt, right?"

She shook her head.

"Where's Weatherby?"

"On top of the TV."

"Hmm." He raised his eyebrows. "Well, I guess if there'd been a loud scary sound in my house, I might have done the same."

She knew he was trying to make her laugh, lighten the moment, but she couldn't even smile.

"We need to call the police." He cradled her face between her hands.

"No."

"Why not?" He frowned.

"I-I just don't want to."

"But—"

"No. Please. Just don't."

He shook his head slowly. "We need to."

"Not-not now."

"Your apartment super will do it if we don't."

Dorey let out a breath. That was true. There wasn't any way she could stop Mr. Nichols from calling. But she wasn't going to. She couldn't. Not after the instructions on the note.

"All right. Well, let's at least call him." Harry pressed a light kiss to her forehead and then stood. "You need that window covered temporarily until they can replace the glass."

Dorey glanced in the direction of the living room, though she couldn't see the window from where she sat. Harry was right. She couldn't leave that gaping hole in her window. Not even overnight.

Overnight.

There was no way she'd be able to sleep. Not with the thought of that hole—that someone could make the opening bigger, climb inside while she was lying in her bed. She gasped.

"What?"

"N-nothing."

Harry frowned. "Listen. You stay here. I'm going to call the building super. What's the number?"

"It's over there." She pointed to her refrigerator. "With a bunch of other numbers."

"Ah, I see it's at the bottom of the list." He nodded. "Under pizza delivery and the veterinarian. Priorities."

She did lift one corner of her mouth in a quasi-smile, but that was all she could manage.

He pulled his cell phone from his pocket and punched in the numbers. After a few seconds, he tried again. He shook his head. "The first time I got a message giving me the hours he could be reached. Which ended two hours ago. I tried the emergency number for him after hours, and he didn't answer. And there wasn't even a voicemail to leave a message. Not great."

"I know." Dorey shut her eyes for a second, dreading the moment Harry would leave, and she'd be alone with that broken window.

"I can at least cover the hole for you. Got any cardboard?" Harry put his phone away and ran his hand through his hair.

At first, she shook her head, then remembered the large box in her closet where she kept old shoes and clothes. She'd been planning to donate them to the homeless shelter. Just hadn't gotten around to it. "Yeah, in my closet."

"Bedroom?"

She nodded.

He left. It was strange to have Harry go in there. He'd been to her apartment lots of times, but she couldn't remember him ever going in there. And why would he have? It's not like they were going to—

When he returned, he eyed the box. "I had to dump some things out. I left them on the floor of your closet. Does that work?"

"Yeah."

He set the box on the floor and went to her junk drawer to get some duct tape. For some reason, it gave her a warm feeling that he knew his way around much of her apartment. Like he belonged there. With her.

While Harry tore off a section of the box and some tape, Dorey ventured into the crime scene area and pried poor Weatherby from the top of the TV. "Come here, baby."

Weatherby usually growled at her when being picked up wasn't his idea, but this time her cat clung to her, pressing against her chest, burrowing under her chin. Just like she'd done with Harry.

Like they were a sort of family. She sighed. Wouldn't that be wonderful?

It didn't take Harry long to cover the hole. He got her vacuum cleaner out of her coat closet. Weatherby tucked himself farther under her chin. He hated the vacuum. Did he think it would swallow him up?

She took him back to the kitchen, hoping he'd be less traumatized if he couldn't see the suck monster.

The vacuum quit. A couple of minutes later, Harry returned. "Okay. Window is covered. Glass is cleaned up."

"Thank you, Harry. I just—I appreciate it."

"Honey, you don't need to thank me. I'm just glad I was here."

Hold on. Harry normally wouldn't have been here to take care of things. "Why did you come?"

"I thought maybe you'd like to take a walk." He shrugged. "'Cause, you know, when I stopped by the other night for one, you'd just gotten back. With your friend."

"Right. Marie." She needed to talk about something besides the brick and broken window. "She thinks you're hot, by the way."

He chuckled. "So, you'd mentioned."

Dorey shrugged.

"Well, like I told you, she's not my type." He took a step closer.

"I seem to remember something like that."

Another step, and he was only a couple of feet away. "And what about you?"

"What about me?"

The next step brought him within a few inches. Weatherby squirmed as if claustrophobic with so much human body heat. Dorey put him down, needing a distraction from Harry standing so close.

He now stood so close she had to tip her head back to see his face.

"Do you think I'm ... hot?" Harry asked in a soft voice.

Dorey swallowed. What she should say was something funny. Something trite. Anything to divert Harry's attention from staring at her lips. But she couldn't. The only thing she could say was the truth.

"Yes."

17

Harry's lips found hers. He tugged her close. The man tasted heavenly. The kiss took control of her entire body. Without her consent, her arms wound around his neck. Pulling him closer. Wanting to press against his solid wall of chest. Her knees buckled. Not sure if she was even breathing, and not really caring. There was nothing besides them. Nothing apart from this wonderful, glorious, all-encompassing kiss.

Heat spread across her back as Harry's large hands massaged her muscles. *I'm kissing Harry!*

As if hearing her, realizing what had happened, Harry ended the kiss. He peered into her eyes. She'd never been this close to him. Well, she had, but it had never been after that kiss.

"Dorey, I—"

"It's okay."

He shook his head. "I shouldn't have. I mean, I'm your boss and—"

She laid her hand flat against his chest, wishing he'd do it again. "But we're not at work, are we?"

He smiled and looked around, like he was checking to make sure. "No. So, you're not going to slap me or anything?"

"Did I act like I hated it?"

"Not from what I could tell." His face reddened.

She wanted so badly to tell him how much the kiss meant. How long she'd wanted to do it. To press her lips to his. But she couldn't. If she did that, the words that went with them would pop out.

I love you.

And even though he'd just kissed her, just done something she'd longed for, he'd never said the words. Never indicated he felt that way. So, in an effort to do what they always seemed to do, she made a joke. "Doesn't every girl kiss a hot dentist in her kitchen when she has the chance?"

He laughed. "I wouldn't know. Don't make a habit of it."

He didn't? Good to know. "Oh, come on. I can see you prowling around, looking for single women, wooing them in their kitchens."

"Wooing?" He raised an eyebrow. "That's deep, Dorey."

"I'm a deep girl. You have no idea."

"I think I know you pretty well."

"So you think." She poked his shoulder.

"I'm guessing I know all your secrets."

No, you don't. Not about the scary voicemail. The dead rodent. She sobered and stepped away. "Listen, I know you came over here for a walk in the park, but—"

"Yeah, probably not the best time after your broken window." He studied her face. "Have you eaten?"

"No. Didn't get the chance."

"I'll order pizza. Okay? Since I know where you keep all your most important numbers." He gave her an exaggerated scowl. "So, why isn't my number up there?"

'Cause I have it memorized. "Hey, dentists can't possibly rate with pizza."

"And veterinarians? And building superintendents?"

She laughed. "Sorry to crush your fragile ego."

"This is the thanks I get." He shook his head.

As he turned away to get the number from the fridge, she shivered, thinking about his strong arms holding her. His body pressed close. Soft lips caressing hers.

"All right." He put his phone in his pocket. "It's on its way."

She forced herself to focus and nodded. "Thanks."

"So …" He glanced into the living room.

"Yeah, I think I need to sit down." They went into the living room. She eyed the couch.

"I ran the vacuum attachment over it, but no guarantee I got all the little shards. Some were really tiny."

"For now, I'll cover it with a blanket, just to be sure. I'd hate for Weatherby to get anything in his paws." She grabbed one from her closet shelf and spread it out over the couch.

Somehow it seemed an intimate act, spreading a blanket with Harry standing right behind her. Like they were going to—

Once she'd tucked the blanket all around the couch, she sat down. Harry joined her. He didn't put his arm around her liked she'd hoped, but he did sit close. He turned to face her. Reaching out, he took a strand of her hair and ran it between his fingers. "I've always loved your hair."

"You have?"

He nodded. "It's so soft. And I love the color."

Dorey rolled her eyes. "It's a mousy brown."

"No. It's chestnut."

"Chestnut? When did you get all poetic sounding?"

"I always have been." He smiled. "You just never noticed."

She snorted. "Oh, please."

"Hey, dentists can be sensitive."

She reached up to touch his face, just wanting to feel his skin beneath her fingertips one more time. Lightly, she stroked his cheek. She wanted to do so much more but stopped herself. If Harry had just been reacting to the moment earlier, she didn't want to go there.

Well, she did, but …

She wanted more than that. More than a roll in the hay with her boss. Her friend. The man she desperately loved. But even if he loved her back the same way, she'd wait until she was married.

Pulling her hand away, she rested it back on her lap. She smiled at him and then changed her focus to the TV. Weatherby was back up there. His tail wasn't puffed out anymore, but his eyes were opened wider than usual. He looked like an owl.

Harry sighed. "Dorey, I don't feel right about leaving you here alone."

She didn't want that either but wasn't sure what to do about it. She nodded.

"So, why don't you stay at my place tonight?"

"I'm not sure that's a great idea." She lifted an eyebrow.

He lifted his hands, palms out. "I'd sleep on the couch."

Both of her eyebrows went up.

"Honest."

"Thanks for the offer, but …"

"What?"

She nodded toward her cat. "I don't want to leave him here. I'd worry whoever did that to the window might…"

"Oh, yeah, I see." He shrugged. "You could bring him with us to my house."

"He'd hate it. If he got away and tried to come back here, I'd be afraid he'd get hit by a car or something."

"Doesn't he wander around all the time anyway?"

"Yes, but … I'd just keep thinking something happened to him, coming across town and all."

He glanced around. "Well, I could stay here tonight." He patted the couch.

She glanced over her shoulder at the cardboard covering the window. If Harry stayed on the couch, she wouldn't be able to sleep. She'd worry that the person responsible might do something to Harry while he slept. No. That wouldn't work either. She shook her head.

"I'd worry about you. Out here." She pointed to the window.

He grinned. "I'd be fine."

"I'm sure you could take care of whatever, but I—"

"You'd still worry. And then you wouldn't sleep."

"Right."

"And knowing that you weren't getting any rest would mean I'd worry about you."

She laughed. "Well, aren't we a pair?"

"How about ..." He rubbed his fingers along her shoulder.

"What?"

"Please don't take this the wrong way, okay?"

She lowered her eyebrows. "What? Just say it."

"We could ..." His eyes slid to the right. In the direction of her bedroom.

"Um ... I don't think—"

He grabbed both of her hands and held them tight. "Just to sleep. That's it."

"Harry ..."

"I promise, Dorey."

"But you won't—"

"I won't. I just want to make sure you're safe."

She sighed. Not the best scenario, but probably the best option. At least for one night. "Okay."

"Good."

"What about ... do you need anything from your house?" She didn't want to be alone. Even for a little while. Until they knew who had done this and the perpetrator was behind bars, Dorey would be on edge.

"Do you have a spare toothbrush?"

She gave a snort. "With all those samples I get from drug reps in the mail, are you kidding? I have like a whole dental store in there."

"Then I'm all set."

She eyed his clothes. "What will you wear tomorrow? We do have to go to work, you know. And you might not have time to drive across town and back to the office."

"I keep a spare set at work in case I ever need to change."

"Oh. Right." She'd known that. "Um ... what about ... pajamas?" Her face heated, thinking about lying in her bed with him there.

He stared at her lips. "I don't wear pajamas, Dorey."

She swallowed. "Oh." Her legs wobbled, like they'd turned to liquid.

"But for tonight, I'll keep my clothes on. Does that work?"

"All right." She bit her lip. What choice did she have if she wanted either of them to get a wink of sleep?

They ate supper and watched a movie. Dorey made sure not to get a chick flick. If Harry was being nice enough to stay with her after the broken window, the least she could do was not irritate him with a movie he'd hate.

Weatherby feasted on pepperoni they had left over. Each time one of them gave him a piece, he carried it in his mouth and took it to the bedroom.

"Does he always do that?" Harry nodded his head toward her room. "Take his food in there?"

"Only with something special. His boring dry food stays in his dish in the kitchen. Sometimes I think maybe it feels a little slighted."

Harry snorted. Then his smile fell. "Does your cat sleep in there too?" He said it like he desperately hoped Weatherby didn't.

"When he's here. Otherwise, I guess he sacks out under a bush somewhere. I'm never sure when he's going to show up. But I really hope he sticks around tonight. I don't want him wandering around out there with ..."

"I get it. If you want to make sure he stays in, couldn't we fasten the cat door closed somehow?" Harry rubbed her shoulder.

She shook her head. "I tried that once. I didn't get any sleep that night. He howled the entire time. There's no one in the apartment next to me right now, but there was then. They called the police about the noise. That was fun."

"I'm sure."

Dorey took their empty plates and set them in the sink. She glanced at the clock. Ten-thirty. She was usually in bed by now. Walking out to the living room, she twisted her hands together in front of her. "It's ... getting late and ..." She vaguely pointed to her room.

He looked at his watch. "Oh, you're right." He stood. "Guess I'll need that toothbrush, then."

"Right." She'd nearly forgotten. "Sure. Come on back to the bathroom." She turned, very aware that he was just behind her. *This is so weird.* The times he'd been here before, they'd just hung out, and then he'd left.

Dorey flipped on the bathroom light switch and opened a lower drawer. She rummaged around until she found a green toothbrush. His favorite color.

"Aww, for me?" He smiled.

"Don't make a big deal out of it. I just knew you wouldn't brush your teeth if I gave you a pink one. And if you have pizza breath, I'm not going to bed with you." She widened her eyes. Going to bed with you. She bit her lip.

"Well, all righty then." He smirked.

Dorey had to squeeze past him to get back out the door. Amazing how small it seemed with him in there too. She closed the door behind her, giving him some privacy.

Pacing up and down the hallway didn't burn off her sudden influx of hyper energy. The dishes. She could do the few things in the sink.

That took all of five minutes. She glanced around. What

else? She made sure the door was dead-bolted. Now what? She filled Weatherby's bowl. Got clean pajamas out of the dryer to wear.

'I don't wear pajamas, Dorey.'

Heat, sudden and fierce coursed through her veins. In a matter of minutes, she was going to be in bed with Harry.

Surreal.

The bathroom door opened, and Harry stepped out. His face looked damp. Must have washed up a little. "All yours."

Dorey smiled and hurried past him to the bathroom doorway. After brushing her teeth and washing up, she changed into her pajamas. She glanced down and groaned. Her only clean pair would have to be the ones with frolicking kittens on them all wearing pink bows around their necks and little blue hats. The fact that they held paws and danced was just a bonus.

He'll think I'm seven again.

She left the bathroom and nearly stumbled the short distance to her bedroom. When she entered, Harry was already under the sheet. Her nerves threatened to cause her to pass out.

But there was Weatherby, lying beside Harry, partially under the sheet.

"I think he likes me." Harry rolled his eyes. "At least I guess he does. What does it mean when they knead your arm with their paws?"

"That you're his person from now until forever." She crossed her arms and leaned against the doorjamb.

"Ah."

She laughed. "Got a problem with that, Doc?"

"Nope. I think I can handle a cat professing his undying love for me." He reached down and ruffled the fur on Weatherby's head.

Dorey tilted her head and studied the pair. But could you handle it from the cat's owner?

Deciding it wouldn't get any easier if she waited, Dorey

walked across the room and climbed into bed. She turned out the lamp on the bedside table, plunging them into darkness. Weatherby must have grown tired of being petted, or else three was too many in a bed. She heard a rustle of sheets and the light pressure of his paws as he tromped across her stomach.

Why wasn't she nervous, lying next to Harry? But strangely, she felt calm. Relaxed. Like they were supposed to be together.

"Harry?"

"Yeah?"

"Thank you."

The sheets rustled as he turned. "Can I ask you something?"

"Sure."

"Would you mind terribly if I just held you?"

Tears threatened to attack Dorey's eyes. She blinked them back. "I would love that." She turned, so her back was to him. When he edged closer and pressed his warm chest against her back and wrapped his arm around her middle, she sighed and drifted off to sleep.

18

The alarm blared, and Dorey smacked the off button with her palm. She stretched her arms over her head, feeling more rested than she ever had. She smiled. The dreams she'd had were amazing. All about Harry.

"Good morning."

Dorey shrieked and whipped around toward the voice.

"I know I have pillow head, but I didn't think it was frightening." Harry smoothed his hand down his hair.

"No ..." She swallowed and moved away from him a few inches. "I—"

"You forgot I was here, didn't you?"

"Well ..."

"What a way to boost a guy's ego." He turned his head but snuck a peek at her from the corner of his eye. Teasing her, as usual.

"Guess you'll have to find a way to get over it." She shrugged as she took a deep breath, trying to slow down her heart rate.

He sat up and crawled out of bed. Angling his head toward the doorway, he said, "Want me to make coffee?"

"That'd be great. I'll hop in the shower."

"Yeah, because you need more time to get pretty than I do."

"Face it, Harry. You're already pretty."

He struck a pose like a model on the runway, chin pointed up, acting like he flipped long hair over his shoulder. "I know."

Dorey laughed, amazed that she wasn't more self-conscious about him staying over.

But nothing happened.

With a sigh, she went into the bathroom and took a quick shower. Wrapping up in her thick bathrobe, she combed out her hair.

Harry knocked on the door. "You decent?"

"Yeah."

He pushed the door open. "As hard as it is to reach your building super, should you call him now? See if he can get somebody in to fix that window today?"

"Good idea." She left the bathroom and got her phone.

"Want me to do it?" He held out his hand.

"Sure. Thanks." She handed him the phone. "I need to feed Weatherby, anyway."

Harry was doing more and more for her. Stepping into what should be her territory. Taking care of everything. It used to irritate her so badly. Why didn't it bother her as much? She didn't want him to treat her like a kid again, but somehow, when he treated her as an equal, she didn't mind him helping her out when she needed it.

What had changed?

Her cat had sauntered into the kitchen, yawning, eyes half-closed. Where had he slept? He hadn't come back to bed once she'd gotten there. Had he gone outside?

Hopefully not. But at least he appeared unharmed this morning. She went to the cabinet where she kept his dry food. "Come on, buddy. Time for breakfast."

His eyes snapped open, suddenly looking wide awake. He

meowed and wound around her legs as she filled his plastic dish on the floor.

She petted him for a minute while he ate. "That's a good boy." She was rewarded with a rumbling purr.

Harry had gone into the living room to make his call. He came back in the kitchen. "All right. Talked to him. He said he'd be here any minute, so we should hurry and get ready."

"Yep." She rushed to put on her scrubs and brush her teeth. Light makeup—all she ever wore—only took a minute. She glanced at her hair in the mirror. Still wet. She needed to stay by the door, though, for when the super came. She didn't have a doorbell and couldn't always hear someone knock from back here.

Deciding to dry her hair after Mr. Nichols came to check out the window, Dorey left the bathroom, passing Harry in the hall. He stepped inside and closed the door.

Something bumped her leg, and she gasped. "Honestly, Weatherby, you shouldn't startle me like that." She sat on the couch while she waited, glad the blanket covered it. A more thorough vacuuming of the cushions would have to wait until after work. Where was the super? He'd said he'd be right over.

She patted her leg, and Weatherby came running. He jumped on her lap and turned in a circle before settling down. "I can only stay here for a minute, okay?"

He gazed up at her and blinked his eyes slowly.

"Yes, I love you too."

"Do you always profess undying love to your cat?"

Dorey jumped. Harry stood there. He rubbed a towel over his wet hair.

"Don't be jealous, Doc. Weatherby and I have lived together for months."

"Okay, I see where I stand." But he gave her a wink. "Any sign of him yet?" He pointed to the window.

"Nope."

"Is he always this unreliable? First can't get a hold of him at all, then he doesn't come when he says he will."

"Pretty much."

"Maybe you need to find a better place to live." Harry flipped the damp towel over his shoulder. "I'll finish getting ready. Maybe he'll be here soon. We need to head to work."

"I can wait for him. You go on ahead to work. I don't want you to be late."

"No. I want to speak to him personally. If he's that unreliable, not sure I trust him to do what he says. I'd like to make it clear that the window needs to be repaired today."

Dorey nodded. She let out a sigh as Harry headed back to the bathroom. If the window got fixed today, then Harry wouldn't have a reason to stay with her anymore. Why did that make her want to cry?

A hard knock came from her door. She called back to Harry. "He's here."

"Okay."

Dorey opened the door. Mr. Nichols stood there wearing jeans, a sweatshirt, and his usual scowl. He wasn't a morning person. Or afternoon, or evening.

"Good morning."

He frowned. "If you say so. Who was that guy who called? You got a roommate? If so, we'll have to raise your rent because—"

She held up her hand. "No. No roommate. Just a … friend who stayed with me last night."

"Friend?" He raised his eyebrows.

That hadn't come out the way she'd meant it. "Just … he was worried about me being here alone. With the window." She twisted her hands in front of her. "'Cause he was worried."

"Call it what you want, Miss Cameron." He gave a snort. "But it's pretty obvious what went on here."

Her mouth dropped open. "Hey, that's not what—"

"Mr. Nichols?" Harry stood right behind Dorey.

Flames of embarrassment rose up her face. Had he heard the super's comment?

Mr. Nichols eyed Harry up and down. Dorey was sure nothing she said would convince Mr. Nichols that Harry staying over had been innocent.

Wait. Why did she care anyway? She was an adult. Free country and all that. She relaxed as Harry motioned the super inside and pointed to the window.

"See here?" Harry indicated the hole in the glass. "A brick was thrown through early last evening. We tried to get a hold of you then, but you were unavailable."

Mr. Nichols shrugged, as if he didn't give a care what happened after five p.m. as long as he didn't have to deal with it.

"We'd like this repaired today." Harry lowered his eyebrows.

"We?" The super narrowed his eyes. "I don't remember any name on the lease besides Miss Cameron."

Harry glanced at Dorey and back. "I'm a friend."

"So you say."

Harry took a step closer, so close Mr. Nichols— a good six inches shorter— had to tip his head back.

"Will this be taken care of today?"

Mr. Nichols blinked, sized up Harry, and gave a single nod.

"Good." He looked at Dorey. "We'd better go. Don't want to be late."

"Right." She grabbed her purse and then crammed her feet into her shoes. Weatherby, seeing Mr. Nichols wasn't leaving with them, ran into the bedroom.

Harry headed toward his truck, then stopped. She had her hand on the door of her car.

"Dorey? Aren't you riding with me?"

She tapped her car window. "Um, it might be better if we didn't ride together. Someone might think ..."

"Don't be silly. I'll want to check that window tonight after work anyway, so it makes more sense for me to drive you."

"I don't think this is a good idea," she muttered under her breath, as she trudged to his truck.

When they arrived at the office, cars were already in the lot. Patients were already there? Dorey checked the clock on the dash. They were running late. She smoothed her hair down as best she could. Still partly wet.

They got out and hurried to the main door. As they walked in, Mae stood at her post behind the reception desk. She eyed first Dorey, then Harry, taking in their damp hair, Harry's wrinkled clothes, and the fact that they stood together. A quick glance out the window likely added to thoughts forming in Mae's head. Dorey could just imagine—They came in together. One vehicle …

Harry cleared his throat to get Mae's attention. "Morning, Mae. What's the schedule look like?"

She raised one eyebrow. "Fairly full today."

Was she disappointed he wasn't offering some excuse as to their appearances and showing up together? Dorey leaned forward over the counter. "In hygiene too?"

Mae held out her hand and gave the so-so motion. "You have a few. First one's already here."

Dorey nodded. It was better than none.

Mae eyed the clock and then Dorey again.

As if that had ignited some spark under Dorey, she gasped. What was she doing just standing here? She had a patient. Dorey rushed around the corner and to her room. Thankfully, she'd already set up the previous evening, so she just stowed her purse away, washed her hands, and pulled her hair into a quick ponytail.

She hurried back out and grabbed the chart in the wall holder. Her shoulders slumped. Mrs. Curtis. The talker.

Don't complain, Dorey. You have a patient.

Straightening her shoulders, Dorey went out, welcomed Mrs. Curtis, and led her back into the room. The woman, somewhere in her forties, set her handbag down and sat in the chair. Dorey put the patient napkin on her.

"Have I told you about the latest from my sister?" Mrs. Curtis started in.

"No, I—"

"Now she wants to come and live with me. *Live* with me."

"Well—"

"I don't think I could stand that. All she does is talk. Can you imagine?"

The sisters must be twins. "Um—"

"I wouldn't get anything done around the house. She'd follow me and just yak, yak, yak."

Gee, couldn't imagine. "Maybe if we—"

"I don't understand some people. Don't they realize when they're being rude? Bothering someone else with their flapping lips?"

Dorey took a deep breath, let it out, and hit the button to lower the chair. Mrs. Curtis never broke stride. "Why just yesterday, I was trying to do my weekly dusting. The phone rang. It was her. I couldn't get her to leave me alone."

Dorey nodded and opened the packet that held her sterilized cleaning instruments. "Uh-huh."

"Then, she started in on how I wear my hair. How it's outdated. Do you think my hair is outdated?" She turned and looked up at Dorey expectantly.

Dorey slid a glance to her beehive hairdo. Oh boy. "Well—"

"That's what I said. What business is it of my sister's to criticize how I wear my hair?"

Dorey reached for her gloves from the box on the counter. Mrs. Curtis grabbed Dorey's hand. Startled, Dorey jerked. *What is she doing?*

157

Dorey tried to pry her hand away, but the woman was surprisingly strong.

"I love that ring. I've never had a turquoise one but always wanted one. Can I buy it from you?"

Dorey thought of Luanne. Why did everyone want the ring?

"Well, I'm afraid not. It's ... I really like it."

Mrs. Curtis frowned. "I see." She crossed her arms over her chest and looked away from Dorey.

Mad because she wouldn't sell the ring? What did she expect? Did she normally go around demanding people sell her their possessions?

The ring wasn't really hers, either. But it was for now. Until the real owner showed up.

As she put on her mask and gloves, she hid a smile. At least it got Mrs. Curtis to stop talking.

19

The next morning, Dorey got to the office a little early, hoping to appease Mae for being late yesterday. Harry's truck was parked in the lot. So was Mae's. Why was everyone already there? And a police car parked across the street. Its lights weren't flashing, but somehow warning bells went off in Dorey's head anyway.

Had something happened to Harry? Heart in her throat, Dorey hurried to the door. Mae stood at her desk, wringing her hands.

"Mae, what happened?"

She leaned forward and whispered, though no one else was in sight. "During the night, someone broke into the office."

Dorey gasped. "What?"

"The police think they might have been looking for drugs. They said that happens a lot at doctor and dentist offices."

"Oh, no."

Intending to put her purse away and talk to Harry about the break-in, Dorey started to her room.

"You might not want to go in there."

Dorey stopped short and looked over her shoulder at Mae. "Why not?"

"It's not pretty. Your room's a mess."

"Oh." Dorey bit her lip. "Do you think I can start cleaning it up? Are the police finished in there?"

"I don't know. You'll have to ask Dr. MacKinley." Suddenly, as if remembering how Dorey and Harry had come in together the morning before, Mae looked her up and down. "That is, if you haven't already seen him today."

Dorey blinked. How rude. Even if Dorey and Harry had been doing something more than Harry just keeping her company, it wasn't any of Mae's business. Nosy busybody. Without giving Mae a response, she pivoted and went toward Harry's office, where she heard a couple of male voices.

Harry stood there, leaned back against the edge of his desk. An officer, a man around fifty or so, stood facing him, writing down something in a small notebook.

"So how long do you—?" Harry eyed Dorey and stopped midsentence. He said to her, "Hey, guess you heard the bad news?"

She nodded. "Mae told me."

Harry motioned her into his office. "Officer Beaumont, this is Dorey Cameron, my hygienist."

Dorey tried not to flinch at the introduction. True, she was his hygienist, but they were so much more than that. At least, she hoped so.

Officer Beaumont nodded. "Nice to meet you. Sorry it's under these circumstances."

Dorey sighed. "Yes. What happened?"

"Sometime last night, the perpetrator busted out a back window."

"My operatory," Harry interrupted.

"Right," said the officer. "He or she then rummaged through every drawer and cabinet. I'm guessing looking for drugs. Dr.

MacKinley said there are some pain killers missing. Whoever did this was very thorough."

"What do you mean?"

He frowned. "I've seen thieves go through offices before, but this is the first time they've just concentrated mostly on one room."

"What?" Dorey widened her eyes.

Harry nodded. "Yeah, my room is barely touched."

"Just damage in the hygiene room?"

The officer stared at her as if noticing her for the first time. "You wouldn't happen to know why they'd do that and not bother with the other room, would you?"

Dorey's mouth gaped open. Was he accusing her of something?

"Just a minute." Harry put out his hand toward the officer. "Why would you think that? Dorey is a valued, trusted employee."

There he went again, making it sound like, if it weren't for work, she and Harry would be strangers.

But what else could he say? He couldn't very well go into detail about their friendship. The fact that Harry had recently spent the night at her apartment. The officer didn't need to know that. No one did.

The officer scowled at Harry and then stared at Dorey expectantly.

Dorey bristled. "I don't know why someone would do that. How could I possibly know?" Her voice had grown shrill in desperation. Did the officer somehow think she was responsible? Had prior knowledge of the crime?

Harry gave her a pat on her shoulder. "I'm sure Officer Beaumont doesn't suspect you of anything." He stared at the other man, unblinking. "Right?"

Officer Beaumont shrugged. "We have to check out every angle. I have my doubts that Miss Cameron or any of your staff

—or you—are involved. Still, it's our duty to check all possibilities."

Harry shrugged but didn't reply. His face had darkened in anger.

"Also," Officer Beaumont tapped his notebook with his pen. "Why don't you have a better alarm system at the office? We might have been able to catch the thief red-handed if an alarm notice had come into the station."

"Because the previous dentist didn't think it was necessary to do an upgrade. And I haven't had the spare funds to have one installed." Harry crossed his arms.

"I suggest you take care of that now." He lowered his eyebrows, appearing stern, like a schoolmaster disciplining his wayward student.

"Yes. Looks like I'll have to."

Guilt snuck up on Dorey at the most inopportune times, reminding her of Harry's lack of extra funds and the fact that she hadn't contributed to the office's bottom line much lately. Harry hadn't voiced her part in it, but she felt it all the same.

Harry let out a sigh. "Officer, if you have everything you need, can we get started on cleaning things up?"

"Certainly." He flipped his notebook closed. "We'll be in touch."

As soon as the officer had left, Dorey launched herself at Harry. His arms went around her.

"How awful. You'll have to cancel patients and—"

"I know. Mae is already doing that. And it will take us a while to clean up the mess."

"What a shame. At least your room wasn't messed up as much." She pulled away and looked up at him. "It's the same thing again, isn't it?"

"What is?"

"They only trashed my room. Just mine."

He shook his head, scolding, reminding her of Officer Beaumont. "Don't go there again."

"Harry, I can't help it. All these things—"

"You mean the patients not showing?"

She nodded.

"Is there something else?"

She'd never told him that she'd started to think all the weird occurrences might be connected.

"What aren't you telling me?" He placed his hands on either side of her face.

She shrugged and averted her gaze to the opposite wall. The voicemails. The dead rodent...

He lowered his hands and grabbed hers. "You can tell me anything, you know. Don't you realize by now that I'd do anything for you?" He squeezed her hand gently.

She met his gaze. How could he be so calm about all the calamities happening at his office?

"But how are you going to pay for the damage?"

"Insurance will cover it. I'm not worried."

"Do you ever worry? About anything?"

"You." He ran his gaze over her face, as if he wanted to touch her every place he looked. "Just you."

She blinked away tears that threatened to fall. No, she wasn't going to melt into a sobbing heap in his office again. "Thanks." She stepped back. "What can I do to help with the cleanup?"

"There're lots of things scattered around in your room. It really is a mess. I'm sorry."

"Why are you apologizing to me?" She took another step back. "It wasn't your fault."

"And it wasn't yours. I know you, Dorey. You're somehow blaming yourself, aren't you? Like you have for all the things happening to your patients."

She couldn't deny it but didn't want to say it out loud.

"For now, let's just concentrate on cleaning everything up,

okay? Let's see how fast we can get everything put back together so we can start seeing patients again."

"Okay." She turned toward the door.

"Dorey?"

"What?" She said without turning.

"Don't worry about this, about any of it."

"I'll try."

When she got to her room, she nearly cried. Every single drawer had been opened and completely emptied on the floor. All her instruments would have to be collected, put back together into groupings, and re-sterilized. Disposable supply packages of paste, fluoride gauze, and floss were opened and dumped on the floor too. She wouldn't be able to salvage any of it. It would all have to be thrown away and replaced.

Poor Harry. As if his money troubles weren't bad enough already.

She snapped on a pair of gloves and got to work. Dragging over her trashcan, she dumped all the disposables inside. After she'd cleaned up, she'd have to restock and then do an inventory of what they'd need to reorder.

Such a waste.

Maybe insurance would cover all of that too. She hoped so. Once she got everything thrown away that couldn't be salvaged, she took out a pad of paper and pen to list what they'd need to replace.

She hoped Harry was right, that they could get everything cleaned up quickly. They'd also have to get someone to replace the window in Harry's room. If not, who knew when they could see patients again? At least, the ones who were able to show up.

After finishing her list, she tied up the trash bag to take out later. Finally satisfied she'd done what she could, she concentrated on the instruments. Dumping all the opened packets on a tray, she carried the load into the sterilization area.

Luanne was already in there doing the same with Harry's

instruments. She turned. "Oh, hi. This is something, huh?"

"Yeah." Dorey made a face. "Pretty awful. I didn't realize you'd have to do Harry's too."

"He said since the person had come in through his room and one or two drawers were left open, we'd better be safe and just re-sterilize everything, just in case." Luanne nodded toward Dorey's tray. "I just filled up the autoclave with some of the doctor's instruments, but if you want to scrub yours and bag them, I'll put them in later when there's room."

"Okay, thanks. It's not like we'll need them for patients today anyway."

"True."

Dorey got to work soaking all the instruments for fifteen minutes at a time in the cold sterilization they used prior to the autoclave. It took several times because there were so many instruments to do. Finally, she took a couple of clean office towels and spread them on the counter. She dumped the instruments on the towel and began the slow process of putting together things for each packet.

Mirror, explorer, probe, and two different types of scalers. Thankfully, the instruments from each pack had a different colored band on each piece, so she knew what went where. But it still took a long time to find them all in the massive pile of instruments on the towels. It looked like a bunch of silver bones, waiting to be buried.

Harry walked into the small room. "The bad news is, they have to special order the window glass since it's an odd size. But," He held up one finger, "they will come and board up the opening for the time being."

Dorey gave a relieved sigh. "Yes, that should work."

As Luanne stepped out of the room, Harry came closer.

"See, Dorey? I told you there wasn't anything to worry about."

I'm not so sure about that. She turned back to her instruments.

20

Harry thought they all needed a break from the upheaval of the office, so he treated everyone to dinner out, which thrilled Luanne and Mae. Much to their husbands' chagrin, they would have to fix their own meals.

It was interesting to see Mae and Luanne in a setting other than the office, but Dorey still wished she and Harry were alone.

After they'd finished eating, Mae and Luanne went their separate ways. Dorey turned to go to her car in the parking lot.

"Would you like some company?" Harry reached out and took her hand.

I never mind being with you. "Sure."

"Great. Want me to follow you to your apartment?"

"I can't guarantee what state it's in. I haven't really been in the mood to clean at home with all that's gone on."

"I don't mind a little clutter."

"Follow me, then."

The restaurant wasn't all that far from her apartment complex, which was good. Dorey found herself looking in her rearview mirror more than the road. What would the rest of their evening be like? More kissing? Hopefully.

Dorey pulled into her space in the lot and got out. She jingled her keys while she waited for Harry to catch up.

"Ready?" He took her hand again.

She smirked, ready to tease him. Ready to not talk about anything bad. Anything serious. "I've been waiting, like, twenty minutes for you to finally get here."

"I don't think so."

"I timed you. What were you doing?"

"Wouldn't you like to know?" He grinned and reached his arm around her shoulders.

Just as she nestled in close, his fingers found her ribs.

She shrieked and pulled away. "Why do you always do that?"

"Why do you always let me?"

"Because I trusted you."

"That was your first mistake."

"You'd think I'd learn."

"Yeah." He raised one eyebrow. "You'd think."

Dorey giggled as they reached her door. She put her key in the lock. The door opened before she turned the key. "What?"

"Didn't you lock it this morning?" Harry frowned.

"Are you kidding? I always lock it. Especially after all that's gone on lately." She grabbed the knob.

"Wait. Let me go first."

"Be my guest." Dorey wasn't afraid to admit she was, well, afraid.

Harry pushed open the door, slowly. Twilight had fallen, so the interior of the apartment was already dark. He fumbled around the wall, finally hitting the switch.

Dorey gasped. "Oh, no."

If a group of circus monkeys had held a party in the room, Dorey wouldn't have been surprised. Furniture tipped over. Knickknacks scattered on the floor, some in pieces. When she peered around the corner, part of the kitchen was visible. Every cabinet, drawer, and cupboard stood open. Even the refrigerator.

Dorey swallowed hard. Why was this happening? First the office, now her apartment. They had to be connected, didn't they?

Harry stepped in first, looking behind furniture and into rooms. Was he afraid the person who'd trashed her home was still around?

"Harry?"

He'd disappeared into her bedroom, but she hadn't heard anything for a few seconds.

"Harry!"

He rushed back to the living room. "What? What happened?"

"I couldn't hear you."

"I wasn't saying anything."

"I thought ... I—"

He grabbed her and hugged her tight, crushing her ribs that he'd tickled moments before. The tickling was more fun. The hug wasn't romantic, but desperate. Having a reason to be desperate was getting to be too much of a habit.

"Dorey?" He kissed her forehead. "Are you all right?"

The enormity of what someone had done to her home registered. As if Harry, by asking, had given her permission to feel, tears, large and hot, streaked down her face.

"I don't ... understand. Why?"

"I don't know, honey. I wish I did." He pulled back a little and kissed her, gently. "We need to call the police."

"We just saw the police."

"Yeah, I know. But we still have to call them. Different crime."

"Does the police department have a frequent flier program?"

Harry chuckled. "If they don't, they should. This is getting ridiculous. Come on."

"Where?"

He took her hand and led her outside. "I don't want to stay in here until the police come."

"Okay. No, wait. Weatherby. What if he's—"

"Right. Um ... I didn't see him in there. Would he hide, or—" Harry wiped a tear from her cheek.

"I'll go in and call him. If he's there, he'll come. If not, he ran outside. Poor guy. His little life is so chaotic. Cats are supposed to lie around all the time and sleep, but Weatherby hasn't gotten many cat naps lately. Too many disruptions."

Harry raised his eyebrows. "I'm a little more concerned about you right now than your cat."

She blinked. "But he's my—"

He held up his hand. "Baby. Yeah, I know. All right. Stand out here, right by the doorway, and call him. Then we'll know one way or another."

Dorey nodded and stuck her head inside. "Weatherby? Honey?"

"Honey?"

She shrugged. "He likes it. Weatherby? Mommy's home." A muffled laugh came from behind her, but she ignored it. "Weatherby?"

"Maybe he's—"

"Shhh."

Heat coursed over her skin as Harry stepped up close behind her.

"Did you just shush me?"

"Do you want me to call him or not?"

"You just did."

Dorey peered over her shoulder at him. "I need to see if he answers. I can't hear him if you're talking."

Harry rolled his eyes but said nothing further.

"Weatherby?"

A faint mew, sounding more like a kitten than a full-grown cat, came from beneath her overturned couch.

"Oh no!" Dorey climbed over a lamp, chair, and end table to reach the couch. "Weatherby!"

"Wait, Dorey. Let me help."

Together they lifted the couch and righted it. Weatherby sat crouched down, ears flat, eyes opened impossibly wide.

"Poor kitty." Dorey bent down and grabbed him beneath his armpits. Before she could tug him closer, Weatherby climbed up her chest and attached himself to the front of her shirt like a barnacle to a boat.

Harry reached over and petted Weatherby between the ears. "You okay, little guy?"

Weatherby sighed and purred.

"We can go back outside now and call the police. Again." Dorey tucked the cat's head beneath her chin.

While Harry spoke to the police, Dorey sat on the curb by the parking lot, giving her cat the once-over.

She pressed her face into his fur. "I'm so relieved you weren't hurt. You weren't, were you? Hurt, I mean. You'd tell me if—"

Something rustled in the grass behind her. She turned.

Harry stood close by. "He'd tell you if—"

"Stop grinning."

"It's dark, how do you even know."

"I know."

Harry sat down next to her and scratched the cat under the chin. "Sorry I made fun of you. Is he all right?"

"I think so. He's just scared. His little heart is beating so fast."

"If he's still that freaked, it makes me wonder if it happened recently, as opposed to this morning after you left."

"It gives me the creeps, thinking of some person in my home, pawing through my things." Dorey let out a breath, weary from cleaning and reorganizing the office, and even more tired at the prospect of doing the same here. She wouldn't even be able to go to bed until everything was put back in order. Even then, would she feel safe?

"What's up?"

"Besides the obvious?"

"I mean, what are you thinking?" Faint illumination from a nearby streetlight cast one side of his handsome face in shadows.

"Just that I'm so grateful you're here with me."

She leaned her head against his shoulder, comforted when he wrapped his arm around her.

"I spoke to someone at the police station. They should be here any time."

"They've barely had time to do reports from the office break-in. We'll give them writers' cramp."

"I'd rather have that than all this."

"Me too."

Car lights flashed, causing Dorey to squint. A police car pulled into the next row over. She couldn't tell what the officer looked like from here. Surely it wasn't—

"Seems like you two should stick to dentistry instead of crime investigation." Officer Beaumont walked toward them through the shadows.

Dorey groaned. Harry stood.

Dorey did too, but it took a little doing since Weatherby was kicking her in the stomach with his back claws. "Stop that." She tried to peel him off her shirt before he scratched her. The cat had other ideas and pushed against her with his hind feet. "I am not a diving board, cat."

As Weatherby scurried behind a bush, Dorey brushed a half-pint of cat hair from her shirt.

Officer Beaumont took out his notepad and pen. "When the switchboard operator said a Dr. MacKinley was calling about a break-in, at first, I'd assumed you had more questions. About the other one." He leaned a little to the side and peered behind them. "Your apartment?" he said to Harry.

"No," said Dorey. "Mine."

"Ah."

Dorey frowned as the officer stepped around them and entered the apartment. What had he meant by that? Almost as if he wasn't surprised it was Dorey's place that had been broken into.

It's not like I planned this!

Dorey stood just inside the doorway while Officer Beaumont took a look around. "Anything missing?"

"I don't know."

He raised one eyebrow. "Usually, people rush in before they know it's safe, to check things out."

"Someone told me not to." Dorey gave Harry the eye.

"Wise man."

Harry smiled at Dorey, as in triumph.

"Whatever," she muttered.

Officer Beaumont made copious notes, took some quick pictures in each room, and then came back. He handed Dorey a blank form. "Take a good look over everything. In case you do find something missing, list it here, along with the approximate value."

She sighed. "All right. Anything else?"

"Keep us posted. I'll have someone do a drive-by every couple of hours tonight, just to make sure the deadbeat doesn't make an encore appearance."

Harry stepped forward. "Should Dorey be worried about staying here tonight?"

The officer narrowed his eyes. "That's up to Miss Cameron. If it were me, I'd get a hotel room for the night, tackle this mess tomorrow. But I can't stop you from staying here. Most folks just want things back in their right place and dive right in. Up to you." He tipped his hat and left.

Dorey followed Harry back inside. She watched through the open doorway as the police car pulled out of the parking lot and down the street. "He sure didn't spend much time here, did he? It seemed like he was at the office forever."

"Maybe it had something to do with the fact that we keep drugs at the office. And you don't here." His lips rose on one side. "You don't have any drugs here, do you?"

"Of course not." She smacked his shoulder.

"I know." Harry laughed. "Okay, I'll help you clean this up."

"You'd do that?"

"Haven't I already told you I'd do anything for you, kid?"

Dorey smiled. Except for the last word, his question was just about perfect.

"Besides …" Harry pulled her close and pressed his forehead to hers. "I happen to know where there's an extra green toothbrush with my name on it."

Dorey sighed as Harry kissed her. Yep, another sleepover it would be.

21

A couple of days later, the office was back to normal. Or, as normal as it ever was. When Mr. Long showed up for his appointment, he was ten minutes late, which wasn't like him. Dorey was relieved to see him. With all the other patients who'd had incidents or been discouraged by Dr. Conners, she'd hoped that wouldn't be the case with him.

She took him to her room and seated him. "How have you been, Mr. Long? Any changes in your medical history since we saw you last?"

He reached up and loosened his tie. "Well, I've been a little under the weather today, to tell the truth."

"Would you rather reschedule?"

"No. I'm here, so ..." He smiled. "We can go ahead."

"If you're sure. But you let me know if you start feeling worse, okay?" She patted his shoulder.

"You got it."

She put on her mask, glasses, and gloves, and took a few necessary X-rays. Then she pushed the button to lay the chair back. Mr. Long looked a little pale.

"Are you sure you're feeling all right? Need a glass of water?"

"I think I'm okay." He took a deep breath. "Let's keep going."

Dorey nodded, but had doubts. She scaled his back teeth, upper and lower, then did the front ones. She glanced at his eyes. His pupils seemed a bit enlarged. Had they been that way when he'd first come in?

But he was responding to her requests to turn his head, open wider, so everything appeared to be normal.

She put her instruments on the tray and picked up her polishing handpiece. "Is cinnamon paste okay? Or would you like mint?"

He opened his mouth to answer but coughed instead. "Oh, excuse me. Not sure where that came from."

"No problem." Uh-oh. Maybe he really wasn't feeling the best.

"I guess cinnamon. It's usually pretty good. As far a dental paste goes."

Dorey laughed. "Exactly." She dabbed a little paste onto the tiny brush at the end of her handpiece. "Ready?"

"Yep." He opened wide again.

Dorey polished the outside surfaces of his top teeth, then sprayed some water and sucked it all up with her saliva ejector. She stole a glance at him. He tugged his tie farther down. Was he sweating?

"Doing okay, there?"

He cleared his throat and nodded. "Yes."

She did the same to his lower teeth, polishing the outside surfaces. Then repeated the rinse and suction.

So far, so good.

In the past, she'd been thrown up on before by sick patients and didn't really want to have a do-over of that, so she kept eyeing Mr. Long to make sure he was all right.

When she had loaded up her brush again with paste, she turned toward him. She stopped short when he covered his mouth with his hand and coughed.

"Maybe I should sit you up for a minute." Dorey reached for the button on the chair.

He put up his hand and shook his head no. The poor guy. That was quite a cough.

Finally, he stopped and wiped some moisture from his eyes. "My goodness, I am so sorry."

"I'm wondering if we shouldn't just stop there and let you go home."

"I'd hate to do that. We're almost finished, aren't we?"

She nodded.

"I'm game if you are." He gave her a little smile, but didn't act as jovial as he had just a few minutes before.

Giving a small shrug, she proceeded with the cleaning, determined to finish quickly so Mr. Long could be on his way. He'd probably come from his place of work. Would he feel well enough to go back?

Dorey finished with the paste, rinsed it out, and used the suction again. "All done. Is that better?"

"Yes. Thank you. Sorry I coughed so much. Probably not pleasant for you."

"Don't worry about it. I was just concerned for you." She smiled. "Here, let's sit you up while you wait for Dr. MacKinley."

He held up his hand. "Um, would you mind if I stayed like this?"

"Of course not."

"I'm suddenly feeling a little tired."

"Sure. You stay put, and I'll go tell him we're ready."

She hurried to tell Harry, not wanting Mr. Long to have to wait longer than necessary.

Harry nodded. "Give me five minutes."

"Thanks."

She stopped by Mae's desk to see if her next patient was going to show. Mae hadn't heard differently, so they were on track. Since Mr. Long had arrived late, it would put her behind for her next patient.

As soon as Dorey rounded the corner into her room, her heart stilled.

Mr. Long's eyes were closed. Mouth open. Body slumped to one side, arm hanging down over the side of the chair, his fingertips grazing the floor.

Dorey ran to him and grabbed him by the shoulders. "Mr. Long! Can you hear me?" She leaned her head down to his chest to see if it was moving. Dorey was shaking so bad she didn't know if the movement was from her or him. She ran to the doorway. "Harry!"

Rushing back to her patient, she removed his tie and undid the top three buttons on his shirt. "Mr. Long!" She reached around to his neck and checked for a pulse.

Come on ... Come on ...

Her heart sure was racing, though. Her mouth had gone dry, and she couldn't catch her breath. Not a good time to hyperventilate.

Harry skidded around the corner into the room. "Dorey? What's—"

"I don't think he's breathing! Do compressions while I do mouth to mouth."

"Call 911, Mae!" Harry hurried to her side, then pumped up and down in rhythm to Dorey's breaths.

"Stop for a second." Harry held up his hand. "Is there a pulse now?"

"I don't know." She held as still as her trembling would allow. "I can't—"

He pushed her hand aside and checked. "No. Nothing. Let's go again. Ready?"

Dorey got close to Mr. Long's mouth. "Yes."

They kept it up for several minutes, though to Dorey, it

stretched out like a year. The front door opened, and there was a commotion in the lobby.

"In there!" Mae yelled. "First door on the right!"

Two paramedics raced in. Harry grabbed Dorey's hand and pulled her back out of the way. She stared, mouth open, as the paramedics worked on Mr. Long. He had to make it. Had to.

One of them glanced at Harry. "How long has he been down?"

Harry glanced at the clock. "At least ten minutes."

The man nodded. "Any pulse at all?"

Harry looked at Dorey. She shook her head. "When I came back into the room, he wasn't moving at all. I checked to see if he was breathing. He wasn't." She swallowed hard. *This can't be happening.*

They tried for a little while longer. One of the paramedics checked for a pulse, then shook his head at his co-worker.

Dorey's heart plummeted. *No-no-no!*

The first paramedic stood. "We'll take him to the hospital, but I'm afraid it's a DOA. Had he complained of any symptoms when he came in? Chest pain? Anything like that?"

She crossed her arms over her chest, still unable to believe that a man had died right in front of her. In her dental chair! "Just that he hadn't been feeling well today. I asked him several times if he wanted to stop or reschedule, but he wanted to keep going."

"Anything else? Sweating? Nausea?"

"He was sweating a little. And, he kept tugging at his tie, like it was ... too tight." She couldn't seem to catch her breath. Was she hyperventilating or commiserating with how Mr. Long had been when he'd started coughing.

They loaded poor Mr. Long on their gurney. Dorey grabbed his tie from the counter and handed it to one of the paramedics, though she wasn't sure afterward why she did. A tie wouldn't do him any good now.

The wheels of the gurney squeaked as the men rolled it out of the office. The main door closed with a thud, like someone had closed a tomb.

Dorey began to shake. Her breathing was shallow. Harry grabbed her by the shoulders. He started to sit her in the patient chair, shook his head, and helped Dorey to his private office. Luanne, Mae, Harry's patient, and Dorey's next patient, in the waiting room, all stood and gaped at them.

Dorey closed her eyes, not even paying attention to what Harry was doing. She allowed him to guide her to his couch. The door closed. Footsteps. This couldn't be happening. None of this. It couldn't be real, could it? Poor Mr. Long. Such a nice, sweet man. And not very old at all. Way too young to die so suddenly.

Her eyes opened slowly when Harry sat down next to her. He pulled her close and rocked her.

"Oh, Harry ..."

"I know, sweetheart. It will be—"

"If you dare say it will be okay and not to worry, I'll hurt you."

He let out a breath. "I hate to say it, but you're right."

"People will say it's my fault. Now no one will want to come here, Harry." She pulled away. "I have to leave the practice."

"What?"

"You have to admit it would be for the best."

He grabbed one of her hands, keeping her from moving too far away. "You're not going anywhere."

"But I can't work here anymore."

"Dorey." He brushed some hair away from her face. "It wasn't your fault, he—"

"You can't keep saying none of this is my fault."

"How can you even think that you're in any way responsible for what's been going on with our patients?"

It was on the tip of her tongue to tell him about the

messages. That they weren't pranks. Had grown threatening. And about the rodent Weatherby had found. The masks that must be somehow tied in to all of this.

No. *I can't.* To tell him would put him in danger too. The note said so.

She sighed. "I can't help how I feel. If you were in my position, wouldn't you feel somehow responsible? Harry, I'm the only common link between all those people. And the destruction in my room in the office. And my apartment. And now poor Mr. Long is dead."

"Shhh ..." He placed his finger over her lips. "Listen to me. Mr. Long's situation is different. He showed up for his appointment. He hadn't had anything strange happen to him beforehand. And didn't you say that he'd complained of not feeling well?"

She nodded. "I should have tried harder to get him to go home."

"Even if you had, I doubt the outcome would have been different. Something was wrong with him before he ever set foot in the office today."

Dorey hadn't considered that. Still, the man was dead. So much worse than scared patients and break-ins.

"Are you feeling sick? Your face went pale." Concern was evident in his furrowed brow and downturned lips.

She blinked. How long had Dorey been sitting there, staring off into space, seeing and hearing nothing, but feeling as if someone large was sitting on her chest, robbing her of oxygen?

Her hands shook uncontrollably. A few seconds later, Harry was crouched down on the floor in front of her. He took her hand and rubbed it between his. Why were her hands, her whole body so cold? Even the inside of her chest felt encased in ice. She shivered.

Dorey couldn't stop shaking her head, as if denying it to herself would make it all go away. Why did these awful things keep happening? The other events were bad enough, but … death?

Had she done anything to bring this on the people she was supposed to be caring for at the office? It must have something to do with her, because she was the only connection all the other people had. There was no other explanation. Was she cursed?

Something soft and warm went around her shoulders and covered her back. A blanket. She glanced at it from the corner of her eye. It was the one Harry's mom had made for him when he'd first gone off to college. So soft. So warm. Muted blues and reds. Would he let her keep it forever? Then she could pull it over her head, act like none of this was happening.

Suddenly, Dorey longed to lie down and sleep. Just sleep. Then maybe all the terrible things would go away. If she could close her eyes, would it go back to normal when she opened them again? Everyone healthy, unhurt, and happy?

Instead of helping her to lie down, Harry sat right next to her again and pulled her close. She rested her head on his shoulder. He rocked her back and forth, gently, slowly, as he touched her face in soothing, smooth caresses. She closed her eyes, longing to absorb his warmth, his caring. To stay that close to him forever. Would anything ever be right again? Make sense anymore?

"Dorey, it's going to be okay."

Her entire body shivered from her forehead to her toes. She couldn't stop. "No, it won't."

"It will. I don't know why all of this is happening. But it will end. It has to. It's just … bad luck. A run of weird things happening all at once. Coincidence."

She shook her head, her hair brushing against the smooth fabric of his shirt. "I don't think so."

"What else could it be?" He tugged the blanket tighter around her.

"Me."

"What?" The vibration of his voice rumbled through his chest.

"It's me. My fault. What else do the patients all have in common?" A hot tear rolled down her cheek, landing on Harry's shirt, the moisture spreading into a larger circle on the fabric.

"No ... Don't be silly. It's not your fault. How in the world could it be?" He ran his fingers from her temple to her chin, over and over.

Something inside her had snapped. Indecision took over her brain. Fear held her captive in its clutches. If she kept seeing patients, kept working at the office, would the accidents keep happening? How long before someone else died?

"I don't know." She let out a sob. "But somehow, I've done something to bring it on. It must have been something terrible. Something unforgivable."

Harry moved away a little bit and lifted her chin with his thumb and forefinger. "Listen to me. None of this is your fault. None of it. Do you hear me?"

"I can't believe—"

"Dorey, listen to what I'm saying. It's not because of you."

"But I must have done something or—"

"No. You've done nothing wrong. You never have. You couldn't. You're—" He stroked his finger down her cheek. "You're the sweetest, most thoughtful, caring girl—woman—I've ever met. Do you believe me?"

She shook her head.

"I told you I wouldn't fib to you anymore, remember?"

"But—"

"I'm telling you the truth. You've done nothing wrong. This isn't your fault. I need you to tell me you believe me."

Blinking away another tear, she gazed up into his eyes. His incredible, dark, soulful eyes. Dorey started to turn away, but Harry captured her chin again.

"Listen to me. Watch my lips as I say this ..."

She lowered her gaze, slowly, so slowly, feeling like she'd never get there, right where she longed to be.

"You are special, Dorey." His lips, soft-looking and full, formed his words. "You are wonderful. I treasure you. You have no idea how-how important you are to me. How much I care."

Dorey leaned closer, longing to get next to him, skin to skin, heart to heart. To feel more. Feel something good, something right. Absorb some of his kindness, his caring.

Gently, so very gently, he pressed his lips to hers. Like the barely felt trail of a butterfly's wing stirring in the breeze. It lasted only a few seconds, but to her, it was forever and not enough, all at the same time.

"Do you believe me?"

"I-I believe you." She couldn't really, but she would try.

"Good." Harry let out a breath. "Now, I want you to rest, okay?" He glanced at the clock on the wall when they heard Luanne bringing a patient past the door to seat him in Harry's operatory. "I need to go. I don't want to, but I have to. Will you be okay here for a while? By yourself?"

She allowed him to lean her back against a small pillow and cover her with the blanket, then let out a sigh. "Yes. Thank you."

He stood up and smiled. On his way out of the door, he turned off the light switch and closed the door with a soft click. How did he have the power to soothe her when she felt her worst? Make her feel better, hopeful, cared for?

Dorey's eyes drifted shut. Please let this nightmare end.

22

"I see two chairs together over there." Dorey pointed to the back row. The seats were at the far end, so they'd have to squeeze by several people already seated.

"Mr. Long must have been popular judging by the size of the crowd," said Harry.

"I'm not surprised. He was a very sweet man."

They headed around a group standing right inside the doorway and to the last row. Harry made his excuses. People grumbled as Dorey and Harry edged past but didn't say much else.

Dorey quickly took her seat. It was only five minutes until the funeral was to start. The room was packed. Of course, the funeral home itself wasn't huge, but still … It looked like she and Harry had taken the last two empty spots. The people by the door, plus several other pockets of mourners, would have to remain standing by the wall. Dorey was so upset, she wasn't sure her legs would have held her up if they hadn't found seats.

Harry pointed to the photo of Mr. Long printed on the front of the service program. "He had such a nice smile."

"Yes, he did." She studied the picture again. "Wait, are you saying that because it just was, or because you're his dentist?"

"Uh, both, I guess. Hard to separate one from the other in our line of work."

"True."

A woman in her forties Dorey didn't recognize glanced at them over her shoulder. Had she and Harry been talking too loudly? The woman whispered something to the man beside her. He turned and openly stared at them.

Dorey frowned. *What's that about?*

The man tapped someone on the shoulder who sat in front of him. Leaning forward, he whispered to him. Within seconds that man turned to glare at them.

Harry tugged at his tie, loosening it. "Does it seem like people are staring at us, or is it my imagination?" He kept his voice low.

"No. They're definitely staring." She pulled at his sleeve, suddenly longing to run away from the funeral home. "Maybe this was a bad idea."

"We've done nothing wrong. I always try to attend my patients' funerals if my schedule allows."

"But this is different." None of those other patients had actually died while in the dental chair.

The first woman, the one right in front of them, hissed at them to be quiet, like an irritated librarian.

Dorey leaned close enough to Harry's ear that she barely even had to whisper. "Other people might not see it the way you do."

"I still don't think—"

"Wait." She grabbed his hand. "The pastor is walking to the front. It's starting."

A hush settled over the room.

The pastor stood behind the podium, giving them a serene

smile. "Thank you all for coming today. Jerry Long would have loved this turnout, don't you think?"

A general murmur of agreement followed as several heads bobbed up and down.

"He was a kind man," the pastor continued. "A gentle man. What a heartbreaking time for his wife, to have lost her husband at so young an age."

Dorey sank down into her chair. She'd never be able to forget that day. How he'd started coughing. Turned pale. Eyes dilated. Tugging on his tie as if he couldn't breathe very well.

I tried to get him to reschedule. Several times. But he wouldn't. If she kept telling herself that, would she ever believe it?

"Jerry made everyone's day brighter," said the pastor, "no matter where he was or how he was feeling. He always put others' concerns before his own."

Was that what he'd been doing in Dorey's chair? Telling her to continue the cleaning because he didn't want to inconvenience her? Poor Mr. Long. If only he'd stayed at home that day. She shook her head. He still would have died, just like Harry had pointed out. Just in a different location.

"He left behind a loving wife, a sister, two brothers, and his parents. He will be greatly mourned and missed."

Dorey could see it all again, the poor man lying in her chair as if it happened just now.

"Is there anything anyone here would like to say about him?" He held out his arms to the sides, an open invitation.

Dorey's gaze swung wide over the room. Would others want to add to the pastor's eulogy? Mr. Long had been such a sweet man. Surely there would be lots of people who might want to speak.

But not me ... If people realized who she was, and that it had taken place under her care ... No.

A dark-haired woman stood up from the front row.

Mrs. Long. Dorey gasped. She hadn't seen her for several

months in the office, but she'd know her anywhere. Salon-styled hair, manicured, polished nails, fur coat.

Dabbing her eyes with a pink handkerchief, Mrs. Long stepped up to the podium. "I just wanted to thank you all for coming. For showing your support and care for my husband. How he would have loved the number of people who cared enough about him to attend his service. He would have been so touched that you all cared enough to stop by and—"

Mrs. Long frowned, her attention caught by someone in the second row. The person was animated, hands waving, head turning frequently to look behind him.

What was going on? Dorey sat forward in her seat.

"What?" Mrs. Long's exclamation was so loud, it seemed to reverberate around the room.

People began whispering and mumbling to each other. Mrs. Long was now bent forward, gesticulating wildly to the person who had gotten her attention.

"What's she doing?" Harry frowned.

Please don't let it be what I think it is. Not that. Not here. *I don't want that for Harry. Or for me.*

The person who had caught Mrs. Long's attention stood and turned. It was a young man, about Dorey's age. He scanned the back of the room, nodded, and pointed.

Right at Dorey.

Her heart nearly stopped beating. She froze in her seat, unable to move. *Oh no ...*

Harry peered over the heads of the row in front of them and then put his arm around her. "You're right. This was a bad idea. Maybe we should just go." He stood, so Dorey did too.

We need to get out of here, now, before they start throwing rotten food at us or get out the tar and feathers.

They slowly made their way down the row, past ten other people who weren't making any concessions to let them pass easily. A couple of women uttered things Dorey was pretty sure weren't used in polite conversation. Thankfully, though, they were almost to the end of the row, the exit door in sight. If they could just make it to the door, go outside, reach Harry's truck and—

Harry stepped into the aisle and waited, hand outstretched for Dorey's. She reached out too, longing to make contact with him, the only person in the room, possibly the world, who truly understood her.

With just two more people for Dorey to pass, a man in his fifties deliberately stuck out his foot. Dorey was already in midstep and couldn't gain her balance.

No!

Shocked, she tumbled to the floor, right in the middle of the main aisle. Her knees hit the floor, and her chin banged against the metal of the last chair in the row. She could feel the eyes from others staring at her back, burning into her skin, wanting her far, far away from them.

Harry reached down and grabbed her upper arm, helping her to stand. When Dorey turned, every single person was glaring at her. If looks could speak words, they'd be uttering: *You're despicable. How dare you come here? I hate you. I wish you'd died instead of him.*

Dorey sucked in a sob, ready to run away. Hide from the stares, the whispers, the accusations. But two large men had moved to block the doorway of the room. She froze in her tracks.

We're trapped.

Rapid footsteps came from behind. Dorey, though she knew who it would be and didn't want to look, couldn't seem to help herself. There wasn't any way to avoid the confrontation now. She swallowed hard and peered into the eyes of Mrs. Long.

The widow pointed a manicured finger at Dorey as if passing judgment. "How dare you come here?"

"I ... It's not my fault, I—" Dorey's hand went ice-cold in Harry's.

The crowd gave a collective gasp. Because Dorey didn't admit fault, or because she dared to speak at all?

Mrs. Long stepped closer. "Then whose fault is it? He died in your care."

Some people were glancing at each other, nodding, affirming that Dorey was the hygienist everyone had heard about after Mr. Long died.

The horrific hygienist. Dental worker of death.

Dorey took a shallow breath, afraid she might faint any second. "No ... I didn't ... I just came back into the room, and he was—"

Stepping even closer, Mrs. Long said, "My husband is gone. Because of *you*."

People in the crowd were starting to stand. Were they leaning toward Dorey? Wanting to get to her, do her harm? Or was she imagining it?

"How can you say that?" Harry edged closer to Mrs. Long. "You've known me for years. Nothing has ever gone wrong while you were there."

Mrs. Long answered Harry but kept her venomous glare on Dorey. "From what I've heard, you weren't anywhere near my husband when this happened. It was her. All her fault."

"It isn't her fault." Harry stood up taller. "She did nothing wrong. I'll stake my reputation on it."

"Even if you did," she spat out, "I'd never quite believe it. Besides, what kind of a health care provider is she that she just stood there and watched my husband take his last breath?"

"No!" Dorey screamed. "That's not true. I did CPR. We called 911. Mr. Long wasn't—"

Mrs. Long held up her hand. "Do not speak of my husband. Don't say his name. You have no right. And you are not welcome here."

Several people in the room nodded, agreeing with the widow.

Harry glanced around the room. "I don't know everyone here, but I do recognize several. Those of you who are patients of mine, if you'll be honest with yourselves, you'll know I would never harm anyone."

"But we don't trust her." It was Mrs. Harkins. "Dr. Conners told me how vile, how untrustworthy she was. Now I'm glad I listened. To think, if I'd allowed her to work on me, I might have been killed too. I might be attending my funeral instead. But I'd be in that box." She pointed to the casket.

Harry pointedly ignored his former, snarky patient. He shook his head sadly. "I'm sorry for your loss, Mrs. Long. I truly am. He was a wonderful man. Dorey and I will both miss him."

Grumbling from every corner followed his statement.

He held up his hand. "That being said, she and I will go now. Just know that neither of us has done anything wrong. If you believe nothing else, please believe that."

They hurried outside and away from the building. As they drove away, Dorey made the mistake of looking up. Several angry faces stared at them from the glass entry doors.

Why didn't we just stay home?

23

A week passed. Dorey went to work, but only because Harry said it might help her to just dive right back in. Since they lived in a small town, word soon got out that a man had died at Dr. MacKinley's office. Some patients canceled right away. Others came, some of them being town gossips, to find out if it was true.

They actually had a few patients begging to come in. Once there, all they wanted to do was ask questions about what happened. Still others showed up but refused to let Dorey treat them. Glaring at her. Pointing with long fingers. Making awful accusations about her. Like those poor women accused of being witches at Salem.

And then there was the reporter from the local paper. Peppering her with outrageous questions. Snapping pictures in the office before Harry threw him out.

She wasn't sure how much more she could take. Harry had commented she looked thinner. Her clothes were looser, so maybe she was. Food had lost all appeal, as if her taste buds had withered and died, leaving her with nothing but disdain for whatever appeared on her plate. Dry, uninteresting morsels that mocked her.

They'd finished up for the morning. Two of Dorey's four patients had shown up and, amazingly, let her clean their teeth. In the not-so-distant past, she would have been elated, finally having someone to work on.

But Dorey now ran on pure instinct. Doing the cleanings, speaking when spoken to, not caring too much what happened and what didn't. She'd been so despondent, she hadn't even bothered to wear the ring. What was the point? It wouldn't bring her joy as it had before. Nothing much mattered now.

Harry came to her room and glanced around. "All set?"

She shrugged. She guessed she was done, barely remembering any of it. It was like her mind was sludge. Heavy, slow, and thick.

"Let's go have some lunch."

"I'm not hungry." She crossed her arms over her chest.

"Dorey, you've said that every day for the past week. You need to eat. Even if you're not hungry." He came closer and rubbed his hands down her arms. "Do it for me? Please?"

She nodded but only to appease him. If it would make him feel better, she'd try her best. He'd been through enough because of her. Didn't he see that he'd be better off if she simply left and didn't come back?

"Thank you." He kissed her forehead and took her hand.

They'd barely gotten out of her room when Mae rushed down the hall toward them.

"Dr. MacKinley, it's the police on the phone." Mae kept her voice low.

"I wonder if it's about the break-in we had." Harry's eyebrows lowered. "Maybe they caught the guy."

Mae shook her head. "They said …" She looked at Dorey and back to Harry. "They said it's about that patient. Mr. Long."

"Why?" Dorey took a step back.

Mae raised her eyebrows. "Because apparently, your patient had been poisoned."

Dorey felt as if she'd been physically slapped.

"That's enough." Harry leaned closer to Mae. "It wasn't Dorey's fault that he died. You know that."

"I guess a man would say anything about the woman he's sleeping with." Mae sniffed.

Dorey gasped. "How dare you?"

"Mae, I don't have time to deal with this right now." Harry put his hand on Dorey's arm. "Rest assured, you and I will be having a conversation. Very soon."

With a glare at Dorey, Mae turned on her heel. She grabbed her purse and left in a huff. Why did the woman hate her so much? She acted as if everything that had ever gone wrong in the office was Dorey's fault. Lately, though, Dorey tended to agree with her.

Harry walked to the front desk and picked up the phone. He spoke for only a couple of minutes. He hung up and came back to her. "Someone from their department will be here any minute. We're to wait for them."

She swallowed hard. "It's too much."

"Dorey ..."

"I mean it. I can't take any more." She looked up at him. "I'll stay and talk to the police, but consider this my notice."

"You don't mean it." He shook his head slowly. "Please, don't do this. I need you here."

"You don't need me, Harry. You never have." She blinked away tears hovering on the edge of her lower lashes.

"That's where you're wrong. I do need you. Here at the office —" he touched his chest "and with me. Can we please talk about this?"

That last note, telling her not to say anything to anyone else. If anything happened to Harry, some accident or worse ... She glanced to her room where Mr. Long had taken his last breath.

Dorey would never recover. Maybe it was best if she severed all ties. But it would break her heart to do so.

Although, if something happened to him because of her, her heart would be broken anyway.

Harry ran his hand through his hair. "Please, can we talk this over? Can we—"

The front door opened. Three men came in. One was her new best friend, Officer Beaumont.

"We meet again." He tipped his hat to her.

Dorey clenched her teeth together, just wanting to get it all over with.

"What's all this about Mr. Long being poisoned?" Harry stepped forward.

Officer Beaumont motioned for the other two, who both carried plastic cases that looked like tackle boxes, toward Dorey's room. Then he said, "An autopsy was performed. Mr. Long was only thirty-nine years old and, according to his doctor, in excellent health. A type of poison was found in his system. It was definitely what killed him."

He eyed Dorey. "So, we'll test everything in your room. And I do mean everything. Let's go in there now. I want you to show me the drawers and cabinets where you got the supplies for Mr. Long. We'll test those first, then go onto other items. I want all bases covered. Nothing left out. If we find traces of anything, then we'll have to test in other parts of the office." With an abrupt turn, he stalked into her room.

Without looking back at Harry, Dorey followed.

The men had put on gloves, much like the ones she used. They also had on masks, disposable gowns, and booties over their shoes. Dorey glanced down at her scrubs. Guess they weren't worried about her encountering anything dangerous. But then, if there was something, she'd already been exposed.

With reluctance, she showed them every cabinet and drawer where she'd gotten instruments, paste, gauze, and floss. It hadn't been that long since she'd had to re-sterilize instruments and throw away disposables after the mess of the break-in. Now she'd have to do some of that again, depending on how much the officers messed with.

Poor Harry. More money down the drain.

Staring at an open drawer that one of the officers was rifling through, Dorey couldn't imagine how someone could have gotten in and placed poison. There was always someone here.

Except for the break-in. Could the person have done it then?

She jumped when Harry suddenly grabbed her hand.

"Does she need to be here for this?" He asked. "Can't you see how upsetting this all has been for her?"

Officer Beaumont narrowed his eyes at Harry. "She's to stay. At least until her name is cleared." He pointed a stubby finger at Dorey. "Don't even think of leaving town, you hear me?"

As she sucked in a breath, the edges of her vision grew dark. Were the police thinking of arresting her? Her hands shook. Did Harry even notice? His face had turned red, his hand not holding hers formed into a fist.

"Cleared? She hasn't done anything." Harry's words came out as a growl.

She was jerked forward as he leaned closer to Officer Beaumont.

"Dr. MacKinley. I'm only going to say this once. Step back from me unless you want to see the wrong end of my gun." He rubbed his hand down his face. "We've gotten quite a few phone calls at the station about Miss Cameron."

Officer Beaumont switched his glare to Dorey. "Some saying you were at the funeral, flaunting the fact you killed him. Also, that several patients have felt threatened by you, even before Mr. Long died. But the one that really got my attention was from Mrs. Long. She swears her husband was fine before he left home to come to this office. Because of all of that, I have reason to at least suspect you."

She stood motionless. Couldn't have moved by herself if she'd tried.

"Hey." Harry startled her by squeezing her hand. "Let's go wait in my office." He glared at the officer. "If that meets with your approval."

"By all means." Officer Beaumont swept his hand out to the side as if giving his royal permission.

Once in Harry's office, Dorey's energy returned. She paced. Too wired to sit still. Wringing her hands, she muttered, "I feel like a caged animal. Some sort of convict. People glaring at me. Pointing their fingers. Accusing me of—"

"The police will get this all straightened out." Harry gave her a brief hug then stepped away. Could he sense she didn't want to be touched?

"Police?" She gave a harsh laugh. "That man out there, Officer Beaumont, already thinks I'm guilty. The way he glared at me ..."

"He's just doing his job. Just like you were doing yours. You did nothing wrong."

"You keep saying that."

"I'll keep saying it until you believe it." His words came out sounding gruff. Dorey knew he was agitated with her, but she couldn't help how she felt. The pounding guilt was relentless.

"Then you might lose your voice because, with all that's happened, I don't see how it's all going to just go away."

Harry took her hands in his. She tried to pull away, but he held fast.

"About before. When you said you'd given your notice—"

"I meant it. I can't stay here. Everything that's happened. It's too much."

"Please stay a little longer. Wait until the police get it all taken care of and—"

"You don't understand." How could he when he didn't know everything?

"Then make me understand."

"It's ... I can't do it."

Harry hugged her tight. "I'm not going anywhere. And neither are you."

Dorey pressed her forehead to his chest. She didn't agree with him, but no matter how many times she said she was leaving, he wouldn't listen. At least not now. Her heart ached for him. How pained he was that she wanted to leave. She wouldn't leave today, after all. But it was coming. Soon. When the time came, she'd just have to go her own way and hope he could someday forgive her.

24

Several more days of running on autopilot followed. Harry scolding her for not eating, mentioning the dark circles beneath her eyes. It might have bothered her before that maybe he didn't find her attractive, but now, simply getting through the day was all she could do. A couple of mornings, she must have forgotten to fill Weatherby's food dish, because he tackled her ankle on her way out the door.

Poor kitty. He didn't understand why Dorey was different. Why she was sad. Listless. Not patting her leg when she sat on the couch to invite him up. He'd finally started jumping on her and nudging her hand until she petted him. Also, he was sticking around her apartment more, not running off as often.

She was ready to leave for work that morning when her cell phone rang.

"Dorey—"

"Harry? I'm just on my way to—"

"Meet me at the police station."

"What? Why are you—"

"Just meet me here. I'll wait for you in the lobby, okay?"

"Okay."

He hung up before she had a chance to say more. Her hands shook as she walked out and closed the door behind her. Was Harry in some kind of trouble? The police hadn't said anything about him when they'd searched the office. Only her. If he got dragged into this mess because of her, she'd never forgive herself.

Heart racing, she tried not to race her car at the same speed. Didn't need to give the police another excuse to drag her to their station, though she'd guess Officer Beaumont would gleefully haul her into a cell.

Once there, she parked and hurried up the walk, stumbling once but catching herself before she fell headlong onto the concrete. Harry was visible through the glass doors, standing just inside. He lifted his hand in a wave when he saw her and then held open the door.

"Harry, what—"

He shook his head, stopping her. "All I know is, I got a call from Officer Beaumont telling me to get down here. When you weren't with me, he got all snarky sounding. Said he'd assumed we'd be coming together. Sorry for the short notice."

She clutched his arm. "No idea what he wants to tell us?" Was it the office break-in, the apartment break-in, the poisoning? It was a sad state of affairs when a girl had so many options linking her to possible crime.

"He wouldn't say."

They walked down one hall, turned left and down another, their footsteps loud against the polished floor. Why did it feel like they were headed to the guillotine?

Harry stopped at the second door on the right. "He's in here." He gave a terse knock on the wooden door.

"Come in."

Dorey would have recognized Officers Beaumont's surly voice anywhere. Something about his smug demeanor made her want to kick him. She sucked in a breath. Better not voice that out loud. At least not here.

She followed Harry inside. The officer sat at the end of a long wooden table. Another man, briefcase open in front of him, sat next to him.

Harry pulled out a chair for Dorey, then sat next to her. Why did it feel like she and Harry were on the wrong end of a firing squad?

Officer Beaumont looked at the man beside him, then back. "We got the preliminary results back for the tested items in your office. I'll let Officer Steele explain further."

Thankfully, Harry grabbed Dorey's hand beneath the table. He rubbed his thumb over the back of her hand as if to say, whatever these men say, you and I are in this together.

But were they?

With determination, she forced herself to sit very still and not tremble. So far, they'd only been interested in her because it had happened in her room. Her chair. Maybe they only asked Harry here too because it was his office. Dorey hoped that was the only reason he'd need to be involved.

Officer Steele pulled a thick stack of papers out of his briefcase. Was all of that the results of their tests?

She wanted so badly to ask the outcome. Scream at the man to spit it out so they'd know, good or bad. But in her mind, she'd bolted from the room, raced down the hall, and run far away. Someplace where there weren't patients having horrible accidents. Where she wasn't blamed for something that wasn't her fault. Where a man hadn't died under her care.

That place, though, also wouldn't have Harry.

Impatient, she watched Officer Steele shuffle through several things in his case. Finally, he produced what had taken his attention for three whole minutes.

His reading glasses.

She wanted to scream. If that was the only holdup, surely Officer Beaumont could have read the report to them.

No, that would have been the considerate thing to do, and Officer Beaumont didn't seem too fond of consideration.

When Harry's grip tightened on hers, she squeezed back, glad he was sitting there with her. Holding her hand. Showing her his commitment and friendship. She worried about Harry's business. His livelihood. Would it recover? Or would he have to start over somewhere else?

Officer Steele had his glasses on now and was perusing the paper on top. He tapped his pen against the table in a kind of drum-like beat until Dorey was tempted to throw something at him.

Just get on with it!

Officer Beaumont took a drink of his coffee and set the Styrofoam cup back on the table. He hadn't even offered her and Harry anything. Not that she cared, but did that signify something? Did you not offer refreshment to someone you were going to arrest?

She took a deep breath and let it out. Jail. Did they really think she had poisoned her patient? Why would she do that?

But someone had. And she had no idea who. Or why. Was it just some nut running around with a vendetta against hygienists? That brought to mind Dr. Conners. But even he, as mean as he was, wouldn't stoop to killing his own former patients just to get rid of Dorey. That was insane.

Officer Steele kept tapping with his pen and perusing the pages. Now he was on page two. And humming.

If it wasn't Dr. Conners, then who? Another patient who'd listened to the older dentist enough that they'd taken it upon themselves to do something about the wicked hygienist in their midst?

And how did the guilty person know who would be coming into the office for future appointments so they could track them down and cause them harm beforehand? The schedule, except for the current day, wasn't posted in her room. Even the current one, she kept at the back of her counter so other patients couldn't see it. New laws governing patient privacy advised dental offices to keep even that information private.

Maybe the government had to keep some kind of eye on public places, so a person's personal business wasn't blabbed everywhere. But what did the powers that be think happened when the patients all sat in the waiting room at the same time? Or passed each other in the hall as they were coming or going to their appointment?

It was a small town. Pretty much everyone at least recognized everyone else. Once they spotted another patient at the office, the jig was pretty much up that they had an appointment there too.

How, then, did the person even find out who would be coming to see Dorey in the future? Mae was always sitting at her computer, guarding the desk like a junkyard dog. And when she was gone at lunch or for the day, she shut the computer down. It was only unlocked with a password.

If the police couldn't figure out who had done this, how in the world would Dorey?

She startled and stared at the two officers, who were talking quietly to each other across the table. Maybe they assumed Dorey had done all those things and weren't even looking for anyone else. What if they intended to arrest her? Today?

"Excuse me." Harry leaned forward.

Both men stared at him like they'd forgotten he and Dorey were there.

Officer Beaumont crossed his arms. "Have something to say, Dr. MacKinley?"

"Yes. I do. You called us down here to give us some information. I don't know about you, but I have work to do. Right now, a patient, probably an irritated one, is sitting in my office in the dental chair waiting for me to fix his tooth. And Dorey most likely has someone waiting as well."

"And your point would be..."

"Either tell us what you thought so important when you called or let us go and get to work." Harry's face reddened.

Dorey had seen him that way before. The man was spitting mad.

Officer Beaumont sighed, as if even taking time to talk to Harry was an inconvenience. He looked at the man next to him. "Do you have everything you need to tell them your findings?"

"I believe so, yes." Officer Steele nodded.

Finally ...

He tapped his pen against the table again. When Harry cleared his throat, the tapping stopped.

Officer Steele set the pen down and picked up the papers. "Mr. Long did indeed die of a type of poison. There was no doubt. It was rampant throughout his tissues. From the operatory where the death occurred..."

The operatory of death. That's what people would call it now. What would they call Dorey? The dental worker of doom?

"... we tested the paste, fluoride, water, floss, gauze, instruments, patient napkins, toothbrushes, and even the spray in the cleaning bottles used for disinfection after a patient was finished."

"And?" Dorey couldn't help it. The word just popped out.

"And..." Officer Steele looked down at the papers again and then back up. "Right after we tested everything and got the results, another preliminary test from the patient's autopsy came back."

Not blinking, Harry sat ramrod straight, shoulders and arms tense, all his attention focused on the officer. Through gritted teeth, he muttered, "Will you please just tell us the results?"

Officer Steele frowned, as if affronted that someone dared to try to hurry him through his meticulous job of delivering important news. "The autopsy finding showed the poison, a slow-acting one, had been in his system for at least twenty-four hours prior to his appointment with Miss Cameron."

She gasped. "So that means—"

"Mr. Long could not have been poisoned while under your care."

Suddenly as limp as a damp towel, Dorey slumped to the side against Harry's shoulder. They didn't think she was guilty!

He stood so abruptly, Dorey nearly tumbled onto his chair.

"It's about time you spit that very important piece of information out. While she and I have been sitting here thinking…" He sliced his hand through the air and glared at the men. "Is that all? May we go now?"

Officer Beaumont gave a nod. With all the pomposity of a king to his servant, he said, "Certainly. You may go."

When Harry reached down and grabbed Dorey's hand, he pulled her up so fast she almost tripped. He gave her a light tug toward the door, and they left the room. He kept hold of her hand until they were outside on the sidewalk. Without a word, he took her in his arms and held her close.

Breathing in his scent, she pressed her forehead to his chest, not caring who might drive by and see them standing there in an embrace.

"Dorey." He rubbed his hand up and down her back. "I'm so sorry you had to go through that. But grateful they didn't …" His chest moved as he sucked in a breath.

When she pulled back to look up at him, she said, "I'm thankful too. I was so scared that they thought … that I'd—"

"It's over." He hugged her again. "It's okay now."

She shook her head against his jacket, her hair making a swishing sound on the smooth fabric. "But it isn't over. A man is dead. All those patients who've had accidents. Someone out there is doing this. We don't know who. Or why."

Giving a sigh, he said, "Whoever did this to Mr. Long is most likely the same one who's committed all the other crimes. The police will catch them."

"Are you sure about that?" She tilted her head toward the police station. "After that circus they put us through in there?"

He shrugged. "I have to believe they'll catch the guilty person. What other choice do we have?"

Dorey wasn't so confident.

25

Once Dorey got to the office, she went into her operatory and slumped back against the counter. Several deep breaths later, it started to sink in. She wouldn't be arrested for poisoning Mr. Long. It was a relief, but she was wiped out. More than anything, she wanted to go home and sleep. Her arms and legs were depleted of energy. Did she resemble Weatherby when he was so tired, he lay on her couch like a boneless ragdoll?

But as luck would have it, she'd ended up with four patients in the morning. And there were some scheduled for after lunch. The first was a man named Robert Keane, and the second was a college student named Daphne Jordan. Dorey hadn't met either one before, but they'd been to the office already to see Harry, since he liked to see all the new patients for their first appointment.

Amazing that she and Harry had been at the police station for what seemed like forever, yet somehow managed to get to the office ahead of everyone else. Maybe waiting to hear the outcome of her possible future in jail made time slow down.

The front door opened and closed. Mae wouldn't be in yet,

so Dorey headed out to the waiting area. A man in his forties, wearing jeans and a polo shirt stood in the middle of the room, tapping his boot.

Dorey cleared her throat so she wouldn't startle him. "Hello."

He looked up. "Oh, hi. Um … I'm Robert Keane."

"Great." She forced a smile, though there was no emotion behind it. If she didn't get her energy back soon, cleaning her patients' teeth might be interesting. "You'll be seeing me today."

He nodded and frowned.

"If you'll give me just another minute, I'll have everything ready to go." She turned away.

"How long do I have to wait?" he muttered.

Going back to her room, she sighed. Perfect. A grumbler. After all the patients she'd had lately who either didn't show or showed but wouldn't let her touch them, couldn't she at least have someone who was pleasant?

Where have all the nice people gone?

The front door opened again. Mae's loud voice floated back, greeting the patient. Dorey got busy pulling out supplies to use. Hopefully, Mr. Keane would be an easy cleaning, and Dorey could shoo him out the door fast.

Harry appeared in her doorway. His face was pale, drawn, like he hadn't slept in a week. "Since my patient isn't here yet and yours is, I'll go ahead and see if we need any more films than what I took at his new patient appointment."

"I'm almost ready to go get him."

Harry nodded. "Come get me when he's seated."

"All right."

Once she was ready, she went to the waiting area and asked Mr. Keane to follow her to her room. Of all days for patients to show up, right when she wanted nothing more than to go home and snuggle with Weatherby.

He sat in the chair and looked around at everything. That wasn't unusual. Lots of patients were nervous about going to the dentist. It might even account for his grumpy mood. She'd seen that before. Some patients, scared about being there, wanted assurance about everything she was doing. Or... was he nervous because of all the talk of a man dying right there, in the hygiene chair?

Harry did his exam and proclaimed Mr. Keane to be in good shape regarding x-rays.

Her patient didn't say a single thing while he was in the chair. At first, Dorey tried to make small talk to hopefully put him at ease, but after a few fruitless attempts, she gave up. After an easy—thankfully—cleaning, Dorey said good-bye to Mr. Keane.

She glanced at the clock across the room. Ten minutes to clean the room and set back up for the next patient. What a luxury. Sometimes she got behind and had to literally run around getting the room turned over for the following person to be seated.

The college student, Daphne Jordan, was a delight. Chatty, cheerful, and easy to work on. Talking to her helped lift Dorey's mood somewhat.

Daphne pointed to the handpiece. "And that's what you polish with, right?"

"Yep."

"And those instruments. Some are for doing a different part of the cleaning?"

Dorey nodded. "Are you interested in being a hygienist?"

"I've been thinking about it. I'd love to do something in the medical or dental field. Do you like your job?"

Dorey bit her lip. Trick question there. Of course, her experience lately had been a nightmare, but that wasn't the norm for dental offices. So, she answered as honestly as she could about the positives. "It's an extremely rewarding, fulfilling occupation. You get to help people, talk to them, see what makes them tick. If you're a people person, you'd love that part."

The girl nodded. As chatty as she'd been so far, Dorey could believe it.

"The pay is great, and lots of times you can choose to either work part time or full time." Though Dorey didn't have much choice now since her rent and food bills demanded she work fulltime.

"Oh, that sounds awesome." Daphne bounced in her seat like a little girl.

With a smile, Dorey said, "Yep, it can be pretty awesome." When your patients show up and allow you to clean their teeth, and no one dies.

What a pleasure to have a patient who was excited to be there. It sure was a far cry from someone terrified, and her having to explain what she was doing to calm them down or reassure them she wasn't a murderer.

Dorey smiled when the appointment was over. This was the feeling she loved when caring for a patient. One of the reasons she went into dental hygiene in the first place—to give dental care to someone who appreciated it. Of course, they hadn't told them in dental school about the high percentage of people who wouldn't want to be there or dislike hygienists simply because of where they worked.

In all fairness though, who would want to be a hygienist if, on the first day of class, the instructors were honest about only a handful of patients who actually wanted to be there in your chair. Batten down the hatches, people. Prepare yourself for an onslaught of unhappy people.

A glance at her schedule showed an hour break before her next two cleanings— little boys she'd seen before. She got out two toothbrushes, one blue and one green. Inevitably, they'd both want the same one. Dorey would let them duke it out and their mom be the referee.

Determined to keep busy until they showed up, Dorey went

to the reception area to file charts for Mae. Nothing like boring busy work to occupy her mind.

After she'd finished the little boys' cleanings and fluoride treatments, Dorey cleaned everything up in her room. Her afternoon was uneventful, with three of her patients showing up. No one glared at her, snarled, or died in her chair.

Before leaving the office, she checked the schedule for the next day. "Not bad. Fairly full." With a smile, she left the building. After having had the police clear her earlier in the day and getting to chat with the friendly college student, Dorey was, for the first time in quite a while, hopeful for the future.

26

For the next couple of weeks, things went back to normal. Patients showed up. No calamites keeping them away. At least, if they had things come up, they hadn't said so. Maybe their run of bad luck was over. Dorey relaxed and tried to get back into the routine she'd followed before any of the calamities disrupted their lives.

Until the following Tuesday.

Dorey checked the schedule first thing. "What in the world?"

"We had five messages on the machine this morning." Mae shook her head. "All canceling. I'm starting to think they're making up reasons just so they don't have to come."

Dorey didn't think so, although with the way Dr. Conners was spreading his lies, it could be possible. The man was a menace. "What kind of excuses did they give?"

The receptionist frowned as if trying to remember. "Some didn't give any, but at least two said something about Dr. Conners talking to them. A couple of them hedged around a little. I got the feeling it had something to do with what happened to Mr. Long.

"In all my years working here, I've never seen anything like it. For the last couple of weeks, things had calmed down. I'd thought maybe it would stay that way. I guess not." She raised one eyebrow. "You wanna tell Dr. MacKinley, or do you want me to?"

"What?" Dorey stared at Mae in a daze. "Oh, I will." She trudged back to Harry's operatory. He was giving his patient anesthetic, so Dorey stood just inside the doorway and waited until he was done.

When Harry looked up, Dorey caught his eye. She angled her head toward the hallway.

He raised both eyebrows and then nodded. "All right, Mr. Davis, we'll let you get numb for a few minutes and then get started."

Harry removed his gloves, washed up, followed her into his private office, and closed the door. "What's up?"

"It happened again."

"What did? You mean the schedule?"

She nodded. "I don't get it. And just on *my* side. Again. I am concerned, but not for me. How can you afford to keep paying me when I don't see patients? Don't make any profit for you? I think it might be best if I ... if I quit."

Harry held out his arms, and she went willingly. When she was little, an offered hug from him meant an ear flick or a rib-tickling.

Dorey wasn't ticklish now.

She sighed as he wrapped his arms around her. When his chin rested on the top of her head, she closed her eyes in perfect delight.

"Dorey, please don't leave. Just ... just don't."

"But why?" She pulled back enough to look at him. "I'd thought things had gotten better, but apparently, I was wrong. It's not good business sense for me to stay here. You're losing money on me."

"I'm not losing ... not losing *anything*."

"What will you do about all the cancelations?"

He gave a sigh and stepped away. Was he disappointed not to be holding her anymore? She was.

"We'll come up with something. We did get several new patients the last few days, right?"

"Yeah, but that still doesn't make up for all the openings on my side since you see the new ones first."

"Listen, after the things Mae said to you, I gave her a good scolding. She seemed to take it to heart. So right now, she's working feverishly out there to get someone in. And I know you help with that too, which I appreciate. I haven't checked your schedule today, only mine. What have you got this morning?"

"No one until eleven." What would she do to occupy herself for all that time?

"We need some supplies for the office, and Mae hasn't gotten them yet. Would you mind? I can give you the company credit card." He smirked. "But if I see purchases on there for a bunch of stuffed animals, I'm coming after you."

She laughed. "Of course, I don't mind. And I'll buy the animals with my own money, thank you very much."

His laughter followed her out of the room. She retrieved her purse and jacket and headed to the local wholesale store where Mae did all the shopping for the office. It was a nice break from thinking about the schedule. At least she was doing something productive. Even if she wasn't bringing in money.

Mae's list was long, but in no time, Dorey had everything in her cart and checked out. She almost wished it had taken longer. She'd only been away a little over an hour. But so early in the day, not many people were out shopping. Now she had no choice but to head back and try to get someone else to come in. She still had a couple of openings in the afternoon too. Dorey's luck had changed once, for a couple of weeks. Maybe it could change again—get things back to normal and *stay* that way.

With her trunk lid open, she unloaded everything inside.

One roll of paper towel was making its escape from the top of the pile. Dorey had to chase it a few feet across the parking lot before it stopped rolling.

Stupid rogue paper product. She grabbed it and hurried back to the car. The only spot for it without putting it on top again was way in the back. There was a narrow opening. The roll might just fit if she pushed hard. Nobody would care if the paper towels were deformed, would they? Mae might squawk, but she'd get over it.

As Dorey leaned inside the trunk, she heard footsteps. A shadow formed over the supplies in the trunk to her right. She straightened and squelched a scream.

A man stood there with a hideous mask over his face. A zombie with blood dripping from his mouth. His hat was tugged low over his head, and his chin was tucked into the top of his zipped jacket.

"W-what do you want?" She took a step back.

He stared at her for a minute, looking her over, then grunted in a gravelly voice, "Your purse."

Dorey froze. Her mind went blank. She couldn't form any coherent thoughts. But she snapped back to awareness when the mugger grabbed her purse. The strap was wrapped around her wrist, and when he gruffly tugged it away, the momentum spun her. She lost her footing and fell, cracking her head on the pavement.

Pain, sudden and fierce, shot through her head and back. She screamed. Retreating footsteps sounded. It took a minute for Dorey to decide which way was up, as stars bounced around in front of her eyes.

Dizzy, she slowly raised her head and looked around. Her stomach clenched as the realization sunk in. Someone had mugged her! And he'd worn a mask! Was it the same person who was behind everything else? It had to be.

She needed help, but no one else was nearby. Her back

ached. Was she bleeding? Reaching gingerly back, she ran her hand across her skin. No, no blood. She'd probably have an awful bruise come tomorrow, though. It already felt like an angry hippo had given her a karate kick.

With care, she stood and held on to her car. Sliding her hands along the side, she held on until she could open the front driver's side door and crawl inside. She only vaguely registered she'd forgotten to lock the door when she went into the store. Dizziness overtook her, but she managed to tug the door shut. Head pounding like a jackhammer, she pressed her forehead on the steering wheel and took deep, slow breaths.

Someone was after her patients, but now, she couldn't deny they were after *her* too. Was the culprit a patient? Dr. Conners? A random psycho who had a vendetta against innocent dental hygienists?

She shook her head but stopped when it made the pain worse. No. Why would someone do that? Nobody liked going to the dentist, but that would be an extreme way to show it. And Dr. Conners was a nasty old goat, but she couldn't see him mugging her and being agile enough to run away.

Her cell phone rang. She blindly grabbed inside her jacket pocket a few seconds before her fingers curled over the hard plastic of the case. She picked it up quickly and hit the button, wanting the noise to stop. "H-hello?"

"Dorey? It's Mae. I might have someone who could come in now for a cleaning, but I didn't know when you'd be back."

"Um ... I ..." Her voice came out sounding like gravel being crushed under something heavy.

"Are you all right? You sound funny."

"I kind of ..." She rubbed the back of her head, then moaned.

"Dorey?"

"Someone ... I had a sort of accident, and I—"

"What?" Mae's screech tore through Dorey's head.

She rubbed her temple with her other hand. "It's o—"

"Where are you?"

"I'm in the store parking lot, but—"

"Stay there." The phone clicked in Dorey's ear. Was Mae leaving the office to come to the store?

This is not good. Dorey would be the laughingstock of the office. Mae, someone old enough to be her grandmother, having to come rescue her. Harry would never stop teasing her about this.

She wanted to start the car and hurry back to the office before Mae had a chance to come, but another round of dizziness engulfed her whole head. She slumped over to lie across the passenger seat.

Without her permission, her eyes drifted shut. She couldn't stay here like this in the parking lot. What if the person who'd hurt her came back? I need to sit up, try to start the car …

All her strength now gone, Dorey pressed her cheek into the seat and let the darkness come.

27

When Dorey opened her eyes, it wasn't Mae who'd come to her rescue.

Harry's brow was furrowed, his face laced with concern. "Dorey. It's Harry. Can you hear me?"

"Of course, I can hear you. You're like three inches from my face."

The muscles in his face relaxed. "You can't imagine the thoughts running through my head when Mae told me you'd had an accident. I just got here, but I'm going to call an ambulance."

"No. I don't need one."

"You have a giant lump on your head. You need to get it checked out. They might need to take an X-ray."

Dorey hated hospitals. Didn't everybody? "You could take an X-ray. At the office."

"With the tiny sizes of film we use?" He smiled. "I'd need at least fifty of them to cover your whole head."

"Please don't call an ambulance." She reached out for his hand, relieved when she found it. "I feel stupid enough already."

"Fine." He closed his eyes for a second. "I'll give in on the ambulance. But you are going to get checked out. I'll drive you."

"But—"

"No. You're going, and that's that. You'll thank me later."

She huffed out a breath. Even that slight movement hurt her head. "I highly doubt that." Dorey fished the car keys out of her pocket, the jangling of the metal zipping painfully through her ears as Harry leaned in and stuck the keys in the ignition.

"Can you sit up?"

"I can try. But I'm …" She rose up a few inches and covered her eyes with her hand. "Dizzy."

"Okay. If we could just slide you over a little bit, I'll get in, and you can put your head on my lap. Like you did when you were little and needed a nap."

Dorey widened her eyes, but that caused a rush of pain as well. Somehow, she didn't think putting her head on Harry's lap would have the same meaning that it did when she was eight. But Harry wasn't going to back down. She'd seen that stubborn set of his clenched jaw before.

"All right." She was too tired, weak, and dizzy to fight about it.

Harry slid his hands under her shoulders and lifted her slightly until he could scoot onto the seat. The light coming through the windshield nearly sent her into orbit. Too bright!

She closed her eyes and concentrated on breathing slowly. In. Out. They'd be there soon. The hospital wasn't too far away. The blessing of a small town. One of the few.

"How did you get that bump on your head? I didn't see any dents in the car. Did whoever hit you just drive off?" Harry stroked her face lightly.

"There was no driver."

His hand stilled. "What do you mean?"

"It was a walker. You know … oh, what do you call those … Umm … ped-ped …"

"Pedestrian?"

"That's it."

"I don't understand. Some person physically ran into your car? Like on purpose?"

"Not the car. Me."

The car jerked as Harry lifted his leg. Had he let off the accelerator? "Dorey, are you sure? A person hit you on the head?"

"No, the parking lot hit me on the head."

The car jerked again.

Dorey took a deep breath and released it. "I really wish you'd quit doing that, Harry. I do have a headache, you know."

"Sorry. I just … I'm trying to understand."

She sighed. It was taking so much energy even to talk. "I was putting away the … oh … you know the …" She raised her hand, flipping it in the air.

"Office supplies?"

"Yes. Office supplies. I was bent over into the trunk, trying to wedge in a wayward roll of uncooperative paper towels, and a man in a mask showed up."

"He wore a mask?"

"Yes. Zombie. Listen. I'm tired. I'm going to sleep now. Wake me when we get there."

"I'm not sure that's a good idea. If you have a concussion, they don't always want you going to sleep."

"But I'm so tired." She turned and nuzzled him again, this time causing him to gasp.

Within a few minutes, Harry turned the wheel sharply to the right. The car bumped a little bit. They must be in the parking lot. When she opened her eyes again, she could see the portico over the drive in front of the building, like a little hair bonnet protecting the main door.

"I could have walked in, Harry."

"I'm getting you a wheelchair." He opened the door. Bright

light nearly blinded Dorey. Harry slowly slid from underneath her and got out.

With a groan, Dorey mumbled, "Oh, brother." But after Harry left, she tried to sit up. Nope. Not happening. Everything whirled, and her stomach clenched. Slumping back down on the seat like a slow mudslide down a mountain, Dorey was once again flat on her back.

The door opened. The loud squeak of the hinges shot through her, making her cringe.

From her vantage point, Harry was upside down. She could see up his nose. He had such a nice nose. Another pair of legs stood next to his.

"This is Dorey Cameron," Harry said. "She has a pretty nasty bump on her head. We need to get her checked out."

"No problem," the other man said. "Let's get her into the chair and inside."

Dorey kept her eyes closed as two strong pairs of hands grasped her from underneath and slid her along the seat. She dared another peek and was very sorry. When she looked to the side from the corner of her eye, she saw blacktop. Way too close.

"Don't you dare drop me! Ouch." Yelling didn't help her headache much either.

"Don't worry," said the man. "We'll make sure you get there safe."

When she was finally in the wheelchair, she angled a glance to her right. There were two hospital workers instead of one. A tall, skinny one and the other short and stocky. So, had they been the ones to pull her from the car? "Where's Harry?"

A warm hand grasped her shoulder from behind. "I'm not going anywhere."

She sighed and slumped down to the side.

"Whoa," said one of the men. "Not too steady there, huh?"

"I'll walk beside her." Harry came around to one side. "She can lean into me."

"Thanks, Harry." Dorey nuzzled her head against his leg like Weatherby often did her.

He chuckled. "You're welcome."

"I'm thinking concussion," one of the other men said. "Is she acting strangely?"

Silence.

Dorey frowned. Why wasn't Harry answering? Coming to her defense. Telling the man she wasn't acting strange.

Finally, Harry muttered, "Um ... yeah, let's get her checked out."

"What? Thanks a bunch. Throw me under the bus, so I'm run over and squashed flat like a—" *Dorey* moaned, as even the thought caused her head to pound.

Whoever pushed the wheelchair was an awfully bad driver. They were going way too fast. Would he lose control and let her and the chair go careening down some staircase? Crash into a wall? She clutched the arms of the chair with everything she was worth.

The fluorescent lights inside the hospital were way too intense. Dorey squinted her eyes closed. That hurt too, but not as much as the lights. This pain wasn't permanent, was it?

She kept her head pressed into Harry, not caring if the men thought she was silly, or acting strangely, or anything else. She just wanted to get to a bed and lie down and never wake up.

It seemed to take forever for them to run tests. She heard voices, felt hands moving her, and mumbled when they asked direct questions. But she mostly kept her eyes shut against the glare. Just hurry up with them so I can go home.

She snorted awake when something tapped her shoulder.

"Dorey, the police are here. They need to talk to you."

"You said I wasn't supposed to go to sleep." She glared at

Harry. "How could you let that happen? Can't you see I have no control over it by myself?"

"The longest you could have been out was forty-five seconds."

"Well, it felt like hours." She sighed and closed her eyes again. "It was wonderful."

"Okay, but I need you to try to focus now." He patted her.

She forced one eyelid open, then the other, and squinted up at the face peering down at her. Officer Beaumont. "You again," she muttered.

"Don't take it personally, Officer, she did get hit on the head pretty hard," Harry said.

"I'll do my best not to get my little feelings hurt." Officer Beaumont scowled.

Dorey laughed. "Little feelings ... Feelings," she warbled out the song. "Nothing more than feelings ..."

"Stop singing." Harry's voice came from right beside her ear.

"All right," she grumbled, but the song was stuck in her head.

"I just want to make sure I have the facts of the story all straight." Officer Beaumont flipped open his notebook. "I'm going to ask you some questions."

"Rock on, Mr. Policeman." Dorey tried to pump her fist but couldn't remember how to do it.

Harry rolled his eyes.

Officer Beaumont lifted one eyebrow. "Dr. MacKinley told me what you'd said. That someone came up from behind you, wearing a mask. Then you fell and smashed your head. Is that correct?"

"Oh .... Don't say smash. That makes my head ache again."

"I'll try to refrain from using such descriptive verbs. Anyway, is that how you remember it happening?"

"Yep. I was bent over, trying to stuff a deformed paper towel roll into an empty spot in the back. Some man in a mask, hat, and jacket wanted my purse. He ripped it from around my wrist, and I fell. I heard footsteps, like someone was running away. By the time I could look around, whoever it was had gone."

Office Beaumont narrowed his eyes. "So, that's your final statement."

"It is indeed." She attempted a salute but only succeeded in poking herself in the eye.

"Dr. MacKinley," said the officer, "would you have any reason to think this incident, the break-in at your office, and what happened to Mr. Long are connected?"

"I don't know," said Harry, his voice agitated.

"With them happening so close together, I can't rule it out. Has anything else odd happened lately?"

"Well ... our patients haven't been showing up."

The officer chuckled. "I'd strike that up to nobody liking to go to the dentist. No offense."

"None taken."

"Offense taken," piped in Dorey.

Harry patted her shoulder. "I can handle this, Dorey, thanks."

"Just keep your eyes open, all right?" Officer Beaumont closed his notebook and stuck it in his shirt pocket. "And call us if anything else occurs. We'll be on the lookout for Miss Cameron's purse."

"Okay."

Footsteps sounded, and the curtain around her bed was closed.

Dorey's eyes drifted shut. Something touched her shoulder, and she opened her eyes. Harry stood over her again. "Would you please stop poking me?"

"The doctor was just here."

"Hooray. Don't forget to invite me to the party."

"He said you do have a concussion but that I can take you home. I'll need to stay overnight with you to make sure you're okay."

"Good. Will you sleep next to me again, Harry?"

He grimaced. "Don't talk so loud."

"Sorry," she whispered. "I really liked sleeping next to you."

"I really liked it too."

"Harry?"

He let out a breath. "What?"

"I love you."

He chuckled. "I love you too."

The ride home was pretty much like the ride to the hospital. Dorey's head on Harry's lap. She tried not to move her head around, though, so he wouldn't jerk his leg again. No use having an accident after her other accident.

Harry parked her car and got out. With care, he slid Dorey off the seat and pulled her to a standing position. She immediately wilted. Harry grabbed her before she hit the pavement. Then he hoisted her up, one arm around her back. They made slow but steady progress to her apartment from the car, her feet shuffling along like those of a drunken sailor.

Once inside, Harry half-carried Dorey down the hall to her bedroom. She could hear Weatherby from somewhere behind them squawking to be fed.

Harry lowered her onto the bed, flat on her back. His face was inches from hers.

"Hi, Harry."

He grinned. "Hi."

She smiled back. "Did you want to kiss me now?"

"I ... I would, but right now, I need to get my arm out from underneath you. I'm stuck."

"Oh." She sighed and allowed him to turn her a little so he could slide his arm out. "A kiss would have been more fun."

"True. But maybe we'll wait until you're over your concussion."

"If you say so." She pouted. This day wasn't turning out very well at all.

Harry pulled the covers up over her and then sat down beside her. He stroked her cheek. "I was so afraid, Dorey, when I saw you there in your car, not moving, I thought ..."

"You thought ..."

"That I'd lost you."

Dorey blinked, wanting to close her eyes so badly but not wanting to miss anything Harry said. "I'm still here."

"I'm glad." He pressed his lips to her forehead. "Now, you get some rest."

"I'm not supposed to."

"The doctor said it's been long enough now since your injury that you should be okay. But I'm going to wake you every couple of hours just to check on you."

"'Night, Harry."

"'Night."

28

Harry had checked on her during the night, though Dorey barely remembered it. Kind of like a hazy dream she wasn't sure was real or not. She'd woken up with a headache the size of Montana, but the dizziness was almost gone. Her bedroom door opened, and Harry came in carrying a tray.

Dorey sat up cautiously, pleased when the movement didn't make her feel sick. "You brought me breakfast in bed?"

"Didn't want you to go hungry."

"You're so sweet." She glanced at the bedside clock. "Oh. We're late for work."

He set the tray down beside her on the bed. "You're not going anywhere. At least not until tomorrow. Maybe not even then."

"What about you, though?" He had on his jeans, but his hair was damp. Probably would change at work again.

"I called Mae, and I don't have a patient until nine-o'clock."

Dorey grabbed a piece of buttered toast from the tray and took a nibble. "It's twenty minutes till. You'd better go."

"Yeah, I know. You gonna be okay here? Alone?"

"I'm guessing I'll just sleep some more. It would be boring for you anyway."

"Are you sure?"

"Yes." She smiled. "Thank you for coming to my rescue. Again." He opened his mouth to speak, but Dorey held up her hand. "Do not say it's what you do."

"All right. I won't say it." He muttered, "But it is."

Dorey slugged him on the shoulder.

"Yep, you're starting to feel better." He smirked, then glanced at her hand. "Hey, you're not wearing your ring. Did the mugger take it from you?"

"No, I hadn't been wearing it. Not since Mr. Long. Didn't see the point."

"Well, I think you should start wearing it again. It looks so pretty on you. And I know you like it."

She sighed. "Okay. I guess. Before I do, though, I need to have a jeweler check it out. The stone was a tiny bit loose."

"Okay." He stood. "Your cell phone is right there. You will call me if you need anything? Right?"

"Yes."

"Now, let's see. Weatherby has been fed, and I'll lock the door on my way out. I have to take your car because mine is still at the store. I'll have to get it later. Besides, you're not allowed to drive anyway."

"Don't worry. I'm so tired, there's no place I want to go."

"Good. Well, I'll see ya later." He kissed her cheek. "Hey ..."

"What?"

"Do you remember any of the stuff you said when you were at the hospital?"

"Not a whole lot. Why?"

He grinned. "Just checking." He turned and walked toward the door.

"Wait. Harry? What did I say?"

The next thing she heard was the front door shutting.

She ate a little more and then slid back down under the covers. What had she said that was so weird?

The next time she woke up, it was to the ringing of her cell phone. Bleary-eyed and feeling sluggish, she answered. "Hello?"

"Dorey!" Her dad's yell nearly sent Dorey into orbit.

"Not so loud."

"Harry called. Are you okay?"

"I was until you woke me up."

"Sorry. Is Harry there? Let me talk to him."

"He went to work."

"And left you alone?"

"Stop yelling."

"I'm coming there. Right now."

"You don't need to come. Honestly. I'm fine."

"You have a concussion!"

If her dad didn't stop yelling, Dorey might hang up. "I was examined by a doctor at the ER. I'm doing everything he told me to. Harry is checking on me. He wouldn't have gone to work and left me alone if he was that worried. Plus, I have my cell phone right here. I'm to call him if I need anything, and he'll come right away. Okay?"

"You're sure?"

"Positive."

"When Harry called, he also filled me in on a few other things. Why didn't you tell me, Dorey?"

"I didn't want to worry you. Look, when it all started, I didn't think too much about it. But things started to … escalate, and then—"

"You still should have called me."

"You're right. I'm sorry."

"I'm glad you have Harry there."

"Me too." She wanted to point out that her dad had taken Harry aside and specifically requested he look after Dorey, but at this point, what good would that do? "Oh, and Dad?"

"Yeah?"

"I don't want Mom to worry. Please don't tell her yet."

"Too late."

Dorey groaned. "Then tell her I'm really okay. Just need some rest."

"Okay. But you'll let me know if you change your mind about me coming."

"I promise."

"Okay, kid. Well, take care. Love you."

"You too."

She ended the call and lay back on the pillow. Just that conversation had worn her out. Maybe Harry was right. She might not feel up to working tomorrow.

Weatherby jumped on the bed and sniffed her uneaten toast.

"Go ahead. Lick off the butter. You know you want to."

As if glad for the permission, he hunkered down on his paws and gleefully licked every inch of the toast.

Poor soggy piece of bread would never be the same.

She woke again an hour later. Someone was knocking on her door. Harry had a key, so he wouldn't knock. Maybe it was Mr. Nichols? Dorey stood up slowly, making sure she had her bearings before walking across the room. Weatherby leaped out at her feet from the open bathroom doorway.

Dorey shrieked, then grabbed her head. "Cat, don't do that when Mommy is still a little dizzy. You might not get fed if I fall and get another concussion, ya know?"

He ran to the kitchen and sat beside his dish.

"Wait. Have to see who's at the door."

When she opened it, though, whoever had knocked was gone.

Well, that was just perfect. She could have stayed in bed. With a sigh, she started to close the door but noticed something stuck under a large rock to the left of the door. That rock wasn't usually there. And something the size of a football would have snagged her attention. Reaching down, careful not to move too fast, Dorey edged the envelope out and stood back up.

Don't let it be another threat. They need to go away. Leave me alone. She glanced around, but no one was nearby. The parking area was mostly empty, with most of her neighbors at work.

Something touched her bare foot, and she gasped. "Weatherby. Stop that."

He whined and pawed at her pant leg.

"All right. Hold on." They went back inside. Dorey closed and locked the door. Weatherby was acting like he might have kittens if she didn't hurry, so she fed him before looking at the note.

She wanted to read it.

Yet, she didn't.

Maybe it was a neighbor who'd heard about her accident and wanted to wish her well. Or the bill for the glass company fixing the window, and they'd left it for her instead of Mr. Nichols.

Dorey, you won't know until you read it.

She opened and unfolded the paper, which read:

Check beneath your bushes for your purse.

Dorey frowned. My purse? She headed back to the porch. With care, she crouched down, hoping not to keel over to the side. There was a plastic bag tucked just beneath the bush. Sure enough, her purse was in there. She darted a quick glance around but didn't see anyone.

After she was back inside with the door locked, she took out her purse and opened it. Her cash was missing, but that was no great loss. She hadn't had much in there anyway. But her credit card was still there, along with her driver's license. Why would they have left her credit card? Still, she'd call the credit card company and report that it had been stolen, even though she got it back. Just in case some weird charges showed up on her account.

What kind of nut mugged someone then returned the item along with a note? She'd have to tell the police she got it back. And Harry would want to know too.

Harry's words right after she'd hit her head, 'I thought I'd lost you,' came back. Well, she'd feel the same way about him. Because she loved him. Did that mean he loved her too? More than as a friend?

Something niggled at her brain. Something she'd said to Harry. Was it when she'd been in the ER? What was it? Love—

Her eyes widened. She'd told Harry she loved him. And he'd said it back, but he'd laughed when he did, like he was teasing her. So, he hadn't meant it like she did. Later, he'd asked her if she remembered everything she'd said at the hospital. He'd been laughing then too.

This is not good.

29

I t was the following Monday before Dorey felt well enough
to work on patients. She could have gone back on the
previous Friday but was still a little dizzy. A dental professional
with unsteady hands wielding sharp instruments wasn't the best
way to reassure patients who were already leery after listening
to Dr. Conners. And hearing about one recently demised
patient.

She got to the office, relieved to discover she had some
patients scheduled. Not a jam-packed day but better than most
had been lately. Trying to force away the scary stuff that had
happened, especially the week before, Dorey went to her room
to make sure it was ready to go. Odd, going in there, since she'd
missed some days last week. Almost like she was a stranger,
walking into someone else's operatory.

Stop it. You belong here. Harry said so.

But with all the notes, messages, unwanted gifts, and the
concussion, did she really believe that?

"Your first one is here." Mae came in the room and laid a
chart on the counter. She eyed Dorey. "You okay? We were all
worried about you."

"Thanks, Mae." Dorey smiled. "Yes, I'm much better."

"If you start feeling woozy during the day, just give a shout, okay?"

"I will."

Warmth surrounded Dorey's heart as Mae left the room. She could be nosy and even rude, but it was nice to know that she did care at least a little.

Mrs. Betters sat in the waiting room with a white-knuckled grip on her handbag.

"Mrs. Betters? I'm ready for you."

Her patient stood but didn't say anything. She followed Dorey to the room, stiff-legged, as if she walked on wooden pegs.

"How are you today?" Dorey waited while her patient placed her purse on the counter and sat in the chair.

"Fine."

She didn't look fine. Her face was pale. Or was she nervous? She never had been before. Dorey had always enjoyed their visits in the past.

Maybe Dorey needed to ease her into the appointment with a little small talk. "How's that cute little granddaughter of yours?"

"Fine."

Dorey frowned. Usually the woman couldn't wait to talk about her family. Whipped out pictures of them and told Dorey all about what they'd been up to.

After putting on her gloves, Dorey leaned the chair back. Mrs. Betters gripped the arms of the chair much like she'd been doing to her purse.

What was going on? Maybe her patient had some health scare recently. Wasn't feeling the best. Concerned, Dorey asked, "Have there been any changes to your medical history? Any problems?"

"Nope."

"Okay." Something wasn't right. If it had been another patient, Dorey would have chalked it up to grumpiness. But not cheerful Mrs. Betters. "Um … any problems with your teeth since I saw you last?"

"No. Not yet." The woman narrowed her eyes.

Uh-oh.

"I see. Well, let's get you checked out, all right?" She reached for her patient mirror, startled when Mrs. Betters grabbed her wrist. "Is something wrong?"

"I … I think I'd prefer it if the doctor did my cleaning."

It sounded like good old Dr. Conners had been at it again. Dorey sighed. "May I ask why? I've cleaned your teeth several times before."

"I'd just rather have him do it." Mrs. Betters dropped her hand, but her fingers fidgeted in her lap.

"If you have some concerns about my care, I can certainly have you talk to Dr. MacKinley, but—"

"Yes. I'd like to speak to him."

"All right." Dorey could see she wouldn't get anywhere with the cleaning. She stood and removed her gloves. "If you'll excuse me." She left the room, trying to ignore the strange look Mae gave her when she walked out into the hall.

Harry sat, talking to his patient. An empty carpule sat on the tray next to a syringe. So, he'd just given the anesthetic. She cleared her throat and he looked up.

"May I speak to you?" Her eyebrows rose.

He darted a look in the direction of her room, and she nodded.

"I'll let you get numb." Harry glanced at his patient. "I'll be back in a few minutes. Would you like a magazine while you wait?"

"Sure." The man smiled.

"I'll get you one." Luanne stood.

Harry followed Dorey to his private office.

"Wow." Dorey grimaced. "We sure are spending a lot of time in here."

"Have another difficult patient?"

"Mrs. Betters. She says she'd rather have the doctor do her cleaning."

Harry ran his hand down his face. "I could just strangle Dr. Conners. Why did he retire and sell me this practice if he wanted to stay so involved with his patients?" He glanced at Dorey. "And cause so much trouble?"

"I don't know. I'm—"

"Don't apologize. This is his doing. Not yours. Well, I won't start doing cleanings just because that old goat has been telling lies. You do a great job, Dorey, and the patients love you. If it weren't for Dr. Conners, there wouldn't be any problem. Come on." He opened the door and briskly walked down the hallway. Dorey almost jogged to keep up.

Once back in Dorey's operatory, Harry sat down in the chair next to Mrs. Betters.

"Good morning."

"Hello, Dr. MacKinley." Mrs. Betters visibly relaxed at the sight of Harry.

Dorey wanted so bad to roll her eyes.

"Dorey has told me you've stated your preference for me to do your cleaning. Is that right?" Harry crossed his arms.

"Yes."

"May I ask why?"

Dorey wanted to sink into the floor. She hadn't done anything wrong but felt like she'd been dragged into the principal's office because some kid had accused her of pushing them down on the playground.

Mrs. Betters avoided Dorey and looked right at Harry. "I've … been told that …" She glared at Dorey and back. "That … I'm much better off having a dentist do my cleaning."

"Can I ask who has told you this?"

Mrs. Betters dropped her gaze to her lap, her hands fidgety.

"I'm going to guess it was Dr. Conners?"

Her head snapped up, and her face reddened.

Softening his voice, he said, "Is that right?"

She gave a slow nod.

"Mrs. Betters, Dorey has cleaned your teeth several times. You've never had any complaints about her care before. Have you had any problems with them? Or trouble with your mouth afterward?"

Dorey held her breath, hoping like crazy Mrs. Betters would say she hadn't. If she said yes, would that affect Dorey's confidence in the future for patient care? She already had to fight an uphill battle because of Dr. Conners.

"No."

Relieved, Dorey let out a breath.

"Then, you know she does a good job." Harry patted Mrs. Betters' hand gently.

"That's true." Mrs. Betters shrugged.

Dorey wanted to run away. She hated being talked about. Her face heated. Why couldn't Dr. Conners mind his own business? Because this business wasn't his anymore. He'd sold it. *Cut the apron strings, Doc.*

"Do you trust me?" Harry smiled kindly.

She nodded.

"Then trust me when I tell you that nothing has changed here. I trust Dorey. Completely. You used to until today, right?"

"Well, yes." She snuck a peek up at Dorey, then looked away.

"While Dr. Conners was a good dentist, for some reason, he didn't see the need for hygienists. That's his opinion and his right to think so. But ..." Harry held up his finger. "I believe hygienists are necessary and important. If you'll think about it, perhaps you'd remember why you used to think so too."

Mrs. Betters blinked and tilted her head, as if she really was considering it. Then, she looked past him to Dorey. "Oh ... I'm

…" She blinked more rapidly as her eyes grew damp. "I'm sorry, Dorey. Would you … Could you go ahead and do my cleaning? You really do a wonderful job."

"Of course. I'd love to."

"So, if we're all okay here?" Harry stood.

"Yes." Mrs. Betters nodded. "We're fine. I'm sorry I listened to Dr. Conners when I knew what a good job your hygienist did."

He smiled. "I'll be back in a little while to do your exam."

"Thank you." She smiled back.

Dorey sat down and grabbed another pair of gloves, her mask, and safety glasses. She picked up her instruments and paused, waiting. Just to be sure Mrs. Betters had no remaining doubts.

The woman glanced up at Dorey. "I'm so sorry. Can you forgive me?"

Dorey grinned. Her patient wouldn't see it, but Dorey hoped she could feel it. "There's nothing to forgive. I'm glad you came in today."

"So am I." Mrs. Betters leaned her head against the headrest, looking relaxed for the first time since she'd arrived.

"Maybe when we're through, you could show me your latest pictures of your granddaughter." Dorey pushed the button to recline the chair.

"I'd like that." The joy that lit the woman's face could have rivaled the sun.

The cleaning went off without a hitch. Dorey was worn out, though, simply because of the nervous tension preceding it. But she was so relieved it turned out like it had.

Harry did the exam and pressed the button on the patient chair. "Everything looks great, Mrs. Betters."

"Good. Thank you."

"Thank you for sticking around today. I'm sorry if my words

earlier were in any way harsh. If so, my attitude wasn't directed at you. I hope you know that."

"No, dear." She patted his hand. "I completely understand."

"Maybe …" Harry smiled. "If the subject comes up with any other patients you happen to talk to, you could—"

"Tell them about my good experience?"

He nodded.

"Of course. I'd be happy to." She left the office with a smile and a spring in her step, looking like the woman who'd had enjoyable visits every other time.

Shame on Dr. Conners for causing so much trouble.

30

The next evening after work, Dorey drove to the mall. The place wasn't much, but in such a small town, they were lucky to even have one at all. She parked near the entrance, not wanting a long distance to walk back afterward because, by the time she was done in the store, it would be completely dark.

Even though the owner of the ring might show up and claim it, Dorey wanted to have the ring professionally cleaned and the prongs checked by a jeweler.

And maybe, if she was lucky, no one would call the office to inquire about it. Then she could have something to remind her of the one her sweet grandmother had given her.

The air inside the mall was stuffy. She fanned her face with her hand as she made her way to the store. Unable to afford much nice jewelry, very occasionally, she treated herself to something they had on sale.

Dorey glanced down at her hand as she waited at the counter. The tiny turquoise stone appeared even brighter under the fluorescent lights. She studied it more closely. Now she could see that the color was deeper, richer, than other turquoise jewelry she'd seen. She'd been surprised when the ring had fit her finger perfectly. Almost as if—

"May I help you?"

She jumped and looked up. "Oh. Um, yes. I wondered if you could clean and check my ring. Make sure the prongs aren't loose."

The saleswoman smiled. "Certainly." And held out her hand.

Dorey removed the ring and gave it to her, almost hating to be without it.

Don't be silly. You just got the ring. And it's not even technically yours.

After the woman turned and walked into a back room, Dorey wandered around, checking out the new necklaces and bracelets they'd gotten in since her last visit. A turquoise pendant was displayed by itself beneath the glass. She'd have to see them side by side to compare but was sure the stone in her ring was slightly different.

Why was she so fascinated with the ring? Was it because it was her favorite color? Because of her grandmother's gift, or because someone might call any day to claim it when Dorey didn't want to give it up?

A familiar voice caught her attention. Harry stood in front of a sporting goods store halfway down the mall, talking to a gorgeous blonde. Dorey started to turn away, but ...

The woman laughed. And put her hand on Harry's chest.

What?

Dorey's mouth dropped open. The woman was flirting very openly with Harry. Dorey's blood boiled. That woman, whoever she was, had better watch herself. Dorey could take her in a catfight. Would tug out the roots of her bleached hair and smear the gallon of makeup she had caking her face. Then she could—

Why did she care?

Because he's ... they're ...

No, you're not, he isn't, and the two of you aren't anything but friends and co-workers.

But that kiss. Maybe it hadn't meant as much to Harry as to Dorey.

She blew out a long breath. It never used to bother her in years past when girls flirted with Harry. In fact, she'd taken great delight in teasing him about it. He'd done the same with her whenever he found out she was dating someone new.

Not lately, though. He hadn't had a reason to tease her about that because she hadn't had a date in—

Who knew? And if she couldn't remember exactly how long it had been, how sad was that? Her love life was non-existent. The well had run dry. If she lived in another century, she'd be a spinster at the ripe old age of twenty-seven. Was it because there weren't that many eligible, nice men in their tiny town to date? Or had she lost her appeal?

Dorey glared at the woman again. Maybe that was the reason. Women like that one took all the men with their long, smooth hair and smiles so white, the glare was nearly blinding. And skin-tight capris, a nearly see-through white top, and four-inch heels.

While Dorey, on the other hand, had never worn an overabundance of makeup and didn't care about the latest style of clothing. Mostly because she was stuck in a rut of always wearing the same things. Jeans, long-sleeved T-shirts, and bare-footed when at home.

At work, she always had on her most comfortable sneakers and loose scrubs. And those didn't look good on anyone. How could Dorey have any appeal when she wore something as formless as a pillowcase?

She squinted and observed Harry and the woman again. Was he flirting back? Dorey's hands tightened to fists at her sides. Harry was smiling and nodding, but from that distance, she couldn't quite make out his full expression.

Were his eyes darting to the side, as if wanting to escape a boring conversation? He did that when Dorey talked about subjects he found uninteresting. Or was he watching the woman's face intently, his eyes focusing on hers, lowering to her lips—

"Miss?"

Dorey gasped. She really needed to calm down. She was as jumpy as a cat. Well, not her sneaky cat, but anyone else's.

It was the jeweler holding out the ring. Where had the saleswoman gone off to? The man held up the ring. Dorey started to take it from him, wanting to feel it in her hand, to keep it near her. But the man shook his head.

Dorey lowered her gaze to the ring. "Were the prongs all right? I was concerned they might snag on something."

"They're fine. It's an exquisite piece."

She nodded. "I think so too."

"If I may ask, where did you get it?"

Was he upset that she hadn't purchased it at his store? Heat flooded her face. What an idiot. Of course, he would be a little irked that she brought in a ring from someplace else.

"I found it." She wasn't going to say where. Let the owner of the ring come to the office, but she wasn't going to give anyone any information to help them.

"Oh." He frowned.

What was that about? Maybe there was something else he'd found when he'd examined it.

"Is something wrong?"

"No. Not at all. As I said, it's lovely. I know we didn't sell it from here." He tapped the glass on the display case and gave her a look that said, why haven't you bought something from us in a while? "But it seems familiar to me. You said you'd found it somewhere?"

Dorey shrugged, hoping to appear nonchalant. If the jeweler had seen the ring before, did that mean the original owner brought it in for repair at some point? That didn't improve her chances for keeping it.

If the owner did show up, she'd have to give the ring back. Her shoulders slumped, and she sighed. When she glanced up, heat crawled up her cheeks. The man was staring at her with one eyebrow raised. She'd been just gazing at the ring, daydreaming.

"Uh, yes. I found it." She needed to get out of here before she embarrassed herself even more.

The jeweler eyed the ring again. "It's so unique. If memory serves, though it was a long time ago, it reminds me of a ring that had been stolen from the museum."

What? She frowned. Surely not. How could a ring stolen a long time ago end up in her dental chair? Suddenly, she wanted to take her ring and leave the store. "Thank you so much for cleaning and checking it. How much do I owe you?"

He gave her back the ring and waved a hand. "No charge. You buy enough from us that we don't mind checking your jewelry when you come in." His gaze flicked down from the ring to the glass case that sat between them, which was full of rings with stones of every color.

Yeah, okay. Point taken. She gave him a smile she didn't feel and turned to leave. *Guess I'll be buying something else from them. Soon.*

With another glance at Harry and the woman, who had stepped even closer and was staring up at him, Dorey gritted her teeth and stomped toward the exit. Was the woman someone he was seeing? If so, wouldn't he have said something to Dorey in the office? But why would he? He was her boss and didn't owe her any explanations.

But that kiss. Did he go around just kissing any woman who crossed his path?

It had grown darker outside. She could still see, but it was tough. Her bright red car was easy to spot. She'd made sure to park under a streetlamp. Someone's car alarm was going off. She took few more steps.

Oh, no. It's mine!

Her car lights were flashing, and the car alarm blared like a fire engine. Pushing on the panic key, Dorey silenced the alarm. She quickened her steps toward the car, key in hand and ready to jump inside. Quickly, she glanced around. There were several cars in the lot, but no people at the moment. As she got closer, it didn't look like anything was disturbed. No broken glass on the ground.

Maybe someone had bumped against her car with a shopping cart. Would that have set off the alarm? When she bent down to insert the key, she frowned. There were scratches around the keyhole. Those hadn't been there before. Had someone tried to break in?

She flung open the door and scanned the front and back seats and floor. After letting out a relieved sigh, she jumped in, closed the door, and locked it.

Her heart raced, thinking of what might have happened if the person had taken her car. Or worse, if they'd still been there when she'd come out.

She'd never driven home so fast in her life.

31

D orey had a productive morning. Thank goodness. At lunchtime, she was famished. The office had a small breakroom. She retrieved her lunch, such as it was, from the refrigerator. As she peered inside the sack at her cheese sandwich and celery sticks with peanut butter, she sighed. If she didn't go to the grocery soon, she'd be out of food. So would Weatherby. And he had a nasty temper when his dish was empty.

Since Mae and Luanne both had errands to run at lunch, that left just Dorey and Harry.

"Busy morning." He strolled in.

"Finally." Dorey nodded.

He grabbed his container from the fridge and nuked whatever it was in the microwave. When he retrieved his lunch and sat down, Dorey eyed the dish. She inhaled deeply. Ah, lasagna.

With a chuckle, he said, "Want some?"

"No. Just … um, no." She widened her eyes.

"Are you sure?" He pushed the dish closer to her. "I know it's only a store-brand lasagna, but it's pretty good."

The rich smell of tomato sauce drifted up to her. Suddenly, her cheese sandwich seemed lame in comparison. But she couldn't. "I'm fine. Really." She took a bite of her sandwich. "Yum."

Harry shrugged. He dug into his lunch like a pig after a truffle. Dorey glanced at the discarded food box sitting on top of the trash. It was a family size. Good grief, the man could eat. Then he ate two pieces of bread from a loaf they kept in the breakroom and a big glass of tea.

Harry always wolfed down mass quantities of food. Yet, he never appeared to gain any unwanted weight. Her gaze slid down to his midsection. No, he was just about perfect.

"Got something on my scrubs?" Harry was peering down at his shirt.

"What?" Dorey snapped her gaze back up. "Oh, no … I thought … never mind."

Dorey, you're an idiot.

"Are you okay?" Harry narrowed his eyes and studied her.

"Sure." She shrugged. "Fine."

"You don't act fine. If something's wrong, you can tell me, you know."

What she really wanted to tell him was that she saw him with that woman last night but couldn't bring herself to say it. Instead, she muttered, "Just thinking about something that happened."

"What?"

"I … went to the mall last night to have the ring cleaned. And I had them check the prongs on it to make sure they weren't loose."

"The mall? I was there too."

"You were?"

She waited to see if he'd say anything about the blonde. But he didn't. Did that mean he wasn't flirting with the other woman? Wasn't interested in her? Dorey desperately hoped so.

But until Harry said how he really felt about her, she wasn't brave enough to come right out and ask.

"When I came out afterward, my car alarm was going off."

He dropped his fork on his plate, the clank like a crashing cymbal. "It was?"

"Yeah, but there wasn't any broken glass or anything."

"That's a relief." He stared at her, unblinking. "Is that all?"

Harry had always been able to read her, darn it. She set down her sandwich, not interested in it anyway.

"When I got ready to open the door, there were scratches near the lock."

"Dorey. Did you call the police?"

"For something little like that?" She frowned. "No. With all that's gone on, I didn't think it warranted another police visit." She was so tired of dealing with that snarky Officer Beaumont, she could scream.

"Someone tampered with your car." He rapped his knuckle on the table.

Her vehicle was so old, a few more scratches wouldn't hurt its value any. "It's not a big deal, Harry." She'd picked the wrong subject to discuss.

"You are too trusting." He shook his head. "Someday, that might get you into trouble."

"All right, Dad." She knew he hated when she called him that but couldn't resist needling him about his tendency to hover.

His jaw clenched. "I'm *not* your dad." He held up his hand. "And me being only five years older than you is not that much."

"Fine. Whatever." With a huff, she finished her sandwich. Even though it didn't taste great, she'd need her energy for the afternoon's work.

"Sorry." Harry reached over and gave her hand a squeeze. "Didn't mean to snap at you. I just worry about you."

"You don't need to. I'm a big girl."

"True. Still, we've known each other for a long time. With

your sister married to my brother, we're practically family. Allow me to worry about you a little, all right?"

She gave him a small smile, glad they weren't arguing anymore. "Okay." While she used to think of them as family, especially before that kiss, now she only thought of Harry as a man. A handsome, built, desirable—

"Better get to my operatory." He stood up. "Luanne said she might be a little late since I'm having her stop at the bank for me, so I'll need to set up for the patient. See ya later." He gave her a mock salute, grinned, and left her alone in the room.

Why did she have to be attracted to him of all people? Someone who was too old for her, someone she spent time with nearly every day. As protective as he was, he couldn't see her as anything but a sister-substitute. Could he? If the kiss had meant something to him, why hadn't he said so? Or done it again? Somehow, she was trapped, swimming in her own confused swirl of emotions. And she didn't like it.

With a sigh, she went back to her room.

32

At the end of the day, Dorey was beat. Not only from the earlier tension with Harry, but physically worn out after her concussion. Guess it would take a few more days before she had all her energy back from lying around for so long. Plus, it seemed like every time she turned around, Harry was watching her. Was that because of their argument or because it was still soon after her accident?

She headed home and fed the cat, took a shower, and changed into comfy sweats.

A knock on her door made her jump. Lately, it seemed to be bad news, an anonymous threatening note, or something dead or beheaded. She shivered as she walked slowly to the door. Unlocking it, she opened it two inches and peered out.

"Dorey?" Harry stood on her step, staring back at her.

She let out a breath and opened the door wide. "Long time no see."

"Why didn't you ask who it was before opening the door?" He stepped inside.

"I think I'm just a little wired after today." She couldn't tell him about the messages, the dead rodent, or mangled roses. Couldn't put him in danger. She closed the door.

He held a grocery sack in his arms. Placing it on her coffee table, he said, "Still feeling the effects of your concussion?"

"I guess." Dorey didn't want to talk about any of that. And she didn't want to think about the scary creep making her so jumpy. She pointed to the bag. "What do you have there?"

"I could tell you had a rough day." He gave her a sheepish grin.

"With all the times I caught you watching me, I'm not surprised."

"Maybe I just like looking at you." He stepped closer and cupped her chin in his hand.

She snorted. "Right."

"Why would that surprise you so much?" Harry tipped her chin up, so she had to make eye contact.

"Because I'm ... me." She shrugged.

"What does that mean?"

"Nothing." She stepped back and waved her hand. Harry's teasing was hitting too close to home. She wished he meant half the things he'd said lately. Wanting a diversion, she eyed what he'd brought. Opening the bag, she peered inside. "Snacks? I think I may love you."

"Yeah, so I've heard."

Dorey froze, her hand in the bag. *Uh-oh.* She'd forgotten that in her woozy state after her accident, she'd said that to Harry. She'd been hopeful that since he hadn't mentioned it again, he'd chalked it up to her being out of her head.

"Well ..." She straightened and looked at him. Looking at his ear instead of his eyes, she muttered, "Um ..."

"So, when you said that, I was really surprised." He took her hands in his.

"Oh, well, I'd just hit my head and all. Didn't know what I was saying." She gave a little laugh, hoping he'd see the humor.

"You didn't?"

She shrugged.

Harry tugged on her hands and led her to sit on the couch. He released his grip but put his arm on the couch, behind her shoulders.

Why did the room suddenly seem to have shrunk?

"I need to ask you something, Dorey."

Not now. She had so not planned on having this conversation tonight. Maybe not ever, if he didn't feel the same way. How could they still be friends? Still work together if he knew she loved him, but he didn't love her back? She couldn't answer, so she simply nodded.

He gently took a lock of her damp hair between his fingers. The gentle tugging nearly did her in. Made her want to fall into his arms. Kiss him again. Releasing her hair, he ran his finger down her cheek. She closed her eyes for a second, savoring his warm touch on her skin. Hiding the memory deep inside for later on. Because if this was it for them, if it wouldn't go any further, she'd want, need that memory someday to hang on to.

"Dorey?"

Her eyes opened.

"I know you'd hit your head, weren't quite yourself but, when you told me you loved me, did you mean it?"

She'd been waiting for that question. Yet, gave a little jerk when he actually said it. Staring at his lips, she wondered if he really had voiced those particular words. Was her mind playing tricks with her, an after-effect of smacking her head on the pavement?

"Will you tell me?" He tilted his head.

"Why?" she finally croaked out.

"I need to know."

Her chest rose and fell as she let out a long breath. This was it. After she told him, things would never be the same. But keeping her feelings for Harry bottled up inside wasn't an option anymore. Time to come clean and worry about the results afterward.

She forced herself to meet his. "I ... meant it."

A slow smile formed on his mouth. Not what she'd expected. Not what she'd been dreading.

Unless ... was he going to tease her about it? That was one thing she didn't think she could take right now. She waited for the familiar ribbing, the glint in his eye when he was ready to deliver a zinger to her, to make her laugh.

But it never came.

"Why are you smiling?"

"Because a beautiful girl just told me she loves me."

Was that all? Were they back to that again? So, this might be like in the kitchen when he'd kissed her. That they were just a man and woman in convenient proximity. Her heartbeat thudded hard in her chest, almost painfully. But she wasn't going to ask him. If he loved her back, he was going to have to say it.

Just say it.

Harry pressed a light kiss to her lips, but she didn't move. Didn't throw her arms around his neck like she'd done before. He pulled back and ran his gaze over her face. Forehead, nose, chin, and back to her eyes. "Isn't that a good reason to make a man smile?"

"I wouldn't know. I'm not a man."

"No. You're definitely not a man. You, Dorey, are a desirable, loving, beautiful, funny, special woman."

He pressed his finger to her lips, making a slow, lazy circle over her top lip, one corner, then down to the bottom lip. "For a while now, I've been feeling ..."

She wanted to ask what, but bit her tongue, waiting.

"I've felt like maybe, I ..."

Good grief. Why didn't he just say it?

"I don't really know when things changed, when I started to see you not as a little sister, but as a woman. And ..."

Dorey clenched her jaws in frustration. If Harry was going to say he loved her, he'd better do it quick. Otherwise, she'd die of unrequited desire. And explode on the couch.

"So, I guess what I'm saying is, Dorey, I love you."

She'd been waiting to hear the words. Hoping. Dreaming. Wishing. Now that she'd heard them, she couldn't be sure if she'd imagined it or if he'd really said it. Maybe the effects of her concussion were still causing her to have warped thoughts.

"Would you mind repeating that, please?"

"What?"

"Say it again."

His mouth curved up on one side. "I. Love. You."

Dorey let out a sigh. "I was so afraid that—that you didn't ... wouldn't ..."

"What, honey? That I wouldn't what?"

She toyed with the collar of his shirt, unable to make direct eye contact. "Wouldn't love me back."

"Well, I do." He chuckled. "So, you're stuck with me. Is that okay with you?"

Pure joy soared through her veins. "More than okay."

He took her face in his hands. Looked deeply into her eyes.

Wait, what about that gorgeous blond Harry had flirted with at the mall? She frowned.

"Hey, what's wrong?"

Might as well just say it. "I saw you. When I was at the mall."

"Saw me? Why didn't you say anything?"

"You weren't alone."

His brow furrowed. "I wasn't?"

"Nope. Some pretty blond was there."

Harry tilted his head, his eyes narrowing. Then, he brightened. "Oh, that was Amy Bates. I went to dental school with her brother."

Dorey poked him in the chest. "You were flirting with her."

"No. I wasn't. Promise. Whatever you saw, that was all her flirting with me and me being polite."

"Honest?"

"Yep."

Relief swept over her. She held her breath. And waited.

Nothing.

"Harry?"

"Hmmm?"

"Are you going to kiss me now?"

He lifted one eyebrow.

Here it came. The teasing.

"Is that something you'd like?"

She wrapped her arms around his neck and put her face so close to his there was only a whisper of space between their lips. "If you don't kiss me right this minute, I'm going to bite you."

He laughed. "Come here." He tugged her up on his lap and pressed his lips against hers.

Soft and warm. Lovely. But it didn't last. He pulled away. Was that it? She knew he could do better than that. Had that time in her kitchen.

Harry grasped her so tight to his chest she was afraid to breathe. His lips found hers again, but this time there was nothing gentle about it. He angled his head and deepened the kiss.

Time slowed down. Now all there was in the world was her. And him.

Something brushed against her arm. She frowned, trying to account for Harry's body parts that were otherwise engaged. Lips on hers. One hand around her shoulders, the other massaging the small of her back.

Something small and sharp, like a needle, caused a zing of pain down her forearm. Dorey pulled away from Harry, gasping for breath.

"What—" Harry stared at her, looking like he was breathing hard too.

She glanced down and to her left. "Oh. It's you."

Weatherby sat to the side and slightly behind her on the couch with one paw, claws visible, extended toward her arm. The wicked feline was grinning.

Harry laughed. "Maybe he's jealous?"

"You think?"

"You did say earlier that you and he had lived together for a while, and you'd professed your love for him."

Dorey grinned. She reached back and petted Weatherby's head and was rewarded with a purr. "There's room for both of you in my heart."

33

Work had returned to normal. As normal as it ever was. Patients, those who didn't seem afraid they'd die in the hygiene chair, showed up. No calls about being chased by a white van, men in masks. Not even runaway poodles. Dorey was relieved. But it was still weird. Like someone had flicked a switch. They'd been okay, then the switch had been turned off. Plunged into darkness. Trouble. Despair. Fear. Switch flipped again. Fine.

It'd been the busiest day she'd had in two months. And she was tired. Not only from the physical work, but she still had the tiniest remnant of slothfulness from her concussion. Thank goodness, the headaches were gone.

Glad to be home, she'd taken her shower and changed into sweats. Weatherby was nowhere to be seen. Since the trouble started, Dorey had been extra protective of him. But there was no way to keep him inside short of locking him in her bathroom. And who knew what mischief he'd get into in there? Hair gel in his fur. Toothpaste on his whiskers. And every roll of toilet paper shredded into unidentifiable bits.

No. He'd be miserable, and she didn't want that for him.

Besides, her cat was quick. If he was outside and someone tried to grab him, Dorey doubted they'd succeed.

Bummed that Weatherby wasn't around, Dorey laid on the couch and stretched out on her back. Time to relax. She took a deep, cleansing breath and closed her eyes. Would Harry come over tonight? Even though she'd just left him a little while ago at work, she missed him already.

Her landline rang. She bolted upright. It wasn't Harry. He always called her cell. What if it was another one of those threatening calls? With the rough-sounding voice? Instead of answering, she stayed on the couch. Her answering machine came on, then the beep. Dorey's heart thudded hard while she waited for someone to leave a message. Maybe they wouldn't. Or it could be Marie, wanting to do something or—

"You have my ring." A voice—that voice—came on the line. "I want it back. Put it in a plain brown paper sack and take it to the town square. Leave it behind the large, pointed rock to the left of the fountain. You won't see me, but I'll be watching. Do not call the police. If I see them there, something will happen to your dentist friend. You have ten minutes. Don't bother showing up after that. It will be too late."

The machine beeped.

Too late? Too late for what? Frozen, Dorey had to remind herself to breathe. The ring? That's what this was all about? Scaring patients away from the office. Her being mugged. Mr. Long poisoned?

Harry! The man had said something would happen—

Ten minutes!

She jumped from the couch as if her butt had been zapped with an electric current, and then stuffed her feet into a pair of old shoes by the door. The ring was on her finger, and there was a crumpled old lunch sack still in her car from earlier in the week. It would have to do.

Grabbing her keys, she hurried from the apartment, shutting

the door behind her. With a quick glance at the kitty-door, she desperately hoped Weatherby would be okay.

It took her three tries to get the car door unlocked. *Come on!* Finally, the key met the lock, and she was inside.

She turned the ignition.

Nothing happened. *Not now.*

Dorey tried again, clenching her teeth together, willing the car to start.

Nothing.

Her mouth went dry. She tried to breathe slower, get her heartbeat to quit racing, but it wasn't working. I have to get to the town square! It was too far to walk and get there in such a short time. No, she'd never make it. Should she ask a neighbor to take her? But how would she explain what she was doing?

Would you mind waiting here while I put this bag behind the fountain? That would lead to questions she couldn't answer. And might very well put that person in danger too.

When she tried to start her car again, it hummed. Was it going to start? Please!

It died again. Dorey banged her fist on the steering wheel. "Come on, you bucket of bolts. I need you to work!"

Another attempt brought a wheeze from the engine. That didn't sound good at all.

"Just get me to the square," Dorey whispered. "After that, you can die. I'll walk home. Once I deliver the ring, it won't matter how long it takes me to get home."

With purpose, willing the vehicle to start, Dorey turned the key again. She yelped when it started.

"Yes!" Putting it reverse, Dorey turned her head to look out the back window. All clear. She stepped on the gas.

And went five feet.

"What? No! Come on, I know you can do it. I need more than a few feet. I'm sorry I called you a bucket of bolts."

When she turned the ignition, it started and then died. This can't be happening. It can't! Why was her car acting up now? It was usually dependable.

Dorey pressed her forehead against the steering wheel and moaned. How was this happening? Her gaze lowered to the dash. She blinked.

The gas tank registered empty.

No, no, no! How had she let this happen? Usually, she was so good to keep an eye on it. Made sure everything was orderly and taken care of. But lately, with all the upheaval, she'd forgotten. And now, of all times, she couldn't use her car.

She'd never make it. Not now. Even if the car somehow magically started and carried her to the town square on determination alone, she'd be too late. Too bad she lived in such a small town they didn't even have cab service. But even if they had, by the time she called and they arrived, it would be too late.

With a sigh, she got out of her car and slammed the door. Mr. Nichols would get her some gas in his can, though she hated to ask him. She'd need it to get to work the next day.

But that didn't do her any good now.

What would the man on the phone do when he didn't get his ring? She glanced down at the piece of jewelry she'd come to admire. What was so special about it that this man went to so much trouble to get it back?

She trudged back to her apartment, unlocked the door, and went inside. Before she forgot, she left a message on Mr. Nichols' machine, begging for him to give her some gas in her tank. That done, she collapsed on her couch.

Dorey gasped when Weatherby appeared out of nowhere and jumped on her lap. "Honestly, my heart is about ready to burst from my chest as it is. Must you scare me like that?"

He blinked slowly and curled up in a ball. She ran her fingers through his fur. Guess cats didn't care about things like cars, rings, and ominous voice messages. "Weatherby, do you have any idea how lucky you are?"

His sigh ended with a loud rush of purr.

"What am I gonna do? That person, whoever he is, wants his ring back. Why couldn't he have just called me or the office about it? I would have gladly given it to him. Then all the mayhem that's been going on wouldn't have happened. And Mr. Long would still be alive."

Pulling Weatherby closer, she pressed her nose into the fur on the top of his head. She hadn't thought it possible, but he purred even louder.

"Should I call the police? Let them know about the call? The threat to Harry? But he'd said not to call the authorities." Would she make things worse by getting their attention?

She couldn't risk it. Couldn't risk anything happening to Harry. Thoughts of the way Mr. Long had lain lifeless in her dental chair merged into Harry's sweet face. "No ... I can't, under any circumstances, go against the orders of the caller."

But she already had. She hadn't shown up where he said, when he said.

What would happen now?

Her phone jangled, startling her, which caused the cat to harrumph and jump to the floor.

Fear coursed through her. Would it be the caller? Did he have her cell number too? "H-hello?"

"Miss Cameron? It's Mr. Nichols. I've filled your tank with gas. I'll put it on your next month's rent."

"Thank you so much. You can't know what—"

The phone clicked in her ear.

Mr. Nichols had never been the warm and fuzzy type. But she'd take that over whoever had called her before. She set the phone down and slumped back against the couch. Since the caller had said she shouldn't bother to come after the allotted time and she hadn't made it, what should she do now? Would he call again? Do something to her? To Harry?

She reached for the phone to call him. To warn him. No ...

She set down the phone. To get Harry involved would only put him in more danger.

But her heart nearly broke at the thought of something happening to him. Although calling him wouldn't work, she could still keep an eye on him. Determined to do just that, she ran to her car, got in, and drove to Harry's house.

There was a spot just down the street where she could park beneath a large tree not visible from his house. She, however, would be able to see him if he went out his front door or backed his vehicle out of his garage. If he did either of those things, she'd be right on his tail. Even though it wasn't safe to tell him what was going on, she'd find a way to protect him. Somehow.

34

Dorey rushed away from work as soon as she was done with her last patient. Mae looked at her like she was crazy, practically running out the door. Would she have a message once she got home? Or would the caller do something out of anger toward her?

This would have been a really good time to have a phone plan where she could call from a different phone to access any messages. A little late for that now. At lunchtime, she'd hoped to run home for a few minutes but ended up working through nearly her entire lunch due to her last patient of the morning showing up way late.

Poor Harry had frowned at Dorey all day. Probably upset because after her sleepless night, she'd hardly spoken to him. But she couldn't. If she'd talked to him more than necessary for patient exams, she might have blurted out something about the ring. The voicemails. That everything they'd been through might somehow be connected.

And she couldn't do that. Not when it might put Harry in danger.

Dorey's tires squealed as she veered into the parking lot.

She'd barely gotten her car into her allotted space before shutting off the engine and running up the walk. Curtains fluttered in the apartment nearest hers, a nosy neighbor seeing who was making all the racket. But Dorey didn't have time to worry about making good impressions now.

Once inside her apartment, she dropped her purse wherever it landed and ran to her answering machine. The light was blinking. Her finger shook as she reached out to press the button, almost as if the button might reach out to grab her.

"You've pushed me too far. You didn't show up when I told you to. Now the plan has changed. Bring the ring to the caves. Go in the entrance to the first cave. I'll find you. I know you'll come. Wanna know why? 'Cause I have your cat."

Dorey gasped.

"If you don't believe me, check below the bush to the right of your front door. You'll see evidence. If you don't bring the ring right now, say bye-bye to kitty."

Her machine buzzed as the line went dead. Then silence.

A scream stuck in her throat. Weatherby? Running back to the door, she flung it open. She dove down into the grass beside the bush, plunged her hands inside the shrub time and time again, not caring that the branches left angry red scratches on her bare arms. What was in there? Please let the evil person not have harmed Weatherby, not have left something—

Her hand brushed something hard and stiff.

No! What is it? She jerked back her hand and peered cautiously down to the bottom of the bush where her hand had been. It was starting to get dark, so she had to squint to see. Something red. Blood?

Please don't let it be—

She checked again. It was Weatherby's collar. Dorey grabbed it and held it close. My poor Weatherby. That man has him.

Wait …

Weatherby was quick. He'd never just let someone pick him up. It would have to be—

An odor reached her nose. She sniffed. Tuna. Weatherby's favorite. Dorey hung her head. Her cat couldn't resist that flavor. Nearly ripped her hands to shreds if she tried to eat a tuna sandwich without him.

That was his downfall. If the man had come close to Weatherby with tuna, her cat would have happily done a river dance, a cartwheel, anything to have a bite.

Even let a maniacal murderer pick him up and take him away.

She raced into the apartment, grabbed her keys, and ran out again. Once in her car, she backed out of her space, tires squealing. Tearing from the lot, she turned the corner to the road too sharply. The screech of her tires was loud, sounding like a woman startled by a spider the size of a buffalo.

Dorey rammed the accelerator to the floor. If the cops saw her, she'd have to outrun them, because having them show up at the cave with the man there would be the end for Weatherby.

Within minutes, she was to the parking lot, barely remembering having navigated the roads to get there. When she parked, she darted a glance around.

Was he here? Did he have Weatherby somewhere close by? She didn't see anybody, but parked at the back of the lot, under a large maple tree, was a white van. Hadn't Mr. Anderson mentioned a white van that had scared him off the road?

She shut off the car and ran halfway to the cave before she realized she'd left the keys in the car. It didn't matter. She had to get to Weatherby. Now! Her legs pumped hard as she ran up to the main entrance of the cave. She had no idea where the man would be once she got inside. Or even who he was.

The question of his identity would be known soon. But would he be the last person she ever saw before she died? Would he hesitate to kill her?

No, Dorey. He's killed before.

A slap of bracing cold air hit her as soon as she entered the mouth of the cave. She shivered. Hadn't even brought a jacket. It couldn't be helped now. And if this all ended like she feared it might, she wouldn't need a jacket anyway.

She felt her way inside the cave, hoping she didn't slip on the damp ground, and ran her hands along the hard, wet rocks that formed the walls of the passage.

Weatherby, where are you?

Heartbeat racing so fast, she feared she'd pass out. *Keep going. Don't think about it. Don't think about anything but getting Weatherby back.*

But her mind sped as fast as her cat biting through a tuna sandwich. This was all because of that ring? The mugging, vandalism, accidents. A man dead? Why would someone do that?

And why did she ever have to find that awful ring in the first place?

Her foot slipped, and she gasped. Wind-milling her arms, she managed to stay upright. Last time she'd slipped, Harry had broken her fall. But Harry wasn't here.

Thank goodness. Because if he was, and something happened to him—

Don't think about it. He doesn't know where you are. Keep going.

The air turned icy the farther she went. There had been decent light from the parking lot for the first couple of minutes she'd been inside the cave, but now it was faint.

Swallowing hard, she forced herself to move. Go forward. Just go! But her mind screamed to turn around and run away.

She couldn't do that to Weatherby. Because she'd seen the evidence of what this man was capable of. If he did something to harm her pet, she'd never get over it.

Water dripped in a menacing beat to her right.

Drip. Drip. Drip. Drip. Drip. Drip.

Come and get me, Dorey …

Drip. Drip. Drip. Drip. Drip. Drip.

Or I'll find you instead …

Drip. Drip. Drip. Drip. Drip. Drip.

And then I'll kill you …

Stop thinking like that, Dorey. She clenched her jaws together, took a deep breath, and let it out. She stopped and pressed her forehead against the rock, not caring that the cold bit into her skin and shot through her head, causing it to ache.

A sharp noise, like someone giving a single hard knock on a door, came from ahead of her. Falling rock? Or was it him?

Dorey had no idea if she was heading toward him. Or even in the right direction. It was so dark now that she couldn't even make out the small openings that led to alternate trails through the cave. Harry had led her down a couple of them when they'd been here before, but she hadn't paid attention. Had been too busy hanging onto his belt loop.

Harry …

How she loved him. And he loved her. A dream come true. Now, though, she doubted she'd ever see him again. What were the chances the mystery man would do what he'd said and exchange her cat for the ring? Let her just walk away afterward?

Not great.

But if there was the slightest chance she could save Weatherby and escape, then she could go to the police. Because if she were lucky, she'd finally know the identity of the murderer.

That would take a whole lot of luck.

A crash came from ahead. It was hard to tell how far away because of the echo that followed. Then, a loud, long howl.

Weatherby!

She picked up her pace, slipping every few feet. Her hand scraped something jagged, and she cringed as a sharp pain raced up her arm. Warmth spread over her palm. Blood? It didn't matter. She wiped her hand on her pants and pushed ahead.

Dorey curled her fingers around every rock that had even the slightest handhold. The soles of her shoes, now slick with water from the path, skated along as if on ice.

Another screech bounced off the walls in an echo. It was louder. She must be close. Had the person already hurt her cat? Is that why he was howling? Tears stung her eyes, but she pushed on. There was no turning back now.

Hazy light came from an opening she could now make out on her left. She swallowed hard and pushed ahead. *I'm coming, Weatherby. Don't be scared. Mommy is scared enough for everyone.*

Something squeaked and fluttered past her shoulder. Dorey held in a scream. A bat. It had to be.

Don't think about that now.

After a few minutes, the trail ended at an opening. A man, his back to her, stood holding her cat over his shoulder. When Weatherby's eyes locked on Dorey, he howled and struggled, digging his claws into the man's upper arm.

"Stupid cat!" The man yelled and turned around.

It was her patient. One of the new ones. Robert Keane!

"About time, Miss Cameron." He glared at her. "Your cat is not very friendly. Look at these scratches on my arm."

Weatherby hissed and struggled, but Mr. Keane held firm.

Her patient. Dorey stared, open-mouthed, at the man. She still couldn't wrap her mind around it. All this time, he'd been causing people harm, even killing, for a stupid ring?

"Why?" She took a step forward.

"Why, what?" He stared at her, looking genuinely confused.

She held her hands out away from her sides. "You frightened people. A man is even dead. You—you're—"

"None of that matters."

Rage coursed through her. "Of course, it matters. They're people. They never did anything to deserve that."

"They were in my way." He shrugged, earning a growl from the cat.

She held up her hand. Weak light from a lantern on a nearby rock reflected off the ring. "For this? It's a piece of metal."

"It's a priceless artifact, Miss Cameron. You've been wearing millions of dollars around on your hand."

Dorey took a step back, pressing her hand to her chest. "What?"

"It was featured at the museum. That is, until I stole it." He edged closer as Weatherby howled and clawed. But Mr. Keane didn't appear to notice. His attention was focused solely on her. "Give me the ring, Dorey."

She stared at him. "I can't believe you did all that—"

"Give me the ring." Another step had him close enough she could see the menace in his eyes. "Now. Or—" His glance slid to her cat. Her precious, loving, wonderful cat. Her baby.

"Please don't hurt him."

"I don't want to hurt him. Just give me my ring."

Dorey reached down to her finger to remove it. Weatherby screeched again and slashed with his paw.

"Ahhhhh!" Mr. Keane dropped the cat as dark, angry welts appeared on his face and four trails of dark blood followed the claw marks' paths.

Weatherby ran toward Dorey. She bent to grab him but froze when something clicked.

The safety of a gun?

Her cat raced past her, stumbled, and ran in place on the slick rock before zipping around a corner.

"Run, Weatherby!"

Her heart beat so fast she thought she'd die, right there on that spot.

You might die anyway.

Mr. Keane pointed the gun straight at Dorey and edged closer.

Dorey backed up until she crashed against something hard and immovable. The wall. There was no way out. She was caught. Done for.

Good-bye, Harry. I love you. Take care of Weatherby.

Mr. Keane took another step closer. He slipped on a wet spot on the stone floor. The toe of his boot caught on a rock, and he stumbled. The gun went flying. Dorey screamed as the bullet ricocheted off the ceiling.

Trying to block out the curses of Mr. Keane, she turned and ran, hoping with everything in her that he wouldn't be able to catch her. That she'd get enough of a head start and maybe, just maybe, she could escape.

Not knowing where she was going and losing what precious little light there'd been from the lantern, Dorey ran and slid, climbing and clawing her way forward.

Where had Weatherby gone? Please let him be safe. Let him escape this death trap.

Cats could see better than people could in the dark and had a great sense of direction. If Weatherby could escape from the confines of the cave, he might be able to find his way home. She let out a loud breath, both from relief and exhaustion.

Now if she could only find the path to the cave opening. If someone hadn't already happened along and found her car door open, keys hanging from the ignition, she could get away too. She'd be free.

A few thuds sounded from just ahead, followed by small rocks trickling down a wall. Weatherby? If she followed the sound, would he lead her out of the cave?

She hurried in that direction, focusing on the sound of falling rocks, and took another step. Her foot came in contact with—

Air.

Dorey screamed as her body tore through the darkness. Cold wind whistled past her ears. With no light, she couldn't tell if her head was up or down. Nothing to grab onto. Nothing below her feet. She tumbled end for end, reaching out her hands, trying to touch something. Feel something.

She crashed onto solid rock, knocking the breath out of her.

Thank goodness, she was— She gasped.

Her foot slid down a sharp incline. The rest of her had no choice but to follow. Rock scraped against her back, sending jolting shots of pain up her spine. She tried to grab onto something, anything to stop her downward plunge, but the rock was too wet. Too slick.

Dorey landed with a painful thud and leaned back against the rock. Her breath, cold in her lungs, came in rapid pants. She tried to push herself against the wall to stand, but gasped when one foot hit nothing but air again. Cautiously feeling along with the toe of her shoe, Dorey reached a frightening conclusion.

She was stuck on a narrow ledge.

With no way out.

35

Dorey's short fingernails scraped against the jagged surface of the rock, chalky bits of stone raining down into her eyes and mouth. She coughed and tried to blink away some of the dust. She didn't dare let go of her skimpy hold on the wall to wipe it away with her fingers.

The toes of her shoes were barely perched on the narrow ledge. Cold air bit into her skin right through her shirt and pants. Was this how it would all end? With her unable to hold onto the wall of the dark cave, her body plummeting to the ravine below?

There didn't seem to be any way out. She'd either fall to her death or stay on the ledge and starve. How had her life come to this?

She glanced up, her heart in her throat. Was he still following her? Would he find her? Her heart rapped against her ribs as if thudding a death knell.

Faint light reflected off the item which had started the whole nightmare.

The ring.

She wished she'd never seen the stupid thing. That he would have lost it somewhere else.

I never asked for this.

Something flew directly over her head. A bat? Dorey jerked and nearly lost her balance. She pressed tight against the wall, the icy temperature seeping into her cheek. Her whole face hurt from the cold—even her teeth ached. Plops of a loud drip from somewhere nearby made her shiver even more. She wished for the hundredth time she'd brought her jacket.

Her jacket.

The one Harry so lovingly zipped up for her before he'd brought her here the first time.

She closed her eyes as hot tears burned their way down her frozen cheeks. Harry. I'm so sorry. All this horror and destruction because of a ring I found.

Her ring shone bright again, when it reflected the ...

Wait ... Light?

Had he found her? Dorey gulped in air so fast she got lightheaded. She closed her eyes and took a slow breath. *Please don't let him see me. I won't get out alive.* Peeking to the right as she kept her movements slow and measured—one, because she didn't want to give her location away, and two, she didn't want to fall—she saw a beam of light coming from the mouth of the cave. A lantern?

It was him! It had to be. Who else would be here this time of night in such awful weather?

Something scratched on the rock a few feet below her. There was a wider ledge there, but she couldn't reach it without tumbling down into the dark.

No thanks.

At least here, she had a chance of getting out. Very slight, but what else did she have?

Whatever it was scratched again. An animal? What would be in the cave? Mountain lion? Bear?

Fresh fear of wild creatures doing her harm got in line behind the terror already racing through her veins.

How would she escape the madman who wanted her dead?

The light grew stronger. Heavy footsteps came from above and to her right. Was he on the same path she'd taken? Where she'd lost her footing and fallen? She'd caught onto this ledge only by the grace of God. Would Mr. Keane be so fortunate?

Part of her wanted him dead. Gone. Another part of her cringed at anyone plunging to their death in the abyss below. Because that had very nearly been her own fate. Her own cold, hard grave.

No. She wanted him caught. Tried for his crimes. But if he found her, he'd simply shoot her. There was no doubt about that.

She shook her head. With her on the ledge, if he shot her, she'd simply fall, tumbling through the nothingness to crash onto the rocks below. There's no way she'd survive the fall. Even if she did …

Dorey shuddered. *Don't think about that.*

But wait. The greedy man wanted the ring. So, he wouldn't just shoot her. He'd have to save her from the ledge to get what he wanted. She wasn't stupid enough to just throw him the ring, hoping he'd help her up after the fact. And he didn't have Weatherby anymore to try to make an exchange. Her cat wouldn't be fooled by him again.

At least not without more tuna.

The steps came closer, and she pressed herself as tightly to the freezing rock as she could. If she got out alive, would she ever be warm again?

Readjusting her grip on the rock, Dorey cringed when the metal of the ring pinged loudly against the stone.

She held her breath. Now he'd be able to find her! But if he didn't help her up, she might be stuck here forever.

Until she died.

Was trusting the murderer her only chance to live?

The footsteps grew louder, the light stronger. He was close. So close.

You can do this, Dorey. Convince him to help you up off the ledge. It's the only way he'll get his precious ring. Then ...

She couldn't think beyond that. Fear clutched her heart, her mind, like she'd go crazy.

Rocks skittered past her as the footsteps were now right above her.

"Dorey?" A loud, whispered voice called.

She frowned. That didn't sound like Mr. Keane. It sounded like—

"Are you here? Dorey! Say something if—"

"I'm here! Harry, help me!"

"Dorey!"

She closed her eyes against the light that now shone in her eyes. She sighed. He'd found her.

"Are you okay?"

Her mouth dropped open as she squinted into the light. "Are you seriously asking me that question now?"

"Sorry. Just habit. Thank goodness, I found you."

"No argument there."

"Don't move."

"No problem."

"Wait a second. I have a rope. I'll lower it down."

"Harry, you have to be the most practical person I've ever met."

"It's what I do."

"That, and take care of me."

"True."

Something tickled her cheek. The rope. She grabbed it like the lifeline it truly was.

"All right. You have the end of the rope?"

"Yes."

"I'm going to lower a little more, very slowly. Wrap the rope around your waist and tie a knot. Make it tight, so you don't fall through."

"Gee, never would have thought of that."

"Sarcasm? Now?"

"It's what I do." She snorted.

"Let me know when you're ready, okay?"

She finished snaking the rope around her waist and tied a double knot. With all the strength she had left—which wasn't much—she tugged on the rope with both hands to tighten it.

Her feet slipped from the ledge— "Harry! I'm falling!"— leaving her dangling over the very dark hole she'd hope to avoid.

"I've got you." He grunted. "Can you grab the rope above you? Hang onto it?"

Dorey reached up but couldn't grasp it. She was swinging around in a circle, bouncing against the wall every so often, but not for long enough to catch the ledge with her fingers. "I can't."

"Don't worry. This will still work."

"I hope so."

"Do you trust me?"

"With my life."

"Good answer. I'm going to pull you up. Don't be scared, I've got you. I'll have to back up several feet so if rocks start falling, close your eyes."

"Okay."

Slowly, the inches going by at the rate of a drunken tortoise, Dorey rose toward the ledge above. She tried not to think about what was below.

Think about what's above. Who's above. My love. My life. Harry.

A shower of small rocks pelted her face. She squeezed her eyes shut and lowered her head. Grunts and skidding boots came from just above her. She was close now. Had to be.

The rope stopped moving.

"You can open your eyes now."

Dorey peered up into Harry's eyes. When she glanced down, the ledge was a few inches below eye level.

"I'm going to give one more tug, and then I think you'll be able to get your arms over the edge. Ready?" He readjusted his grip on the rope.

"You have no idea." She took a deep breath and let it out. Come on, Dorey. You can do this.

She rose with the rope again, arms outstretched, fingers searching for a handhold. Another few inches, and she found it, grasped as tightly as she could, though her fingers slipped a little on the damp surface. Another try, and she dug her fingernails into the rough surface of the rope.

Harry tied the end of the rope on a thick outcropping of rock and then crouched down. He crawled over to her and took her hands in his. "I'm going to pull you up. Try to use your feet to walk up the rest of the way on the wall."

She nodded, not sure if Harry could make it out in the near dark, but not caring. It didn't matter. Harry had found her.

Strong hands wrapped around hers and tugged. He let out a sharp breath with the effort of pulling her weight straight up.

The lip of the ledge bumped against her knees, and she crawled up. And into Harry's arms.

He held her close, raining kisses down her jaw, across her forehead, then her lips. Time and time again, as if he couldn't get enough. Would never get enough. "I'm so— I was so—" He pulled her tight against his chest. So tight she couldn't breathe very well. But it didn't matter. He had found her. Rescued her.

A tiny thaw began in her chest, her shoulders, her arms as Harry's body heat flowed into Dorey.

"Couldn't we stay like this forever?" She snuggled under his chin and sighed.

He chuckled. "While I like the holding part, I think I'd rather get out of this cave first."

"Wait." She frowned. "Why are you *here*, anyway?"

"'Cause I knew you were here."

"But how?"

He let out a sigh, his warm breath fanning across her face. "I went over to see you. When I got there, your car was gone, but you'd left your door wide open."

"I did?" She barely remembered running from her apartment and driving to the cave.

"Yeah, scared the crap outta me too. I went inside, and Weatherby's collar was on the floor. When I picked it up, it smelled like—"

"Tuna?"

"Right. I called out for you and searched your apartment, hoping you were there, even though your car wasn't. I got suspicious. And there was the flashing light on your answering machine."

She clutched the front of his shirt, so relieved he'd come for her. "So, you heard …"

"I was so scared." He squeezed her tight. "I got here as fast as I could."

"I'm so glad you did. But wait … you brought a rope. Did you stop off somewhere? Like a store?"

"It was in my truck."

"You keep a rope in there? All the time?"

"I was a Boy Scout, remember." He tapped her nose.

But this time she didn't mind. She smiled. "I'd forgotten that. Well, I salute you, former Boy Scout. Job well done. And even more appreciated." She kissed his cheek.

The scratching sound came again from below. She swallowed, nearly forgetting about Mr. Keane. She pressed closer. "Harry, I know who's behind this. All of it."

He tensed. "Who?"

"It's one of our patients."

"What?"

Dorey cringed when his loud-voiced echoed off the walls. "Shhh. He's still probably around here somewhere."

"What do you mean?"

"You listened to the message, so you know he'd taken Weatherby."

"Yes, but ... Dorey, why didn't you tell me? I would have come and—"

"Because I didn't want you to get hurt. He said I had to come alone. I love you. I was worried that—"

Harry pressed his fingers to her lips. "Okay, we can talk about that later. Who was it?"

"Mr. Keane."

"You're kidding."

"I wish I was. He wants this ring." She held up her hand.

"The ring you found in the chair?"

"Exactly."

"What for?"

"He said it's very valuable. He wanted it back."

"Why didn't he just ask?"

"Because he stole it. From the museum."

"Wait. Are you telling me he did all those things to our patients? Mugged you, broke into the office, your apartment. And poisoned Mr. Long?"

"Yeah, I'm afraid so."

He gripped her tight. "Dorey, he murdered someone."

"I know." She blinked away tears, thinking of poor Mr. Long. "It's terrible." She clutched the front of his shirt. "But Harry, he's probably still here."

"Does he have Weatherby?" Harry glanced behind them and back.

She shook her head. "No, he got away, thank goodness. I'm not sure where he is, but—"

Something moved right behind them. "What was that?" she whispered. Slowly, they both turned and peered into the near darkness. Was it what Dorey had heard scratching before? A wild animal?

Two glowing eyes stared at them. Dorey clapped her hand over her mouth. Was it a mountain lion hoping for a snack? Were she and Harry going to be someone's dinner right when they'd found each other again?

The animal slunk closer. Gave a spine-chilling growl. Hunkered down like it was going to spring—

And licked Harry's hand.

"Weatherby." Dorey slumped against Harry, relief flowing through her, making her weak.

Her cat climbed onto her lap and turned in a circle, getting comfy for a nap. She ruffled his fur. "Honestly, selling me out for tuna?"

He glanced up at her, eyes large and unblinking. He gave a growl.

"I know you didn't do it on purpose. I bet after he grabbed you, you knew you'd been snookered."

Harry shook his head. "Do you always have these conversations with him?"

"Why not?" She shrugged. "He *is* my roommate."

Harry lifted one corner of his mouth. "I've been thinking about that. What if—"

"There you are."

Dorey jumped as Mr. Keane stood a few yards away, gun pointed at them. How had he snuck up on them? Of course, it would have been easy for him to find them. They'd obviously been talking loud enough for the echo to reach Mr. Keane wherever he'd been.

"Like fish in a bathtub." He smirked.

Oh, no. *What have I done? I tried to keep Harry safe, but now he'll die anyway. I'm sorry, Harry ...* She clung to him.

"Get up." Mr. Keane motioned with his gun. "Both of you."

Dorey tried to hold onto Weatherby, but he skittered away and hid behind a large rock. At least he was safe. For now. But Mr. Keane wouldn't need her cat to get the ring anymore. The gun would do that for him.

She tried not to look at the weapon trained on them but couldn't help it. Her eyes were drawn to it. Would their end be quick? Painless? Who would look after her cat?

Maybe she could stand in front of Harry. Then if the gun went off and hit her, he might have a chance to run toward Mr. Keane, knock him down.

Either way, Dorey wouldn't make it out of the cave alive.

Right when the man she loved, loved her back, it was all going to end.

Mr. Keane waved the gun around. He'd set his lantern down next to him. The dangerous glint was visible in his eyes. How had she not seen it before? When he was in the office, he'd acted grumpy, but so did lots of patients. He must have been good at hiding how little he cared about all those people he terrified. The man he killed. And it was obvious that any second, he planned to kill again.

36

Dorey grabbed Harry's hand, glad for the small comfort it gave, but still so sorry that he'd followed her. Now his life would end tonight too. Dorey blinked back tears, determined not to let their insane patient see her fear.

"It sure took me long enough to find out where the ring was." Mr. Keane took a step closer. "I tried every way possible to get in the office during business hours."

"So, you're the reason so many of my patients were terrorized? And another is dead." Harry shook his head.

"That's not my problem." Mr. Keane shrugged.

Dorey gasped at his total disregard for human life. "You're a monster."

"No, just someone who wants his ring back."

How unfeeling could someone be? To cause harm to others because he wanted to get back a ring? That he'd stolen?

"You can have the ring." Harry glared at his patient. "Just let us go."

"I really don't want to hurt you."

Harry sputtered a laugh, but there wasn't an ounce of humor in it. "Now why can't I believe that? Was there a reason, besides the monetary value, you did so much to other people for the ring? Or are you just that greedy?"

Mr. Keane narrowed his eyes at Harry. "I have a very good reason. That ring belonged to my wife."

"What?" Harry glanced at Dorey, eyebrows raised, and looked back.

"That's right," he said. "It was her wedding ring."

"You let your wife wear a stolen ring around?" Dorey frowned. "Weren't you afraid she might be arrested? Was she in on the theft from the museum too?"

"No. No, never. Marlene was too good for something like that."

"Didn't she know you'd stolen it?"

"I never told her. You see, by the time I met her, I'd decided to reform from being a thief."

"You expect us to buy that?" Dorey stared at Mr. Keane.

"It's true. Marlene only got the ring because she happened to find it in my pocket one day. We'd just gotten engaged, and she assumed … well …"

"That you'd gotten it for her."

He nodded.

"Why doesn't she have it now? Why were you carrying it around?"

"Marlene passed on only a couple of years after we married." Mr. Keane glanced away for a second. "Had a bad case of pneumonia. Never recovered."

Dorey's first inclination was to offer condolences, but on second thought, it hardly seemed appropriate now. "Weren't you worried someone would recognize the ring as stolen?"

"You have no idea. I broke out into a cold sweat every time she left the house with it. Thankfully, she didn't travel in circles where someone would have given the ring that close of an inspection. Like an appraiser. Or jeweler."

When the jeweler mentioned the ring resembled one stolen

from the museum, why hadn't she listened? Taken it to the police?

Because selfishly, she'd wanted to keep it. Well, not anymore.

"So," said Mr. Keane, "that ring holds sentimental value for me. As well as its monetary value." He motioned with the gun as nonchalantly as someone would flip their hand. Had he forgotten he held it?

"How did you happen to lose the ring in the office, anyway?" If Dorey kept him talking, maybe she or Harry could figure something out with a little more time.

"I'm an upholsterer. I discovered the ring wasn't in my pocket anymore, and that I must have dropped it somewhere in that room."

Harry stared at him. "You were one of the people who brought back the dental chairs?"

"Unfortunately." He scratched his cheek with the dangerous end of the gun, like he had no fear that anything bad would happen to him.

Dorey glanced at Harry. "You were there that day. You didn't see him?"

"Not until he came in as a patient. I'd unlocked the front door when their van pulled up. I talked to an older man and told them where to put each chair. Then I went into my office and shut the door, so I wouldn't be in their way. Too bad I never laid eyes on Mr. Keane that day. Then maybe at least some of the pain he caused others could have been avoided."

Mr. Keane ignored Harry's comment. "That older man was my boss. A jerk if there ever was one. I hated him."

She couldn't imagine ever saying that about Harry. But then, she was in love with him, after all.

"Wait." Dorey focused on Mr. Keane again. "If you were the one who caused some of our patients not to make their appointments, how did you even know who'd be coming in weeks in the future? Mae's computer would have been inaccessible on her day off."

"I kept opening drawers, hoping I'd find something to help me out. Lo and behold, I found your little list. Conveniently labeled at the top with what the list was for and the dates they were each coming in. That came in handy. Thanks for that."

Dorey's face heated, and she ground her teeth together.

"But how could you just go through drawers?" Harry squeezed her hand. "There had to be someone else helping you unload that huge chair into the hygiene room. Didn't they say anything? Try to stop you?"

"He left to go help another guy unload the chair for your room." Mr. Keane shrugged. "So, I had a few minutes to poke around."

There still wasn't a way out of their predicament. She had to keep him talking. Maybe he'd say something they could use.

"So ... how did the ring end up in the chair in the first place?"

Mr. Keane rolled his eyes. "Like an idiot, I'd had the ring in my shirt pocket. When I'd bent over to do the final installation for the chair, it must have slipped out. I checked all over the floor around it but couldn't find it. The only place it could have been on the chair was down in that crevice between the seat and the back."

"Yeah, that's where I found it." Dorey couldn't help giving him a little verbal jab.

"Dorey ..." whispered Harry.

"Well, aren't you just special?" Mr. Keane's face turned an angry red, looking eerie in the pale, yellow light of the lantern. "I checked there but couldn't feel anything."

But Dorey was on a roll, wanting to give him a good earful. Make him feel stupid. If he was going to shoot them, it was the least she could do. She shook her head slowly. "What a shame. I was able to get it easily with a pair of long forceps.

Guess you have to have the know-how in certain situations, huh?"

"What are you doing?" Harry tugged her closer.

"He has a gun pointed right at us, and you're scolding me for making him mad?"

"I'd like for him not to be mad because he's holding that gun."

She turned back toward Mr. Keane. "I'm pretty sure he was already that way when he lured me to this cave."

Really agitated now, Mr. Keane started to pace back and forth, but the gun stayed trained on them. "I tried to get back into the office to retrieve the ring. Called several times to get in with you, Dorey. But your receptionist wouldn't hear of it. Said the dentist evaluated all of the new patients for their first visit."

"Glad to know my office procedures did some good for someone." Harry barked out a laugh.

Mr. Keane's eyebrows drew together. Now who was ticking him off?

"Anyway, I couldn't get in." He shook his head. "And after I saw Dr. MacKinley, I still couldn't get in to see you, Miss Cameron. Your schedule was full up. So, I had to make room for myself. Move the other patients out."

"Move them out?" Dorey stiffened. "You caused a lot of harm."

"That's neither here nor there. Oh, and by the way, you hurt me when you were cleaning my teeth."

"Good." Dorey wanted to kick him.

Mr. Keane made a noise that sounded a little like Weatherby's growl. "You'll be sorry about that, I promise you." He rolled his shoulders up and down. Was he getting tired from holding out the gun for so long?

"You caused all of that trouble." Harry huffed out an indignant breath. "All the pain and heartache and left a woman a widow, because of a ring?"

"It happens to be very rare." Mr. Keane stood up straighter, as if glad to know something Harry and Dorey didn't. "Very old." He said it like he was proud of being a thief.

"How in the world did you steal it?" Dorey stared at him. "I was at the museum recently, and they checked everyone going in and out."

"Yeah, I heard about that." He laughed. "They started that after I took the ring. But it was a little late by then, wasn't it? I took the ring more than thirty years ago."

Dorey opened her eyes wide. "And for all that time, you had it? Didn't they notice that one of their prized museum artifacts was missing?"

"Of course, they did. Eventually. You have to remember, though, computers weren't in use everywhere then like they are now. The ring wasn't noticed to be missing at first. And their security system wasn't what it is now."

"How do you know all of this? You don't work at the museum, do you?"

"An acquaintance of mine does. His father was a friend of mine, also a thief way back when."

Was his acquaintance's son that French guy with a New Jersey accent? Oh, no. What if Marie had actually dated him?

"We've got to figure out a way to get out of here," she said in a low voice, hoping their patient wouldn't hear.

Harry leaned close, "I know, but—"

"Stop whispering over there!" Mr. Keane pointed the gun toward the ceiling and pulled the trigger.

Dorey screamed and covered her face with her hands as dust filtered down onto her. The ear-shattering noise went off again and again as it echoed off the stone walls. She leaned into Harry. "Okay, point taken."

"Now, let's get down to business, shall we?" He pointed the gun back at them. "I want that ring. I really had no intention of hurting you, or anyone else, for that matter. Since I knew from your schedule when that man had an appointment, and I'm friendly with a custodian where he worked, I was able to sneak in and put the poison in his coffee.

"I only intended to make him sick enough to cancel, so I could hopefully get into the office in his place. Unfortunately, that didn't work out so well."

"Especially not for him."

Mr. Keane ignored her comment. "Of course, now that you know my identity, you'll both have to die. Such a shame. If your mangy cat had stuck around, I'd kill him too. But I guess it doesn't matter since he can't talk."

Dorey's mouth dropped open, "Why, you—"

He held up the gun and pointed right at Dorey's face. "Toss me the ring. You have what you wanted. That furry rodent you call a pet got away from me."

"I can't believe you went to all the trouble, frightening people, scaring me, killing ... For a piece of metal." Dorey slipped off the ring.

"Don't forget the sentimental value since my late wife wore it. I need that ring back."

"Give the ring to *me*," Harry whispered close to her ear.

"Why?"

"Trust me."

She pressed the ring into Harry's open palm.

"What are you doing?" Mr. Keane's face contorted. "Give it to me now, or I'll shoot!"

"You're going to kill us anyway." Harry shook his head. "You already said that. But come any closer, and I'll toss it over the ledge. It doesn't mean anything to me. And then *you* won't have it either. Sorry about your luck."

"You wouldn't." His face paled.

"Try me."

"How do I even know you'll get the ring to me? It might land somewhere else, then I'll lose it. Again." Mr. Keane glared at Dorey like it was her fault he'd dropped the ring in her chair.

Harry tossed the ring up and down in the air, catching it easily each time. "I used to be a baseball pitcher. I'll get the ring right to you. No problem."

"Fine," Mr. Keane spat out, eyeing the huge black hole close behind Dorey and Harry. "Toss it here. But make it good, doc. Or I'll shoot Miss Cameron first, and you can watch."

Harry pulled back his arm like he was going to throw it right to Mr. Keane's waiting hand. Instead, he repositioned his hand at the last second. The ring shot straight up in the air.

It's a popup!

"Hey!" Mr. Keane shouted. "Wait!" He ran toward them, his attention focused up.

Harry grabbed Dorey's arm and yanked her to the side.

Dorey screamed as Mr. Keane, still grabbing at air and trying to get the ring, plummeted over the edge, his shriek, an eerie sound as it collided with its own echo.

That did not just happen. Dorey's mouth dropped open.

From behind them, something rustled. Dorey gasped and turned. Weatherby ran across to them. He started for the edge. She reached out to grab him but missed. "Oh no! Wait, don't—"

Weatherby's paws slammed on the brakes. He slid a few inches, his toes hanging over the edge. Then, he peered over and hissed loudly at the empty blackness of the hole.

Dorey let out a breath and crumpled into a wilted pile. Weatherby had just wanted to tell his catnapper his opinion, which wasn't much. Not that she blamed him. She grabbed her cat and hugged him close.

As Harry picked up the ring and slipped it on Dorey's finger, he laughed. "I think I just found a reason to like your cat."

37

From a safe distance, Dorey peered down into the darkness of the huge hole. It was so creepy to realize Robert Keane was down there now. Surely, he was dead. If not, he would be soon. He'd either succumb to his injuries, die of cold and starvation, or some animal would—

It was all so senseless. For a piece of jewelry. She shook her head.

The ring.

She glanced down at her hand. Even though the ring was barely visible in the dim light, she couldn't ignore its presence. It seemed to grow hot, longing to burn her skin. It was a symbol of death.

"Dorey? We need to leave." Harry stood behind her, his hands on her shoulders.

"I'm more than ready." She turned and wrapped her arms around his waist. "I'm so thankful you're here. Alive. With me."

"Honey, I feel the same about you. I thought that just as soon as we'd really found each other, it was over. Our chance was gone."

Tears she didn't even know wanted to come out ran down

her cheeks. Harry kissed them away, then pressed his lips lightly to hers. "Come on. Let's go home."

He leaned down and grabbed his flashlight, which had ended up on the ground during the altercation with Mr. Keane. He handed it to her, its light winking in and out.

"Uh-oh, Harry. I think the battery is almost gone."

"Let's hurry, then. Before it does." He grabbed her hand and led the way to the left, taking them through a narrowing tunnel. Was this the way she'd come in? She was so turned around. But once she'd been trapped on that ledge, with Robert Keane coming after her, she hadn't been concerned about which way was out. Only which way to life instead of death.

She clung to Harry's hand, not letting go for anything. Something brushed by her leg, and she shrieked.

"What?" Harry stopped midstride, and she crashed into his back. He focused his flashlight beam down.

"Weatherby." Dorey let out a breath and laughed. "You crazy cat."

"That crazy cat better never forget you risked your life to come save him."

Weatherby stopped, turned, and sat down, right in their path.

"What's he doing?" Harry whispered.

Dorey crouched down and reached out her hand toward the cat. Weatherby rubbed the side of his face against her fingers, time and time again. A loud rumble came from somewhere deep inside him.

"He's saying thank you." Dorey smiled.

"Really?"

"Yeah." She stood. "Come on, kitty, it's time to go home now."

Weatherby jumped up like he'd been bitten in the tail and rushed ahead of them.

Hoping their flashlight lasted just a little longer, Dorey kept it pointed ahead. They had to be close, didn't they? She remembered the narrowed path, and if they were on the right track, very soon they should see—

There it was. The carved heart.

Harry stopped and stared up at it. "I'll admit I was wrong before."

"About what?"

"I can see now why a guy would carve a heart in stone for the girl he loves." He wrapped one arm around her and tugged her against him.

"See, doc?" She sighed. "I knew there was more to you than someone who only wants to tease me."

He laughed. "That might be true, Dorey, but don't think for a second the teasing part is gonna go away."

"I hope it doesn't. 'Cause that's a part of who you are. The real you. The one I've loved forever."

"What?"

Hmmm. She'd never said that part before.

"What do you mean, forever?"

Even in the frigid temperature of the cave, her face heated. She turned away. "I ... well ... it's kind of—"

"Are you saying you've had feelings for me for a while?" He placed his hands on her shoulders.

"Yep." Dorey sighed. "Does that freak you out?"

"No." He placed his chin on the top of her head. "It warms my heart. I only wish—"

Dorey turned toward him. "Harry, you're five years older. I was a kid. It's not like you could have seen me for anything else back then. Besides, you've finally wizened up. Seen the error of your ways."

"Oh, boy." He grinned. "I can see you and I are going to have a very interesting time together."

"You ever had doubts?"

Her flashlight stuttered intermittent light. Then died.

"We really have to go." Finding her hand again, Harry tugged her along the path. She skidded a few times, trying to keep up.

They were in complete darkness now. Dorey edged closer to him. "You're in the lead, Harry. I sure hope your sense of direction is better than mine."

"It would have to be."

She smacked him in the back. "You're such a guy."

"Why, thank you."

They stumbled down an incline. Was it the one where she'd fallen on top of him before? Harry pulled on her hand as the path went back up. Dorey stuck the dead flashlight in her back pants pocket. Then she placed her other hand along the wall, helping her keep her balance. Hard to tell which way was up in the total darkness. She desperately hoped the icky bats were asleep now and wouldn't swoop at her head.

A strange glow came from up ahead. "Harry? Is that—"

"Yeah. Almost there."

They stumbled out of the mouth of the cave. Even though the night was cool, the warmth compared to the inside of the cave was as welcoming as a loving embrace. Through the fog that now encased the parking lot, their vehicles were visible beneath a streetlight.

Dorey looked down at her hand. "We need to go turn in the ring."

He nodded. "Yeah. We'd better go do it now. Besides, we need to tell them about Robert Keane. Where he ... is now."

She swallowed, not wanting to dwell on the man's crumpled body lying at the bottom of a deep, cold ravine. "Let's go."

Weatherby was waiting at the foot of the path, tail lashing, as if impatient they'd taken so long to find their way out of the cave. They all climbed into Harry's truck.

"We can come back and get yours tomorrow. For right now, I want you beside me. That work for you?"

She smiled. "Perfectly."

Once outside the cave, Harry retrieved his cell phone from his pocket. "I should have reception now." He punched in three numbers, spoke on the phone to an operator, and described where Mr. Keane was.

"Do you think he might still be alive?"

"I doubt it. But I wouldn't be able to sleep tonight if I hadn't at least called about him."

They drove through town, not saying much. Dorey leaned her head on Harry's shoulder, not caring her seatbelt pressed tight against her middle as she did. Any discomfort was worth being right next to Harry.

He parked the truck on the street in front of the police station. The fog, so heavy at the caves, was just a slight mist here in town.

"I'll be back in a little while, okay?" Dorey kissed Weatherby on the head. She closed the truck door and waved at him as he pressed his pink nose to the inside of the window.

I sure hope what I told him is true. That I will be back soon. Or at all. Who knew what would happen once they were inside the station, turned in a stolen ring, and mentioned a dead body in a cave. Would the police lock them up?

As they walked up to the building, hand in hand, the ring Dorey was anxious to return caught the reflection of a streetlight.

Something she'd liked so much, that had given her pleasure with its simplistic beauty, and reminded her of the sweet gift from her grandmother, now felt as heavy as a large millstone. She didn't want it anymore. There was no room in her life, her heart, for something that represented greed and death. Dorey slipped it from her finger, wishing she'd never laid eyes on it.

They went inside. A lone officer sat behind the desk. "Evening, folks. Can I help you with something?"

"I'm Harry MacKinley." Harry stepped forward. "This is

Dorey Cameron. We have a crime to report. Actually, several of them."

"That so?" The officer's eyebrows rose to his hairline.

Dorey edged up next to Harry. She placed the ring on the desk, relieved beyond words to be done with it. "I found this ring. It belongs to the museum."

"You don't say?" His eyes widened. He turned his attention not to the ring, but to his computer. He tapped away for a couple of minutes. Finding what he sought, he turned the screen toward them. "This ring?"

A paragraph at the top of the page gave details of the missing item and where it had been stolen from, and when. Below the description was an enlarged photo of the ring.

Her ring. No, not anymore. The museum's ring.

The officer turned the laptop back around then and picked up the ring. "We've been searching for this item for a long time now, but no leads. Mind telling me how you came to have it?"

Dorey hadn't thought that far ahead. Sure, she'd tell him everything that happened. But would he believe her? For the first time, the possibility that this nightmare wasn't over yet became very real. If the police didn't believe what she and Harry told them, would they arrest them for something? Possibly the murder of Mr. Keane?

"Would it be okay if we all sat down?" Harry pointed to a grouping of chairs near the corner. "We've been trapped in a cave. We're cold. Tired. And ..." He glanced at Dorey and back. "Probably still in shock."

"Oh. Of course. Have a seat. I'll be right there." He placed the ring in a small plastic bag and locked it inside his desk. After pocketing the keys, he hurried into a room behind the desk.

Dorey sank down on the couch and slumped against Harry. He wrapped his arm around her shoulders.

"Harry, I'd thought we'd just turn in the ring. That it would all be over and—"

"It will be. Nothing worse will happen."

"You can't know that. What if they don't believe us?"

"Whatever happens." He let out a long breath. "We're in this together. All right?"

"Yes." She was no longer alone. Now any obstacles facing her were sliced in half. The threats lessened. The battles weakened.

The officer returned, carrying a tray of steaming coffee in Styrofoam cups and some individually wrapped cookies. Were they from a vending machine? Dorey didn't even care. She was so hungry. And thirsty. But mostly just cold.

Taking one of the cups, she nodded her thanks to the officer and held the drink between her icy fingers. Welcome steam rose, warming her nose and cheeks.

Harry was doing the same. His contented sigh brought a smile to her lips. Poor guy. He'd only been at the cave for her. Because he loved her. She still could hardly believe it.

"Now, let's start at the beginning, shall we?"

The officer's voice jerked her from her musings.

Dorey took a sip of her coffee and nodded. "I found the ring inside a dental chair."

"Beg your pardon?"

"I'm a dentist," Harry said.

The officer addressed Dorey. "Were you the patient?"

"No, I'm a hygienist."

"Ah ..." He scratched his chin. "Go on."

"Well," said Dorey, "I found the ring. We had no idea who it belonged to. I checked with our most recent patients, but no one claimed it, so ..." She glanced at Harry. "I kept it."

"I see. Mighty expensive ring you've been wearing lately."

She swallowed. "Yes. I know that. Now. Anyway, around the time I found it, I started getting these weird, anonymous messages."

"Several of them?" The officer leaned forward. "Threatening in nature?"

"Yes."

Harry looked at her sharply. "You'd said those were just pranks."

"I'd hoped they were. But ..." She looked back at the officer. "I really didn't take them seriously. And there were some voicemails."

Harry frowned. "More than just the one I heard?"

She nodded.

"Dorey—"

"Not now," she whispered. Then she tilted her head toward the officer. "And there were a dozen beheaded roses. Oh, and a dead rodent left on my porch."

Harry's mouth dropped open. "You didn't tell me that."

"Sorry." She cringed.

"Tell him about the patients." Harry shook his head.

The officer sat up straighter, as if glad to be back in the conversation. "The patients?"

Dorey took another sip of the coffee, relieved to have something to do for a minute. With Harry and the officer watching her, she might as well have been a dragonfly stuck on a kid's display board for show and tell.

"Also, around that time, our patients, um, mine specifically, started not showing up for appointments."

The officer smirked. "Can't say I blame them." He held up his hand when Harry started to speak. "You two have to admit, the dentist's office isn't most people's idea of a party."

"True." Dorey shrugged. "But these patients weren't showing up for strange reasons."

He held out his hand. "Such as?"

"Someone scaring people with masks, running a pedestrian off the road, making a prank phone call, trying to keep people away from the office," Dorey said.

"And ..." Harry added.

"Death," he and Dorey said at the same time.

The officer stared at them. "We've been getting so many reports lately of some crazy person wearing scary masks, at least one incident of running someone off the road, among other things."

Dorey sat forward. "By a white van?"

"How did you know?" His eyes grew wide.

Harry pointed his thumb toward the front door. "The van in question is parked in the lot by the caves. The owner, Robert Keane, was, unfortunately, a patient of mine. And the man responsible for all for those crimes."

"He … was?"

"He's lying at the bottom of a deep ravine in the main cave." Dorey shivered. "I assume he's dead. If not—" If some animal didn't get him, cold and starvation would.

The officer eyed her. "We got the 911 call. An officer was already dispatched to the scene. The search and rescue team will need to get down there, try to find the body."

Find the body. What an awful image that was.

Dorey was relieved when Harry gave the officer directions on the path he'd taken to find Dorey at the ravine. There was no way she'd have been able to tell him. She wouldn't have gotten him any farther than, *Well, you enter the cave …*

"Also, you need to know that Robert Keane mugged Dorey, though we didn't know it was him at the time," Harry said. "He grabbed her purse. She ended up hitting her head on the pavement, resulting in a concussion. Today, he lured Dorey to the cave and held her there at gunpoint. I followed. We both ended up nearly shot by him. But when he tried to get the ring from me, he fell over the edge of the cliff."

The officer leaned back and clasped his hands in his lap. "So, you're telling me this Robert Keane caused all that mayhem to get the ring you found in your dental chair?"

"That's about it." Dorey nodded.

"And just how did he lure you to the cave? What did he threaten you with?"

Dorey looked at Harry. He shrugged and nodded.

"He kidnapped Weatherby," she said.

"Is that your son?"

She avoided the officer's gaze. "My, uh, cat."

"Cat? You went to meet a murderer at a cave because of your cat?"

Dorey glared at him. "Obviously, you're not a cat person. He's a very special animal. I happen to love him, and—"

"I think he gets the picture." Harry grabbed her hand.

The officer blew out a breath. "All right." He sliced his hand through the air. "No matter the reason for you meeting him there, the fact remains, you did. And a man is dead because of it."

Dorey gasped. He made it sound like she'd killed Mr. Keane. "But—"

"It's getting late." He held up his hand. "And I have a report, a very long, detailed one, to write. Since I have the ring in my possession now, you two can go. For now." He stood and pointed at them. "But don't give any thought to leaving town. Are we clear?"

Dorey swallowed hard and peered up at Harry.

"We're clear," he said.

When Dorey opened her eyes the next morning, Harry was watching her.

His lips stretched into a slow, lazy smile. "Sleep okay?"

She glanced down at her pajamas. She'd been so tired when they'd gotten home, she barely remembered changing and collapsing into bed.

"I sent Mae a message last night." Harry sat up and tilted his head toward his cell phone on the nightstand. "Told her to reschedule all our patients for today. I'm sure she was thrilled about that, but oh, well. Besides, I didn't figure either one of us would have the energy to go to work today."

"I sure don't." She yawned. "Thank you."

"It was nothing. All it took was a phone call. Dorey? You all right?"

"Yeah." She nodded. "But my thanks weren't just for that. I ... Harry, if you hadn't come to get me last night ..." She ran her finger down his chest.

He grabbed her finger to stop her. "I'm just thanking God that I came by your apartment. Saw Weatherby's collar. Listened to the voicemail."

RUTH J. HARTMAN

"Me too." She wiped away a tear.

He wrapped her in his arms. The beating of his heart was steady. Strong.

Just like Harry. "If we stayed here all day, like this, that would be okay with—"

Harry's phone rang. He eyed Dorey. "It might be Mae."

Grumbling, Dorey slid away from Harry as he sat up and answered it.

"Hello?"

Whoever it was on the other end talked for several seconds. Was Mae that put out about having to call the patients and reschedule? The woman was on thin ice with Harry as it was. Dorey had never seen Harry so mad as when Mae had dared to say something about Dorey and Harry sleeping together. Which, of course, they hadn't.

She bit her lip and studied Harry. His eyebrows lowered, and his other hand clenched into a fist. Was he going to fire Mae now? Over the phone? She must really be telling him off.

"Fine," Harry muttered, "we'll be there as soon as we can."

Dorey sat up. "We're going to the office? Was Mae—"

He put his phone back on the nightstand. "That wasn't Mae. It was the police station."

"What?" Her entire body went cold.

"We need to hurry and get ready. He's waiting to see us down there. *Now.*"

Dread trickled down Dorey's back. No. Were they going to charge her? Harry? For the death of Robert Keane? For being in possession of stolen museum property? Fear clutched at her heart. She couldn't move.

"They found Keane." Harry rubbed her arms. "He's dead. I know it's scary, but we have to go to the station now. Maybe it won't be bad news."

Dorey raised her eyebrows but said nothing.

After taking the fastest shower of her life, Dorey dressed

while Harry showered. Poor guy had to wear the same clothes from yesterday. But they were in such a hurry, he didn't complain.

They hadn't had time to retrieve Dorey's car from the cave parking lot, so they raced to the station together in the truck.

Once there, Dorey opened the passenger door but couldn't make herself move any farther from the seat. She stared through the windshield at the police station. If she went in, would she ever come out again?

"Honey," Harry stood in front of her. "We're together. Don't forget that. Whatever happens ..."

She took his outstretched hand, and he closed her fingers around hers. Strong. Safe. Warm. With a glance up at him, she nodded. Together they could do anything.

Their shoes on the cement steps to the police station door sounded too loud. As if they were the only people on earth. Alone. Headed to the unknown.

When they stepped inside, Dorey stopped in her tracks.

"Glad you two finally made it." Officer Beaumont stood in front of the desk, arms crossed over his chest, a menacing glare on his face.

"You did get us out of bed, after all." Harry, still holding Dorey's hand, started toward him.

Dorey bit her lip. Harry's words had made it sound like he and Dorey had been—

"Have a seat." Officer Beaumont pointed toward the same couch where they'd been only a few hours before.

She and Harry sat down. Too bad there weren't coffee and cookies. She could have used the sustenance. Also, the diversion of having something to do with her jittery hands, which, like the rest of her, couldn't seem to stay still.

Officer Beaumont took the chair opposite them. "First of all, I need to, uh ..." He cleared his throat. "That is ... it seems I owe you an ..." He coughed.

What was wrong with him? His face was so pale, he looked ill.

The man leaned forward and placed his hands on his knees, but stared at the table between the chairs instead of them. "I've been told that I have to …" He huffed out a breath. "Ah, I don't want to have to say it."

Dorey's mouth dropped open.

"I owe you an apology." Officer Beaumont shifted in his seat. "I-I'd had you both under suspicion ever since the office break-in."

"What?" Harry clamped his hand hard around Dorey's.

Officer Beaumont shrugged, seeming relieved he'd finally gotten his apology out. "It wouldn't be uncommon for someone to rifle through their own property for the insurance money."

"But I didn't—"

"We know that." He raised his hand. "Now. Anyway, I really had my antennae up after that patient was poisoned and died in your dental chair." His focus shifted to Dorey.

Having a policeman as an enemy wasn't the best scenario. She slid down in the seat, wishing he'd stop glaring at her.

"But after you came in last night and returned the ring, we went out and found Keane's van. Your story checked out. The registration inside had his name on it. And we found his cell phone. He might have left it in the van, knowing there isn't any reception once you're in the cave. His phone had a few voice messages back and forth with a man who apparently worked at the museum. A man with a New Jersey accent."

Dorey's eyes widened. The guy that Marie liked? Poor Marie. First, Harry wasn't interested in her, and now this.

"So," Officer Beaumont said, "considering all that, you two are no longer under suspicion."

Dorey nearly wilted. "Are we free to go now?" She looked at the front door longingly. Their nightmare had seemed to go on forever. She wanted out.

"No." He stood. "There's one more thing. Don't move." He stalked off, going into the same room where the officer from the night before had gone to get them refreshments.

Dorey's stomach growled. A cookie sounded like heaven right now.

Harry didn't seem to notice her bodily protest. He frowned at Dorey. "Is there still something they're concerned about with Mr. Keane? I can't imagine what it would be. It sounded like everything was taken care of and—"

When Officer Beaumont returned, he wasn't alone. Another man stood to his left. "This is Mr. Bolden. He's the curator of the museum."

Harry stood, so Dorey did too.

Mr. Bolden, a tall thin man in a sport coat and bow tie, gave them an encouraging smile. The first one anyone had sent their way for a couple of days. It was nice, comforting.

"Dr. MacKinley. Miss Cameron. On behalf of the museum, I wanted to thank you for returning our stolen ring."

It's my ring, Dorey wanted to shout. *No, it isn't. Under the circumstances, would you even want it to be?* Dorey pushed aside the thought and focused on Mr. Bolden.

"You're welcome." Harry gave him a nod.

Dorey nodded too. Should she say something? *Sorry it took so long. I didn't know where the ring had come from. That it had to do with my mugging, a poisoned patient, patients not getting their teeth cleaned, a man lying dead in a cave.*

"And," said Mr. Bolden, "along with our thanks, you also get the reward."

"Reward?" Dorey frowned. "But we don't deserve anything for—"

He held up his hand. "Nonsense. If not for you, we never would have recovered the priceless ring."

It wasn't right. Guilt tore at Dorey. A reward for happening

311

to find something that led to the harm of so many people. No. She couldn't accept. "I'm not sure that—"

"I insist." He stopped her again, handed Harry an envelope, shook their hands, and left.

Harry blinked and looked at Officer Beaumont. The man didn't smile, but at least he'd stopped glaring at them.

"You're free to go." He tilted his head toward the door. Without another word, he turned and walked away.

A slow smile pulled up the corners of Harry's lips. "Dorey, I think the nightmare is finally over." He wrapped her in a tight hug and then leaned back to look at her. "Let's get out of here."

She laughed. "Right behind ya, doc."

Even though Dorey had no desire to even see the caves again, they made one more trip and got her car. She climbed behind the wheel, amazed that her keys were still hanging in the ignition.

I bet if Robert Keane had seen them, he would have stolen my car like he did the ring.

Police tape had been strung across the mouth of the cave, and several officers were talking and pointing at it and the white van. She shuddered.

Harry had backed out of his spot and was waiting on her. She started her car and followed him.

They drove to Dorey's apartment and went inside. Weatherby frantically paced around the kitchen. They'd left so suddenly she hadn't filled his food dish.

"Thanks to you, little man, the bad stuff is over." She knelt down and ran her fingers through his fur as he ate.

"Thanks to him?" Harry stood in the doorway.

"If Mr. Keane hadn't stolen him and taken him to the cave and left that message for me and—"

He held up his hand. "Okay, I get it." He came in and sat next to Dorey on the floor, then took the envelope out of his pocket. "I haven't opened this yet. Wanna see what's inside?"

"I have to say, after the notes I've gotten recently, I'm a little leery of opening anything." She eyed the envelope.

"I'm pretty sure whatever he gave us won't be threatening. And it won't contain dead roses. Or a dead rodent, or—"

"Fine. I get it." She huffed out a breath. "Just open it, will you?"

Harry took out the contents. His mouth dropped open.

"What? Is it bad?"

He shook his head and handed it to her.

Dorey let out a loud squeak. It was a check. For twenty-five thousand dollars. "I—"

"Yeah." He ran his hand through his hair.

"What should we do with it?" She handed it back to him.

"I have no idea." He shook his head and stared at the check.

Dorey rubbed his shoulder. "That's a lot of money. Maybe … let's think about it for a little while. Not make any hasty decisions about it."

"You're right." He grinned. "Good idea."

"I'm right? Can I get that in writing, doc?"

"Hmmm. I don't seem to have anything to write with at the moment so, I guess you're out of luck." He dropped the check and lunged at her, tickling her ribs.

She squealed.

With a growl, Weatherby abandoned his food dish and fled.

39

Stretched out on the couch, Dorey leaned her head against Harry's chest. "Hard to believe the nightmare with Robert Keane is finally over."

He kissed the top of her head. "I know. Those poor people he frightened. And killed. Poor Mr. Long. But at least his wife has acknowledged we had nothing to do with the poisoning. We have Officer Beaumont to thank for that. I'm still shocked he went to the trouble to speak with Mrs. Long himself on our behalf. Maybe other people will go along with her and stop being so hostile."

"I know we didn't actually hurt any of those people," she ran her fingers over his shoulder, "but I still feel like it's my fault somehow."

"Dorey, it's not. How could it be? You didn't drop the ring in the chair."

"But I found it. I wore it."

"Even if you wouldn't have found it, he still would have tried to get in the office. Made sure all those patients didn't make their appointments so he could try to get back in."

"But for most of that time, I wore the ring. It wasn't even in the chair. Think of all the people he wouldn't have tried to keep away if he'd known the ring wasn't even there."

"But he didn't know that. And you never knew who was doing it. Or even why."

Dorey shook her head. "Speaking of why someone would do something, have you ever wondered why Dr. Conners caused so much trouble for you in the first place?"

"And for you."

"Yeah, but I was always more worried about you and your practice. And your patients not showing up. That's your livelihood, Harry."

"That's one of the things I love about you. The way you care for others." He kissed the top of her head. "As for Dr. Conners, we may never know why he's so antagonistic toward hygienists. Maybe he's jealous of the way patients seem to like how you clean their teeth."

"I doubt that's it."

"Or maybe one time a hygienist told him he was a big old meanie with a bad haircut and crooked teeth."

Dorey grinned. "That sounds more like it." She sighed. "Thanks for trying to cheer me up. It's hard not to think about Robert Keane and how, if I'd done things differently, maybe none of those bad things would have happened."

"Stop. You did nothing wrong." He stroked his fingers down her arm, making her shiver. "Besides, once he did figure out you had the ring for sure, look what happened. I nearly lost you."

"I nearly lost *you*. That's why I didn't tell you."

"Don't ever do that to me again. Got it?"

"Do what—find a ring? Save my cat? Or meet a murderer in a cave?"

"Let's not do any of that."

"If Weatherby is ever in trouble again, of course I'm going to save him."

"Hopefully, he'll never be seduced with tuna and lured away to a cave again."

"I don't know." She smirked. "He has a really hard time saying no to tuna."

"Dorey, I didn't know what to do." Harry ran his finger down her cheek. "When I came here, and your door was wide open, but you were gone, I-I thought I might die right there."

"Oh, Harry." She slid up closer to his face and pressed her lips to his. "I'm right here. You didn't lose me. You'll never lose me."

He kissed her lips, her jaw, her cheek, until she felt drugged. Was Harry really hers? He actually loved her the way she did him? All those years tagging along behind him, watching his every move, wanting to be where he was, do what he did. Now they were together. But as equals, this time. A man and woman. In love.

"Now that things have settled down," he smiled, "Have you considered what to do with the reward money?"

"I have. It's just ... I hope this doesn't sound weird but, I don't think I could spend any of that money, Harry. Because I'd think about all that happened to our patients every time I did. It wouldn't seem right. And I was thinking ..."

"Go on."

"What would you think if we gave it to Mrs. Long and her family? I know it won't bring back Mr. Long, or make up for what everyone else went through, but—" She shrugged.

"I'm so glad you said that." Harry tilted her chin up and pressed a warm, slow kiss to her lips. "Because that's exactly what I wanted to do too."

She let out a breath and snuggled into his chest.

The kitty door squeaked, and Dorey smiled. "Guess who's home."

Weatherby trotted into the room and sat next to the couch.

"Hey, trouble." Harry glanced over at him.

"That's not his name."

"After giving in to his lust for tuna, so you had to risk your life to save him? Yeah, I think he deserves that nickname."

Dorey shrugged. She couldn't really argue with Harry's logic. She looked closer at her cat. "Weatherby, whatcha got there?" She leaned over and tried to see what he had in his mouth. "Harry, can you grab him? I can't quite—"

Reaching out, Harry snagged the cat under the chest. He pulled him up onto the couch.

"What is that?" Dorey rose up a little so she could see what the cat had. Something curved and smooth. A piece of metal? Harry still had his hand on Weatherby so the cat couldn't bolt. Dorey tugged on whatever it was. Weatherby tried to hide from her, growling low in his throat. The object finally pulled free.

Her eyes widened. "Hey, look. It's a bracelet."

"Your cat drags in the weirdest stuff." Harry raised his eyebrows. "Although, I guess nothing is weirder than that giant bra."

Weatherby growled. Because of Harry's insult or just that he was irritated Dorey had confiscated his prize, Dorey wasn't sure. The cat squirmed until Harry let him jump down.

She turned the bracelet over and studied it more closely. "There's some sort of— there's writing on the back. Like a code. Or a message. Maybe it's a—"

"No, Dorey. We're not going down that road again. No more mysterious jewelry."

"Yeah, but it might be—"

"No. Think about what almost happened to us in that cave."

"It could be a—"

"You are not an amateur detective. Stop thinking there's a crime around every corner. Honestly, your imagination is unparalleled."

"What if it's a—"

Harry's lips on hers squelched the rest of her words. His kiss, so warm, so inviting, made her melt against him. The bracelet slipped to the floor as Dorey clutched the front of Harry's shirt in her fingers, kneading his chest through the fabric.

Kneading. Like Weatherby did.

Weatherby finding that bracelet ... Dorey opened her eyes and slid a glance to the piece of jewelry on the floor.

What if the writing on the bracelet were some kind of clue?

ABOUT RUTH J. HARTMAN

Ruth J. Hartman spends her days herding cats and her nights spinning mysterious tales. She, her husband, and their cats love to spend time curled up in their recliners watching old Cary Grant movies. Well, the cats sit in the people's recliners. Not that the cats couldn't get their own furniture. They just choose to shed on someone else's.

Ruth, a left-handed, cat-herding, farmhouse-dwelling writer uses her sense of humor as she writes tales of lovable, klutzy women who seem to find trouble without even trying.

Ruth's husband and best friend, Garry, reads her manuscripts, rolls his eyes at her weird story ideas, and loves her despite her insistence all of her books have at least one cat in them. See updates about her cozy mysteries at Ruthjhartman.com.

NEW FICTION FROM SCRIVENINGS PRESS

September Shadows

Book One - Justice, Montana Series

A mystery

After the sudden death of their parents, Jess Thomas and her sisters, Sly and Maggie, start creating a new life for themselves. But when Sly is accused of a crime she didn't commit, the young sisters are threatened with separation through foster care. Jess is determined to prove Sly's innocence, even at the cost of her own life.

Cole McBride has been Jess's best friend since they were children. Now his feelings are deepening, just as Jess takes risks to protect her family. Can Cole convince Jess to trust him—and God—to help her?

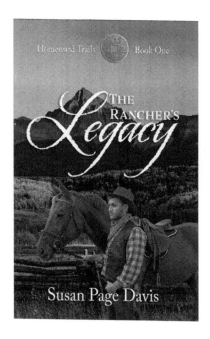

The Rancher's Legacy

Homeward Trails - Book One

Historical Romance

Matthew Anderson and his father try to help neighbor Bill Maxwell when his ranch is attacked. On the day his daughter Rachel is to return from school back East, outlaws target the Maxwell ranch. After Rachel's world is shattered, she won't even consider the plan her father and Matt's cooked up—to see their two children marry and combine the ranches.

Meanwhile in Maine, sea captain's widow Edith Rose hires a private investigator to locate her three missing grandchildren. The children were abandoned by their father nearly twenty years ago. They've been adopted into very different families, and they're scattered across the country. Can investigator Ryland Atkins find them all while the elderly woman still lives? His first attempt is to find the boy now called

Matthew Anderson. Can Ryland survive his trip into the wild Colorado Territory and find Matt before the outlaws finish destroying a legacy?

Books Afloat

Columbia River Undercurrents - Book One

Historical Romance

Blaming herself for her childhood role in the Oklahoma farm truck accident that cost her grandfather's life, Anne Mettles is determined to make her life count. She wants to do it all–captain her library boat and resist Japanese attacks to keep America safe. But failing her pilot's exam requires her to bring others onboard.

Will she go it alone? Or will she team with the unlikely but (mostly) lovable characters? One is a saboteur, one an unlikely hero, and one, she discovers, is the man of her dreams.

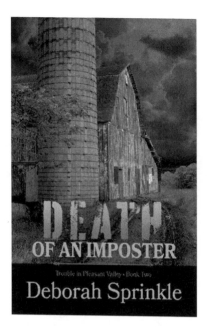

Death of an Imposter

Trouble in Pleasant Valley - Book Two

Romantic Suspense

Rookie detective Bernadette Santos has her first murder case. Will her desire for justice end up breaking her heart? Or worse—get her killed!

Her first week on the job and rookie detective Bernadette Santos has been given the murder of a prominent citizen to solve. But when her victim turns out to be an imposter, her straight forward case takes a nasty turn. One that involves the attractive Dr. Daniel O'Leary, a visitor to Pleasant Valley and a man harboring secrets.

When Dr. O'Leary becomes a target of violence himself, Detective Santos has two mysteries to unravel. Are they related? And how far can she trust the good doctor? Her heart tugs her one way while her mind pulls her another. She must discover the solutions before it's too late!

Scrivenings
PRESS
Quench your thirst for story.
www.ScriveningsPress.com

Stay up-to-date on your favorite books and authors with our free e-newsletters.

ScriveningsPress.com

Made in the USA
Monee, IL
22 March 2021